About the author

Terence F. Jones was born and raised in London. He served in the RAF as an aircraft instruments mechanic, including two and a half years on active service in Singapore and Malaya. Subsequently, he was employed in the head office of a drinks manufacturer, where he worked in various managerial roles for fifteen years. From 1978-1986 the author was a councillor in the London Borough of Greenwich. He and his family have been active members of a historical group involved in the re-enactment of medieval jousting tournaments. He lives in south-east London.

Hidden Hamlets, Dancing Trees

Terence F. Jones

Book Guild Publishing
Sussex, England

First published in Great Britain in 2015 by
The Book Guild Ltd
The Werks
45 Church Road
Hove, BN3 2BE

Typesetting in Centaur

Printed and bound in Great Britain by
CPI Group (UK) Ltd, Croydon, CR0 4YY

A catalogue record for this book is available from
The British Library.

ISBN 978 1 910508 23 7

I

A New Home

Leaning into the incline away from the dankest part of the forest, Egen became aware that the wet, cloying smell of decaying grass and vegetation grew fainter, and the spongy soil beneath his feet became firmer as the ground levelled and daylight filtered more profusely through the trees. He re-adjusted the weight of the carcase about his shoulders and quickened his pace.

The young boar that he had fortuitously found snuffling around in the mud at the base of a large oak had proved to be an easy kill. Just why it had been alone he did not understand and consequently kept a wary eye on the surrounding area, listening carefully for unwanted sounds. Despite its small size it would nevertheless be tiring to carry it all the way back to his village, and once again he silently expressed his gratitude for the half-sleeved leather hunting jacket given to him by his father; the rough, hairy skin of his burden would have chafed unbearably through any lesser material.

He had set out early that morning, just as the first rays of the sun began teasing vapour from the grasses and foliage. The only other person abroad at that time was Josin, the metal worker's daughter, going about her duty of preparing the first meal of the day for her father and herself. Her mother had died of a sudden and mysterious illness several years earlier. When she saw Egen she hesitantly offered him a drink of warmed goat's milk and said, 'This should help to keep you going today.' His eager acceptance was not entirely due to a desire for the milk, it also gave him a chance to speak to and be near to her.

'Thank you,' he said. 'It used to be your mother who would be up at this time doing the chores, you and your father must miss her greatly, as indeed we all do.'

They were both shy and awkward in this short exchange, despite the fact that as young children they had played together completely devoid of inhibitions; but as they had grown older both were aware of feelings within themselves which they found difficult to admit to or conceal. They found it less disturbing to avoid close association especially when other people were near. As he grasped the rough-surfaced bowl, Egen allowed his fingers, as if accidentally, to momentarily touch the back of her hand, he then gulped down the warm drink. He was self-consciously aware that this was the first time he had touched her since those early childhood days. He was embarrassingly tongue-tied as he said, 'Thank you, I must be off or I will not be back before sundown.'

'Good luck,' she called after him, and her voice trailed off as she added, 'and please be careful.'

Egen was now more determined than ever to bring back fresh meat for all, and in his renewed determination he hurried away in a direction that was not of his usual choice and further than he would normally have ventured.

Now a feeling of unease arose within him which he could not readily explain. It was not the unfamiliar surroundings, nor the unseen eyes he could almost feel watching him; had those eyes been Roman or those of Romanised natives, or hostile in any way, they would have shown themselves by now and challenged him for his prize. Yet he had to admit to himself that had he retained the improvised lance used to fell his prey he would have felt more secure. That would, however, have contradicted his normal practice of travelling as unencumbered as possible, except for his well-greased knife and dry, wrapped fire-making materials which hung from his belt. For him it was but the work of a few heartbeats to choose, cut, strip and sharpen an appropriate rod or branch to use as a stabbing lance or throwing spear as required, a skill he had practised very many times. This skill had served him well, allowing him to cover long distances quickly and unhindered; but on occasions such as this he would have welcomed another defensive weapon to hand.

He also felt that he should have been experiencing a sense of satisfaction rather than the vague apprehension disturbing him. For many days his habitual hunting grounds had for some reason yielded little, and the village had existed on a few dried fish and leathery strips of preserved goat's meat, supplemented by whatever they had been able to gather close by in the meadows and woodlands. As he strode purposefully onwards, still keeping a watchful eye on his surroundings, he allowed himself to muse on his hidden hamlet, its inhabitants among which he had been raised, and how it had come to be so hidden.

Many seasons ago his parents had explained that they had been elders in a much larger community known as the Cantiaci well to the south, but with the coming of the Roman invaders many of them had been driven out. Some had fled in the direction of the setting sun, past the great stone circle used by the druids to preach and teach. Some had fled north across the great river, hoping to join up with the Trinovantes. His parents, with a few companions, had determined not to be driven too far from the lands which they considered to be their own by right. They had lived there from time immemorial; they were neither squatters nor invaders; they would, when it pleased the gods, return and reclaim their inheritance. But until such a time, without an unforeseeable and dramatic change in circumstances, they would have to live mainly hidden lives, forever on watch and without the freedom to farm, hunt or live as they had previously.

For many days they had blundered north, across difficult ground and into ancient woodlands of oak and elm bordered by tracts of birch, eventually sighting a small dry cave at the foot of a high ridge, the mouth of which was almost entirely hidden by thick undergrowth. It was late in the evening and drawing towards the end of the year and too overcast to examine the locality closely. Consequently, cold, hungry and exhausted they had all crept into the opening and huddled together for warmth and rest. Elred the fish catcher had pulled more loose shrubs across the entrance in the hope that it hid them from prowling animals, as well as helping to keep out some of the cold night air. At first light it was agreed not to continue their journey without searching for food and exploring the surrounding terrain.

Elred, with two companions, volunteered to climb the ridge, which in daylight proved to be higher and steeper than had appeared the previous evening; they would then report on what lay beyond the crest. The rock-face was yellow-white and largely covered with hanging greenery, mostly ivy, and small tufted plants which softened its appearance. About fifty paces to the left of the cave was a small pool fed by a narrow stream scuttling down the cliff front. It appeared to have no definite origin, but seemed to be formed by the coming together of many trickles exuding from various points in the cracked and porous stone at differing heights. A second group comprising two men and three women agreed to investigate the local area and forage for anything which might be edible. The remaining adults stayed close to the cave, keeping watch and tending the needs of the younger children.

It was mid-morning before the climbers returned to fall ravenously on the root vegetables, small apples, nuts and berries garnered by the foragers and saved for them. As they ate both groups described what they had discovered. The climbers, having scrabbled and pulled themselves to the visible top of the ridge, found that it continued to rise gently as a long wide meadow but the ground was very wet and soft, making it difficult to walk upon. About two hundred paces further on it crested, then dropped gradually down and away to a barrier of trees at a considerable distance, not much above sea level. Beyond the trees the ground was obviously marshy and reed covered, right up to the wide estuary of the great river which then stretched away to a misty horizon. To the west, whence the river descended and was narrower, the terrain was similar. The very wet soil beneath their feet was certainly due, not only to rain, but to moisture carried in by easterly winds being unable to climb higher; it also explained the stream, formed as the water filtered its way down through chalky sub-soil. At first they were alarmed to see a Roman galley moving in with the flowing tide to the new port at Londinium. The great square sail clearly silhouetted figures busily working the ship onwards, but they quickly realised that against the mottled and varied backdrop of long grass and scrub they themselves would be indistinguishable shadows. The foraging party described a mixture of ancient trees interspersed with patches of open ground and shrubs, and an abundance of root plants, most of which were recognisably edible, plus wild fruit, berries and nuts. Small mammals had been seen, but other than traces of fox fur found on brambles, there was no evidence of larger creatures. To their mounting relief, it dawned on the entire assembly that, with due vigilance, hard work and perseverance, here was a place where they might be able to stay and settle, at least temporarily.

By the beginning of summer five dwellings, roughly equal in size, had been erected, each with wattle and mud walls and roofed with overhanging thatch. They were round houses, typical of those built in open villages everywhere, but here hidden and, their owners hoped, safe. Arranged around a central open space, they built to measurements taught them by Athan the druid, whose initial appearance had at first caused great alarm. He was a tall, imposing figure with a flowing beard and long hair tied back, and he carried a staff a little taller than himself. That staff had a strange appearance: it was a straight piece of ash but tapered from a near pointed top to a thick, club-like base. He had a disconcerting ability to arrive and disappear without warning. His unannounced appearances would bring news of the outside world, as well as preaching, teaching and prophesies.

By common consent the home nearest the cave was occupied by Gwain the metal worker and his daughter Josin. Gwain was thus able to set up a forge just inside the cave entrance with a protective porch. The porch, together with small trees and overhangs from the cliff face, effectively dispersed excess smoke from the furnace, so that by the time it had reached the height of the tallest trees in the surrounding woodland, it was so thin as to be all but invisible from any great distance, and easily confused with the mists which hung almost constantly over the cliff face. He would also take responsibility, on behalf of the group, for storing the type of fuel that produced a glowing flameless fire with little smoke, knowledge which he passed on to each family that they might use it on their own central hearths.

Each family or neighbour proved to have a particular skill or attribute that contributed to the smooth and successful running of the little commune. Elred, who had found his own easier paths over the ridge and down to the water's edge without fear of being seen, would return with a sufficiently large catch of fish to share with all. Beren was a carpenter who had had the foresight to bring his beloved tools with him. Hugin was both a tanner and builder, while Eadulf, Egen's father was a skilled and experienced hunter. Unlike his son, to whom he had passed his skills, he believed in always having to hand well-crafted, long, lance-like spears, tipped with sharp iron points. Smooth and highly polished, they were bound at the centre of balance with a soft piece of goatskin for comfort and grip. When properly launched they would glide silently to the target without the slightest sign of whipping.

Life in the community was not, and could not always be, entirely harmonious, but for the sake of all, disputes had to be resolved quickly and quietly. Such settlements were undertaken by Nestin who, being the oldest and most experienced group member, was automatically accepted as the village elder and chief. He had a particular gift of being able to take a squabble between two persons into his own hut and, without embarrassment to either, resolve the situation. More bitter disagreements would be decided by the whole village under his direction and to the satisfaction of all.

Some, especially among the womenfolk, had multiple skills and most needs were covered by someone.

For the sake of safety and seclusion, it had been mutually agreed that domestic or farm animals would not be kept, with the exception of four or five communally owned goats on which they would depend for milk and, in emergencies only, meat and skins. The first two of these creatures had been acquired through a dangerous and stealthy incursion into a distant Roman settlement by Eadulf and two companions, who snatched them from under the noses of sleepy herdsmen. There had followed a chase in which the more nimble and wily villagers, outran and outwitted the enraged keepers in the thickets bordering the settlement. At that time Egen was far too young to have taken part, but he revelled in the telling and re-telling of the story, including the exaggerated embellishments each time it was repeated.

For several years the hamlet's comfort had improved, and life for its inhabitants fell quietly into a routine of active self-sufficiency. Always watchful and careful, they nevertheless remained unaware that the metalled road and its attendant paved villas and forts was relentlessly creeping nearer. Increasing movement from the coastal ports drove on towards Londinium. intending to meet up with river traffic, then cross the river to a further extension of the road leading to the Roman capital of Camulodunum.

This was the environment in which Egen and Josin and several others had been raised, and into which new children had been born, most of their knowledge of the outside world having been provided by Athan on his unexpected and irregular appearances.

2

A Legend is Born

Nearer home where the surroundings were much more familiar, Egen's earlier unease changed to anxiety as he detected the sharp smell of smoke drifting towards him. With each stride it became stronger, until at a distance through the trees he perceived the flickering of flames. Throwing down his burden he charged unheeding through the undergrowth towards them, and as he broke clear of the trees he was confronted by a sight that would stay with him for the rest of his life. So great was the horror and shock of what lay before him that he temporarily lost even the ability to breathe; his chest was suddenly so filled with a mixture of violent emotions that he felt as if a huge rock had developed within him; then, as his mind translated the scene, his breathing returned in huge laboured sobs.

Every home was ablaze, every villager, every living thing appeared to be lying slashed and hacked to death in the open square at the centre of the village. Everyone, from Nestin down to the youngest child had been brutally slaughtered; even the goats had not been allowed to live. Everywhere blood reflected the consuming flames. Nearest him lay his father with his mother face down across his outstretched legs, her head smashed in. One of his father's long hunting spears lay close to his lifeless hand, while a second was buried deep in a Roman auxiliary a little further on. That auxiliary wore no upper armour or helmet, and his dirty linen tunic was only half tucked into his studded leather skirt and belt. A second auxiliary lay across the clearing with one of Gwain's small knives protruding from the side of his neck. Never had Gwain deliberately manufactured an offensive weapon as such, only tools and knives that were necessary to the life and work of the community. Even above the acrid smell of burning wood, skins and fabric, he could easily distinguish the aroma of the thick, red, sweet wine favoured by the Roman militia, and imported by them in vast quantities.

Crouched in a state of shock and disbelief, his hand reaching out uncertainly towards his parents, he heard an angry roar; a third similarly ill-attired soldier lurched out of the cave towards him, his hand raised with his gladius, or short sword, ready to strike. This apparition, covered in a mixture of grime, blood and dribbled wine, made a terrifying spectacle. Instinctively, although had there been an observer he would have sworn that it was a practised move, Egen waited until the last possible moment, then stamped his foot onto the rearmost end of the spear lying close by, kept it there, and raised the metal tip chest high. The roar changed momentarily into a scream as his would be attacker, realising too late that he could change neither the impetus nor direction of his charge, impaled himself on that deadly shaft. For a few long moments spear and man supported each other in a grisly tableau, which, as the victim's legs buckled, toppled sideways in a cloud of dust.

The fact that he had now killed his first man did not even enter Egen's head. From the moment that he had first beheld the carnage around him, his cruelly slaughtered family and friends, the total destruction of his village and home, all things Roman became, in his mind, less worthy of consideration than the animals he hunted for food, or even the insects that attached themselves to his kills, which he brushed aside rather than crush. In the moments that it took for his victim to die, he had resolved that from this instant onwards he would oppose and destroy anyone or anything that in any way represented Rome, even if he had to do it alone. And at this moment he was very much alone, for there appeared to be no other being alive to whom he could turn for help or solace. In the desperate moments when the doomed soldier had realised his fate, he had let fall his weapon which bounced and spun and came to rest by Egen's foot; seizing hold of it he searched around for any further threat. He crept quietly towards the cave, from which as he neared it another drunken Roman hero emerged, staggering and rolling in his inebriation, and leaning heavily on the rock wall, his linen tunic soaked in wine.

This time there was no roar or scream; it was doubtful if he even saw his attacker as he squinted against the sunlight, and the blade in Egen's hand was thrust deep between his ribs. Not knowing who else might be inside Egen wasted no time in trying to wrench it free. Instead, he let it drop with the body and, as he entered the darkened space, allowed his hand fall to the more familiar handle of his hunting knife. Slowly, as his eyes adjusted to the reduced light, he moved carefully around, trying to see anything threatening; his foot kicked an unseen but still dripping wine flask, yet all else appeared to be normal, untouched, and eerily quiet. The small stone forge which should have been the only thing burning in the village was unlit, which indicated that the raiders had arrived early, and spent a great deal of time satisfying their bloodlust. Stored tools and implements rested against the walls as normal, logs and peat used for fuel were still there in alternate layers, surmounted by some rough woollen blankets; only they looked as though they could have been disturbed from the neat pile in which Josin usually laid them to air by the heat of the hearth. As he turned to leave he thought he heard the faintest of whimpers behind him. Silently retracing his steps to the pile of fuel he swept the blankets away, then nimbly stepped aside as a hand frantically waving a small but viciously pointed knife shot upwards. He grabbed the wrist and hauled Josin from behind the log pile. Her face was pale with terror until she recognised him, whereupon she dropped the knife, threw her arms about his neck and clung to him.

'Egen it is you,' she sobbed. 'Thanks be to the gods.'

For a considerable time past he had longed for this moment of closeness between them without daring to speak of it, but now was not the time or place to enjoy it. There might be more danger and more to be done. Gently, he guided her towards daylight, keeping his hand on his knife.

Neither was completely surprised to see Athan with his long staff striding about outside, assessing the extent of the slaughter, putting together a picture of what had occurred. He had arrived soon after the bloody confrontation at the cave mouth and knew, without checking, that it was not empty so warily chose not to enter; had those inside been hostile he would not have had sufficient space to swing his staff freely.

The two young persons blurted out their stories to him, confirming much of what he had already calculated for himself. Josin had escaped the massacre only because she too had been away from the village when the attack occurred. Her father had assured her that Egen was certain to return with fresh meat for all; consequently, she had gone alone to forage for suitable vegetables to accompany the expected meal.

While searching some considerable and inadvisable distance from home, she had seen the drunken group of ten making their way towards the hamlet. It was clear from their shouted conversation that they had not the slightest idea where or in what direction they had travelled, or that they would happen upon a habitation. At first she hid from them, then realised that she should try to warn the village, but by the time she got there the horror was nearly complete. Standing over her father's body with his back to her was a massive, dishevelled assassin looking for whatever else might amuse him, or for anything of value to steal. Shock and emotion destroyed any sense of discretion; she simply launched herself on to his back, fastening with her legs and one arm while stabbed frenziedly with her pruning knife into the left side of his neck. Fortunately for her, the first thrust completely severed the vital artery; the others merely added to the certainty of his demise. He shuddered momentarily and collapsed into the most untidy heap of human flesh she had ever seen. His companions were so intent on looting on the far side of the square that they had seen neither his fate nor his attacker; at this point, suddenly aware of her vulnerability, she had fled unseen into the cave to hide, only stopping to grab one of her father's unfinished knives. There she had waited in fear and trembling, hearing, but unable to see, the two auxiliaries shuffling about, until rescued by Egen. The six unharmed imperial heroes, still bemused by wine, and disappointed by the lack of valuable plunder, had long since started back the way they had come, unaware that their number was now reduced by four.

Retrieving his father's spears from the bodies, Egen cleaned them and prepared to leave. Josin was puzzled and upset, but he advised her and the druid that he had further hunting to do and would return as soon as possible. Athan's understanding nod and advice to be careful quelled any further questions from her; he also indicated that work was still to be done in the settlement and he required her help.

Loping along at a steady pace, Egen knew he would soon overtake his quarry; they were not woodsmen and had come across the hamlet by accident. The slaughter and destruction they had wrought upon it was, to their befuddled brains, an unexpected diversion, adding to the celebrations of their imminent release from military duties. Having served their twenty-five years, they were looking forward to retirement in a civitas, where they would be able to live in comparative luxury and lord it over the civilian population. Hearing their voices even before he saw them, he crept slowly forward until he could discern them clearly through the undergrowth without being observed. On a steep grassy bank five men sprawled untidily, chuckling in response to the sixth who stood before them, haranguing them. Clearly, the events of that day were now merely a subject for merriment; the standing figure saw himself as some sort of heroic leader poetically dramatising their earlier actions, which he now translated into a last great battle and victory on the very eve of retirement. Still unseen but not more than twenty paces away, their pursuer quietly raised the first javelin and sent it thudding into the back of the orator. Even before his stricken target was halfway to the ground he had run forward and lunged the second into the torso of one of the prone listeners. Using his momentum, allied to the full length of the shaft, he vaulted over the lying victim to land lightly at the top of the grass bank. Without hesitation, he turned in his crouching position to wrench his weapon free from the body, then hurled it at a third man who was confusedly struggling to his feet. For the third time that day, that same projectile, originally intended solely for hunting food, sank deep into the flesh of a Roman invader.

Apart from his small knife he was now unarmed, unlike the three dazed murderers facing him, each of whom still had a sword attached to his belt. His only advantage now lay in his intimate knowledge of his surroundings. Before any of the three had time or wit enough to climb the bank to give chase, he had disappeared into the trees. Keeping to the higher ground, he moved swiftly on to a point where he knew a rivulet ran alongside a hardened track. It flowed smoothly for about two hundred paces then turned away when obstructed by a stony outcrop. Thus impeded, it swirled over the soft compost to form a small lake, edged by an area of marshy ground full of weeds and long grasses. On his way to this spot he delayed only long enough to pick up a fallen branch, about as thick as his arm and nearly twice as long. It was a poor defensive weapon, but better than none. Only the haziest of action plans had formed in his mind when, as he had hoped and expected, he saw his three adversaries crashing through the bushes on the lower far side of the lake searching for him. Somehow he had to put them at a physical disadvantage, and to do so he would have to utilise his watery surroundings. As they arrived opposite his viewpoint he feared they might crash on without seeing him, and on an impulse jumped up dancing and yelling, waving two slender branches hastily torn from an adjacent birch tree. His sudden appearance and implied challenge so startled and infuriated them that they turned and, with unsheathed swords. charged straight at him. The rearmost, in his haste, trapped his foot under an exposed tree root causing him to fall face down just short of the reeds. That mishap effectively saved his life, if not his sanity. The other two plunged on, hoping to rush across and destroy their tormentor.

It was then that Egen, and the prostrate auxiliary, were to witness the unfolding of events in a way that could not have been better planned by the young huntsman. The still, reflective water was not only deeper than it appeared, but the bottom was more bog-like. The one fact that he had calculated and relied upon was that those well made studded sandals strapped firmly on, such a boon on stone roads and firm paving, would in this situation prove to be a deadly trap. The leader, about one arm's length ahead of his companion, came to a sudden halt as the glutinous mass underfoot quickly oozed over the wide welt of his sandals. It was then impossible for him to raise one foot without transferring his full weight to the other, thus sinking that one ever deeper. With the water, now turned brown and opaque from the debris stirred up from the bottom, swirling about his thighs, he was delicately balanced, feverishly trying to asses the situation and extricate himself from it when his comrade, similarly stuck, but struggling more desperately, dropped his blade, stepped on it with his free foot and fell forward wildly grasping for any form of support. All his flailing hand found was the empty scabbard hanging from the belt of the man ahead of him, which he grabbed and hung on to. Being firmly rooted short of the bank was bad enough for the leading attacker, but to be suddenly subjected to a strong backward pull which threatened to unbalance him completely was intolerable. Unable to turn to see the cause of this new danger, he swung his arm back to dislodge the threat to his uneasy equilibrium. In the desperation of the moment he forgot he was grasping a sword in that hand, the blade of which sliced deeply into the neck of his hanger on. As the stricken body of his erstwhile companion floated slowly away his own situation grew more dire by the second. Vainly, he tried to shuffle forward to throw himself onto the firmer ground ahead of him. At full stretch, his feet unable to release themselves from the cloying mud, his head and hands just about reached across the reeds at the same moment that Egen's improvised club connected with the left side of his head. Now freed from the weight bearing down on them, his feet floated slowly to the surface, and the rest of his torso slid face down back into the water.

The entire spectacle was watched open mouthed and with increasing terror by the warrior who lay prostrate on the far side of the marsh. In any other circumstances he was as brave as his fellows; he had fought shoulder to shoulder with them in the field, thrusting and parrying against an enemy just as mortal as himself. Here, however, in the dappled light of a bewitched wood, where a demon could appear, float above ground casting all too real and very solid spears, then vanish, to reappear later as a dancing tree luring trained imperial soldiers to their doom; this was an experience far beyond his understanding, and even farther beyond the bounds of his courage. Looking up from the two bodies now floating together face down, he saw that same demon resting on its bloodied club returning his gaze. With trembling legs and pounding heart he managed to stagger to his feet and, without looking back, fled south to the fort that he and nine time-served drinking companions had left earlier that day.

His arrival was greeted with laughter and derision as he babbled out his story to the garrison guards – a story of unearthly beings waging war on innocent woodland wanderers – but even in his ravings he managed to avoid mention of the raid on the unknown hamlet. Regardless of how much ridicule they heaped upon him, it could not be denied that ten battle-hardened and experienced fighters had ventured out that morning but only one had returned, and he was now virtually witless.

His mental balance never returned, and to maintain their own self respect the members of the garrison were obliged to scoff at his crazed utterances. Nevertheless, the legend of an avenging green man of the Cantiaci was born. As time passed, it became magnified and distorted in the oft repeated telling. Travellers, whether military, mercantile or other, when nearing that point in the forest which was constantly shrouded in mist, and from which the tormented man was reported to have emerged, never found cause or need to stray from the road and the company of fellow travellers, especially those who carried arms.

No way could this veteran be released into a civilian population as was his due, and it was soon obvious to the fort commanders that having a member of the occupational army ranting and trembling wildly, uttering fears of floating demons, was scarcely conducive to discipline and morale, and deeply damaging to the Roman image of invincibility. He was therefore re-classified as a Gallic slave and chained to an oar in a galley bound for Gaul. That vessel, under the influence of a gale from the north-west, foundered unseen, short of its destination – there were no survivors. The tales of magic, dancing trees and the green man lived on.

3

Chariots and Swords

From his vantage point Egen watched as that representative of the might and power of Rome crashed headlong whimpering and moaning through the trees; desperate to get as much distance as possible between himself and that dancing demon. It would have been easy for the hunter to overtake his prey, but in the long run, although at that moment he was not at all sure how, allowing it to survive in that broken state could prove to be more advantageous. He was also tired beyond measure; with that last lethal swing of his club all remaining physical strength seemed to drain from his body. Sinking to his knees he allowed his forehead to rest against the bloodied branch; he had, after all, despite having travelled a great distance, neither rested nor eaten since setting out early that morning, and the sun had as yet but two hand-spans to move before dipping below the horizon. In all that time he had not only killed his first man but five others also, was directly responsible for the death of another and probably for the complete mental breakdown of an eighth, who even now was fleeing to the protection of his fellows at the garrison stronghold. He had seen his home and village with all its inhabitants, including his parents, completely destroyed. He had lost everything – but perhaps not everything, as he guiltily remembered Josin and Athan waiting for him; he had been away from them for too long.

Forcing himself upright he retraced his steps to the grassy bank where he had surprised the orator and his audience. Discarding the club, he retrieved his father's weapons. They were precious to him now, for, apart from the two persons waiting for him, they would be the only reminders of his life up to today. Previously, he had not seen a Roman warrior up close, but as a boy, from a distant hiding place near to the edge of the forest, he had watched one of their ceremonial parades. As any youngster would be, he had been in awe of the colour and precision, the pennants and symbols, the stamping of feet and beating on shields; today he had seen another side of the makers and guardians of empire, and this time he was not impressed.

Arriving at the still smouldering remains of what had been the village, he noted a new look about Josin. She had rescued a new shift and was wearing it, and she was no longer crying, but a sterner expression had appeared where previously there had only been innocence. Gwain's finest bone handled knife, the only one Egen had ever seen with a bone handle, hung by a cord from her girdle; even so, she did not hide her relief at seeing him return. The pair had not been idle in his absence; the Romans apart, all the dead had been carefully laid within the cave. The raiders' remains had been dragged to one side, and their clothing ripped open to leave them mostly naked. This last action had puzzled Egen, and while he and Athan pulled at the two porch supports to allow it to crash down across the entrance to the cave, he asked why it had been done. The old man chided him gently as together they gathered large rocks to reinforce and cover the cave mouth.

'You have either forgotten or not fully understood my teachings,' he said. 'When a man dies and is buried, the spirits slowly remove the flesh to be stored and purified. At a later time it will rejoin the bones to rise up and enter the kingdom of the sun for a new and better existence. Some believe that by cremation of the whole body that process can be hastened. If, however, the remains are left unprotected to be devoured by wolves, dogs and carrion crows, and the bones are broken and scattered far and wide, that flesh is so defiled it can never be reunited with the broken frame. Therefore, in no way can the spirit, without the body, ever enter the kingdom far beyond the great horizon. Doing what I have done will help speed that scattering, for surely such men as these were completely devoid of honour and deserve no better fate.'

Each having paid their final respects to the dead of that desecrated site, they retrieved the pig's carcase and moved to a clearing well away from the ruined hamlet, where they cooked and attempted to eat it. Josin could manage only one or two mouthfuls; Egen, without any pleasure, satisfied his long fast; Athan, less personally affected and, despite being full of anger, more used to such happenings, ate hungrily. While eating he advised them that after the meal he would guide them to a spot which he had used many times, well west of where they now sat at the base of the extended ridge, a good safe place to spend the night. Josin had had the good sense and foresight to gather up the stored blankets before the cave was sealed.

On arrival, the spot proved to be an overhung depression in the cliff face, not exactly a cave, but almost totally fronted and protected by young birch trees interspersed with large clumps of bramble, quite dry and secluded. Completely overcome with emotional and physical exhaustion, the two young people wrapped themselves tightly in the rescued blankets and, assured of safety by their guide, slept soundly. Their self-appointed guardian never seemed to sleep as others did, but rather dozed lightly, possessing the ability to be fully awake and alert should anything be even slightly amiss. This attribute was doubtless the result of many years of lone travel through dangerous and often hostile countryside. It also allowed him to tend a small fire which provided warmth against the chill night air, as well as keeping unwelcome nocturnal wild life at bay.

At first light he gathered edible roots from the surrounding area, and reheated some of the left-over meat on a flat stone in the fire. He then gently woke his two companions, offering them breakfast and fresh clean water from his skin water bag which he had refilled at a nearby spring. Egen was at once concerned about their next move, where to look for more permanent shelter and safety, especially for Josin. The older man did not allow him to fret further, but informed them that during the night he had given the matter much thought. About half a day's walk south-west from here, not a great distance from where Egen had made his catch was another village, larger but in many ways similar to that which they had just lost. He was quite certain that they would be welcomed and sheltered there. In the absence of any clear alternative, although with some trepidation, they agreed to meet with the villagers and investigate the possibilities. Up to that day they had led a very secluded and self-sufficient existence, not relying on anyone from outside their hamlet other than Athan, indeed not even knowing much of others, apart from a few glimpses from the edge of their woodland and whatever information was given to them by the druid. Quietly and thoughtfully, they picked up their few belongings, smothered the fire with earth and moved south-west.

The old man talked almost incessantly as they walked; he was fully aware of the mental turmoil his charges would be suffering, and hoped his words would help focus their minds on the future rather than the recent past. Much of what he said was a reiteration of previous teachings and prophesies, as well as a description of their destination and the people who lived there. He revealed that it had existed long before their own was begun, that its residents had known of the newer habitation but, under his instruction,s had not shown themselves openly. He had reasoned that, being longer established and owing to their even greater isolation and the protection provided by the dense forest, they were less threatened by the invaders. It also had a more balanced population with a larger incidence of young active men, while the newer had had only Egen and one or two others in that category. Accordingly, they had felt it would be more beneficial to allow the newer settlement to remain undisturbed. Egen, vaguely recognising the area they walked through as similar to that which he had traversed during yesterday's hunt for food, recalled that feeling of being watched while returning home. Those younger males, full of bravado, were often engaged in opposing the new rule whenever the opportunity arose, and they frequently suffered losses. Had Egen and his friends been persuaded by contact with them to engage in those activities, it could have resulted in a much more serious loss for his little commune. Egen bitterly countered that such a loss was now of little consequence to his family and friends; and feeling less exhausted than last evening, the desire for retribution that had goaded his pursuit the previous day reasserted itself.

'If I can do anything to aid the fight to repel these alien monsters I will do it,' he vowed.

This interruption did nothing to stem the flow of instruction, which continued with a repetition of a much earlier prophesy that now startled Egen. As they walked, Josin had remained very quiet; she did not appear even to notice the prediction, much less to be surprised by it. She had always been present during the orations in her father's home where the elders gathered to listen in respectful silence. This repetition of a much earlier portent was merely part of the stored information in her memory and of no particular significance now. But to the young hunter who had been away from the village when it had been voiced, and had not heard it repeated, it held a particular relevance at this time

'It has been foretold that of a direct blood line from a living member of your tiny hamlet would, very many summers hence, be born a powerful leader whose fame will be lauded to the end of time itself,' intoned the druid solemnly.

If true, which Egen did not doubt for a moment, it meant that Josin, as the only existing survivor, would be the certain progenitor of that line. As far back as he could remember he had always admired her and thought of her as special; in any circumstances would have done all in his power to protect and care for her. This new revelation served only to add to the pressure of his self assumed responsibility on behalf of future generations. The fact that he too was of the blood line referred to never for a moment entered his head. That he also was a survivor of the massacre he did not even consider, probably because he had not been present when the main part of the evil had been perpetrated. He had never regarded himself as an important being in the community, despite the fact that all had relied on his work and loyality; he actually felt a sense of guilt that he had been absent when the attack was initiated. In his own mind he was simply an integral part of an extended family, having a duty to help and support it with any particular skills he possessed. The important personages were the elders, and Josin who was always in attendance on them when Athan spoke. Keeping her safe was now his destiny and duty to future generations.

As he struggled to come to terms with these jumbled thoughts, they broke clear of the woodland to see a shallow valley stretching down and away before them. The grass was very long, especially further down in the dip of the meadow where it swayed gently in a westerly breeze. On the far side where the ground rose again, and at about the same level as where they now stood, the trees re-commenced but were much more dense and continued as far as the eye could see. To the east, the undulating grassland swept away to a point where, just discernable, were a few moving figures.

'There,' said Athan, 'is the nearest part of Rome's newest road, being pushed nearer each day towards Londinium.'

Despite their distance from those figures they moved as unobtrusively as possible across the vale to enter the far forest. Reaching the cover of the trees they were met by a band of young men wearing sheathed swords. They appeared to have been expecting Athan's arrival and greeted him vociferously. With this escort they moved deeper into the woods until they came to the settlement they had been told to expect. Both Egen and Josin realised the description they had been given had considerably understated its extent. The roundhouses were similar to their own in size and construction but far more numerous, at least six times as many. This accounted for the large number of people whose curiosity the newcomers found more than a little disconcerting. Situated in the centre of the village was a much larger construction, unlike the others in that it was rectangular, though with a similar thatched roof, and supported by stout posts, but devoid of walls. The building had no additions apart from some rough benches placed at its extremities; it was obviously a communal facility or meeting place. Waiting in the centre of that hall was the council of elders. A thick set man with a friendly smile was introduced as Jodoc, Chief of the Council, who motioned to them to be seated on one of the benches while Athan addressed the council a little further away. He related the story of the young couple's misadventure with all the consequential details and begged shelter for them.

The council did not take long to reach a decision, whereupon Jodoc approached Egen and Josin and spoke for the whole group.

'You are very welcome, as is anyone who opposes the occupation, but doubly welcome is a man who despatches seven Romans by his own hand in one day, and a woman who avenges her father thus, We will do all we can to help you.'

Egen, embarrassed, modestly replied that those that he had killed were witless from the effect of imported wine.

'Not so witless,' Jodoc responded, 'that they were unable to slaughter an innocent hamlet in its entirety. May their flesh be devoured by the dogs of darkness, may their bones be consumed by the ravening bear, may their eyes retain sight to observe their fate.'

This last curse was almost chanted, as if it were an oft repeated incantation. 'Athan, as always on his visits, shall stay in my own humble dwelling. For yourselves there is an empty house vacated by a family who wished to move further west, away from the encroaching enemy and its accursed road. They deemed it would be safer, especially for their two children. I have already given instructions that it be cleared, cleaned and spread with fresh rushes. You will also find there sufficient food for several days.'

This was much more than either of them could have expected and they thanked him profusely. They were then escorted to the entrance of their new home. Athan indicated that they should enter, after which he raised his staff high with outstretched arms and muttered inaudibly for a short while. Once inside, they found not only all that had been promised, but in addition a small fire glowing brightly; even their own blankets and Egen's spears had been placed inside for them. Meats hung from the apex of the roof where passing smoke would help preserve them as it filtered through the thatch.

They spent the first two days learning about their new friends and their customs. They also learned about food which they had not known or tasted before. Among those things were chicken meat and eggs, and, to Josin's delight, a rough bread, a food she could eat with her fingers without soiling them. That bread they learned later was made from grain seized from merchants and as such was in scarce supply. At one end of the site was kept a row of about nine chariots, all lightly constructed, their sides and backs made of wicker and open at the front. Centrally a pole or shaft was fixed to which a pair of ponies could be harnessed, one on either side. Close by were several more either under construction or being repaired. The ponies were kept in an adjoining paddock, enclosed by wattle fencing. These creatures were attractive animals, small with long coats but possessing incredible strength, stamina and speed which belied their diminutive proportions. With them in that same paddock were three larger horses wearing halters which indicated that, like Eadulf's first goats, they had been liberated from Roman domination. Never before having had experience of either type of animal, both Egen and Josin were eager to learn how to handle and ride them, with and without chariots. The young men of the village were only too happy to demonstrate their abilities and would gallop the vehicles repeatedly around a clearing; while doing so they frequently leaped onto the shaft, then to the ground and back without missing a foothold. Even while performing these feats they showed remarkable control of the whole outfit. Such a high degree of skill could only have been acquired by constant practice from early childhood. In no way could the newcomers hope to achieve such agility in a short time, nor could they see, except in very limited circumstances, a practical use for it other than as a form of entertainment or sport. It was, however, apparent that such excellent control of horses and chariots would be very useful indeed, and with the willing co-operation of those young men, both set out to master it as quickly as possible.

It was not many days before Egen was considered sufficiently proficient to take part in a planned attack on the road builders. A chance to strike at the monsters responsible for the deaths of so many of his kith and kin was almost all he had thought about since his arrival. Although equally advanced in these new skills, Josin had to abide by this tribe's custom of not encouraging women to participate in these attacks. Egen returned from that first skirmish both elated and disappointed. The disappointment was due to a number of things he experienced that day which he thought could have been better executed. The attack was effected, as it had always been, by employing two men in each chariot, one as driver and one as a sort of foot soldier. There would be a fierce charge and a great deal of noise and screaming as soon as their quarry was sighted, which was usually a long way off. When almost upon the enemy the fighting man would jump out to attack a chosen opponent, and if he appeared to be in any danger of being overcome his team mate would drive in to hamper his adversary, thus allowing him to jump aboard and escape.

On this occasion Egen was chosen to be driver for a heavy man who was not as agile as most, which caused some near fatal encounters for both of them. Without a sword of his own he was hard pressed to use his newly acquired driving skills to protect his partner. Little damage was inflicted on either side, and the road-building was delayed for only a very short time. His elation was a natural result of heightened excitement from the heat of battle and escape from injury, but it was supplemented by a mass of ideas for alternative methods that he was convinced would have produced a more profitable outcome. His fellow fighters behaved as they had been taught by their forebears; but as a newcomer he saw the whole episode with fresh eyes and he was aware of greater possibilities. When asked, he reported his experience to the elders who were amazed and disappointed that he had been encouraged to take part without weapons of his own. Jodoc at once ordered him to be given a spare chariot to implement his own ideas, and a choice of any of the stored weapons not immediately being used.

Cadeyrn, the member charged with the care of those items, led him to the store and showed him inside. To Egen's surprise, even in the dim light, he could see an abundance of fighting equipment piled everywhere, mostly swords but also a large collection of other weapons. Cadeyrn explained that in most encounters, if nothing else, they were able to capture arms which were then stockpiled here together with locally made items, he then invited him to choose whatever he required as his own. Looking all around the hut and from one side to the other he recognised Roman gladii alongside longer locally made swords, Roman pili (heavy javelins), a few bows and stout staves similar to the one relied on by Athan. In the deeper shadows he noticed a single sword quite unlike any of the others there and moved towards it. On closer inspection, even in the low light, it proved to be a particularly handsome piece craftsmanship. The grip was bound with soft, dark tan leather and gold wire, the pommel large, heavy and well decorated, helping to balance the longer yet more slender blade which glittered in the shafts of light which filtered through tiny gaps in the walls. Distinguishing it entirely from the other weapons was a longer cross-guard which would more effectively protect the hand and wrist; this was intricately decorated with flowers and dragons.

'I see you are attracted to the witching sword,' observed Cadeyrn.

'It is a very fine object,' replied Egen, 'but why do you call it the witching sword?'

'It has earned that name for several reasons,' replied the older man. 'Most admire it, as you obviously do, but will not use it. Primarily because no one knows whence it came. It is self-evidently the work of a master craftsman; there can be none finer, but there is nothing to indicate whether it is of Roman or native origin. It is different from anything we have seen elsewhere, and it just seemed to appear one day when the stock was sorted. It could well be that it was in a bagged bundle freed from an itinerant merchant, but if so it should have been noticed by its length, and if not it should have been discovered when removed from the bundle for stacking. No man admits to having obtained it as a prize in battle, which any of them would have been proud to boast of. Its mysterious appearance alone makes them wary of it. Moreover, it never needs care, never shows marks of neglect, merely requiring to be dusted to restore it to pristine condition – a very useful, though unnatural, attribute. But, more than any of these things, when a small lad, more daring than the others, once carried it out and held it by its tip high above his head, the shadow cast by the setting sun was exactly that of the feared and despised Roman punishment of the crossed trees, on which they affix convicts or their most hated enemies, there to die slowly and in agony. This so affected all who saw it that none have dared go near it since.'

'That being so,' said Egen, 'I will with your permission use it. I can think of nothing better than to turn the symbol of their barbarism against the Romans themselves.'

'If that is what pleases you, take it, although it does not have a scabbard of its own. And if there is anything else you would have, like a gladius or pilum perhaps, take them also.'

'For myself,' he replied, 'I have my hunting knife which serves me well, also my father's spears, more of which I have crafted in the same fashion. The pilum I consider a clumsy implement; it is heavy and inaccurate, suitable only for the type of warfare the Romans have devised for themselves – that is in massed ranks against a close packed enemy where, once thrown, it will almost certainly find a target without the need for careful aim. I do not believe we should play into their hands by adopting their preferred tactics. We must choose our own methods which do not allow our foes to profit from their training. Now I have this,' and he gave the weapon a deft swing, 'I feel happy and secure, but I would like to take that lighter local sword and scabbard for Josin.'

Caderyn showed some concern at this and reminded Egen that it was not customary for women to go on strikes against the road builders.

Egen reassured him, saying, 'We are well aware of that and, in deference to your customs as well as your generosity towards us, she will not attempt to do so. However, since the attack on our own village she has desired a means of self defence. Her little knife would be of use only at very close quarters and she would not wish to repeat that experience but rather be able to keep an opponent at bay. That said, should she consider another type of venture was not prohibited by the conventions of your community, I would find it hard to restrain her, since her hatred for the invaders knows no bounds.'

Cadeyrn was satisfied with this response and stooped to collect the weapon himself.

When Egen returned to Josin she showed herself well pleased. He had chosen well: it was of a size and weight that she could handle with ease. So pleased was she that she worked for him a new belt and sheath, covered in leather almost identical in colour to that on his sword's hilt, and which she embroidered beautifully and skilfully.

The following morning he selected the two-wheeled chariot promised to him by Jodoc. In that first skirmish he had been unsettled by clods of mud thrown up by the ponies' hooves and, having no wish to emulate the acrobatic feats of his comrades, he reversed the shaft, thus bringing the wicker transom to the fore, and adjusted the harness accordingly. Immediately, it took on a more purposeful appearance, more like the descriptions he had heard of Roman racing chariots, which they did not use for warfare. That, however, was not his aim; to be protected from soil and perhaps other flying missiles while in a charge was more important. He also deemed it more practical to be able to dismount from the rear if the need arose, apart from the fact that in a frantic gallop it would provide a more secure handhold for the driver. Taking it in turns as driver and passenger, he and Josin found the new arrangement much more to their liking, more comfortable, manoeuvrable and, therefore, faster.

A few days later he was invited before the council to expand on his thoughts about different tactics for delaying the road builders; they had been observed moving forward at a faster rate and there was a corresponding need to impede their progress.

'I am not,' he said, 'a trained fighter, but I believe my instincts as a hunter make up for a lot and I am concerned that in the past you may have suffered losses which may not have been entirely necessary. There seems to be a lack of firm leadership before and during the attack. It also appears that your men regard an attack too much in the light of a game or sport, which it is not; it is warfare on a small scale, but, nonetheless, warfare on which more lives than merely their own depend. In those circumstances it does no good to concede even the tiniest advantage, and that wild screaming charge does just that. Whilst terrifying to behold, especially when the warriors are bearing down on you, from such a distance it gives trained soldiers time to gather their arms and adopt a defensive stance. We have thus lost the advantage of speed and surprise. We also lose the advantage of numbers when one of each team leaps out to do combat on a one to one basis; here the better armour and discipline of the trained soldier takes over. I believe it would be better for both men to remain within the vehicle. That way the fighting man has the advantage of elevation. In most cases the Roman has only a short sword immediately available to him and to reach up to try to thrust or cut is unnatural and not what they are trained to do. When I hunt for food I do not allow the prey to know that I am there until the last moment, and, if accompanied, I do not send my partner some distance away to watch – we each take part in overcoming the beast. As well as swords, our fighters should be equipped with lances that would give them the added advantages of both reach and height; it is then the duty of the driver to keep his animals away from the danger of injury while sliding or skidding the chariot round close to the face of his opponents. Nearly every one of your young men has more than enough driving experience to do this. We must be constantly aware that the object is to inflict as much damage as possible with the least loss to ourselves.'

'You have obviously observed well and learned much in that one action with us,' said Jodoc. 'We respect and understand your views but they need to be proven. Would you be willing to lead another foray using those ideas?'

'I would not only welcome the opportunity, but be honoured by the trust you place in me,' answered Egen. 'But I would insist that all who go with me observe strict discipline and obey all orders.'

'Then so be it,' declared Jodoc, and the entire assembly murmured agreement.

As he left that meeting Egen found his mind a jumble of confused thoughts. He hoped he had not sounded too pompous or too critical. Nor did he wish to be thought ungrateful for the hospitality they had shown Josin and him. But he reminded himself that they had invited his honest opinions, they had listened carefully and not questioned his views, and they had offered him the chance to lead the next attack without prompting. Surely, he was being over critical of his performance before the council.

4
Athan Departs

On foot Berrim was probably the only man in the village capable of keeping pace with Egen, which was not the only reason he had been asked to accompany him, for although he was liked by all, he was less excitable and had more self control. It was mid-morning and the two made their way eastwards, keeping to the cover of the trees at the edge of the forest. The grass in the open valley to their left was now very high and heavy with seed, and when they got nearer to the road and its builders, provided they kept low and remained quiet, would provide easy and sufficient cover. He was to lead the attack and Egen wished to be certain of the best approach to the site, making success that much more likely. As they loped along he enquired of his companion concerning the conditions of the slaves used in the building programme and why, given the opportunity, they should not free them. Berrim countered that he had partly answered his own question when he used the words 'given the opportunity'; unlike Egen's own experience in his previous home on that fateful day, they rarely eliminated sufficient of the captors to make that possible.

'In any case,' he said, 'few in the work gangs are from local tribes or even this land. They are from beyond the seas. Constructing roads to imperial specifications requires knowledge and experience that few natives possess. Consequently, most are brought here in prison galleys from similar sites in other lands. They would not want to be released. You will see that although they wear the iron rings of bondage they are not actually chained; chains would not allow them to labour well. All that are employed on the road, or any project far from base camp, have chains of another kind: they are selected because they have wives and children who are also slaves and are brought here on the same prison galleys, but retained in the forts and villas of their masters. Should any worker not return, even in the event of death while labouring, those families would be put to the sword or, even worse, given into the care of those that find a perverted pleasure in buggery before disposing of their victims. No rational being would wish that upon his kin. Even if that were not so, to release them would mean that we had a duty of care for them, and we do not have the resources for that.'

'But you took both Josin and me in readily enough, and treated us better than we had a right to expect,' commented Egen.

'That was different in every respect,' answered Berrim. 'There were only two of you. We had a recently vacated home, and you had both proved yourselves, even before coming to us: your hunting and fighting prowess, the knowledge of which preceded you, made you both very welcome. That debate between the elders and Athan while you were made to wait was for appearances only. When he makes a request or suggestion only a fool would deny him. Even as you slept on the night of your ordeal there was contact between him and one of our messengers. If freed, those slaves, with or without families, would have nowhere to go in what is to them an alien land, and if eventually re-captured they would have to face the punishment of the crossed trees. Although the life of a slave is not to be sought after, it is at least life. Provided they remain totally subservient and do nothing to cross their captors they have little to fear: their masters need a constant supply of labour.'

Now the workers could be seen in the far distance and the line of the forest curved away to the south. Dropping low, they moved from the trees into the long, swaying grass and edged slowly forward, disturbing the natural movement of the pasture as little as possible. It took time but, eventually, they were within about sixty paces of the work site and could see and assess the details clearly, including the fact that the road ran close to the woodland on the far side and the higher ground there was obviously very firm.

Egen suddenly stiffened and clutched Berrim's arm fiercely, motioning him to be quiet, and pointed ahead. There, and a little to the left, only a short distance away, a guard squatted in the grass with his back towards them. Screened from his colleagues by a large gorse bush, yet keeping his eye on his comrades and their charges, he was answering a need that could not be ignored. Berrim put his finger to his lips and silently drew the gladius from his belt. Very gently and quietly he crept towards the unsuspecting warrior, then from behind clapped his left hand over his mouth and with the other slid the blade diagonally across his throat. The man momentarily stiffened and thrust up before collapsing face down into the gorse, the whole episode was completely noiseless. Egen edged forward to praise him on the quietness of his action, but Berrim scowled and replied that he should have kept his feet further apart as, without rising, he strove to remove a foul smelling mess from his sandals by rubbing them on tufts of vegetation. They counted four guards, apart from the one now despatched, and fifteen captive workers. Keeping low, they turned east to follow a path parallel to the road so far completed. They covered two thousand paces before sighting the base camp from which the working party must have started that day. Here many more soldiers were overseeing the stacking of stone slabs and other materials by about forty slaves.

'This will do,' Egen said. 'We can now get back to prepare for an attack on the forward party tomorrow.'

'But surely, when they discover the body they will have a bigger force out waiting for us!' exclaimed Berrim.

'*If* they find the body,' corrected Egen. 'That is a vast meadow for a few men to search whilst they have captives to watch. Even should they find him it would be a mystery to them. All previous attacks have been preceded by a screaming charge, never silently as this today. It is much more likely that it will be assumed to be an act of vengeance by a fellow guard for some unknown grudge. It is my own guess that he will not be found. His fellows will not look too assiduously because they will believe he has deserted for some reason of his own. The only way they will trace it back to us is if you do not rid yourself of that vile smell in the first pool or stream we come upon'.

That night he did not sleep well. A great deal of trust was being placed in him by people who, a short time ago, did not even know him; the venture just *had* to be a success.

Long before the sun rose he woke Berrim who had volunteered to be his driver and who also preferred the new arrangement devised for the chariot. Together they woke the ten men who were to take part in the other five vehicles. Breakfast was a quiet and hurried affair, after which he led them to that point overlooking the valley where he had first crossed it with Athan. Yesterday he had noted the closeness of the trees to the road works on the far side. Provided they arrived there undetected, it would be a good starting point for a short charge from an unexpected direction. While it was still dark they made their way across the valley and down to a point inside the line of trees, well hidden but from where they would be unhindered in the initial rush. He had given strict orders that no one was to move a hair's breadth until he gave the signal. No guard was kept on the site when it was not being worked, as this was deemed by its constructors to be unnecessary. The sun rose as a bright ball of golden light merging into a brilliant blue and turquoise sky behind the construction party advancing from the east. Egen realised that had they opted for their previous tactics they would have started the long charge straight towards, and completely dazzled by, the rising sun; it was a fortunate, though uncalculated, feature of his plan.

The advancing group consisted of fifteen slaves wearing shackle rings but no chains, two ox carts heavily laden with stone blocks with two captive drivers leading them, and six armed auxiliaries with a commander. Egen and his men held back, watching as the carts were unloaded and turned around, now with the drivers and one guard all riding on the empty carts. When they were well out of sight and the six remaining soldiers separated to perform their various functions, he gave the awaited signal. Hurtling simultaneously down the short slope and screaming hideously, they were upon a surprised and panic stricken enemy in moments. As instructed, they had each selected a specific target and kept well apart as they drove down on their chosen victim. Seemingly, within a few heartbeats it was all over: four Romans lay transfixed by long spears used as lances; two, having avoided those weapons, had been cut down by long swords wielded from the chariots without any need to dismount – as Egen had forecast, the shorter gladii could not reach high enough to threaten the riders. So short a time had elapsed between the signal to charge and the demise of the last imperial warrior that the attackers were hardly out of breath. Even the horses appeared fidgety, as though expecting more, and the captives were left standing open-mouthed and uncertain.

When the initial euphoria among his men had abated a little, he approached the slaves to assure them that no harm would come to them. It would be obvious to their masters that they could not have taken part or aided in the action, but as he did so one of them excitedly exclaimed, 'Of course not, it will be attributed to flying demons and dancing trees', 'Or even the green man,' interjected another. Not understanding these outbursts Berrim asked them to explain. A legend had grown up among the military personnel and their servants concerning demons, dancing trees and a green man, which story was related to all new arrivals from other parts of the empire, and as naturally happens, it was embellished with each telling and now repeated to Egen and his companions.

Ignoring the exaggerations and fantasies, the similarities between his own exploits after the destruction of his home and the wild story now being related, slowly made Egen aware that it was he himself who was the subject of the legend. That twisted tale conjured up in the deranged mind of the man he had allowed to escape that fateful day was actually having a deleterious effect on the morale of the superstitious army mentality. He was, for the first time, glad that he had not given chase as the man fled. Now a new possibility entered his mind.

Turning to the captives he said, 'Surely you have no love for your captors but, having taken no part in this, you and your kin will fare better if you wait for the relief party which will assuredly arrive later. At what time do you expect it?'

'When the sun is at its zenith,' replied one.

'We have time therefore to enhance the myth, if you are willing. When it arrives, if you behave as though terrified and add to the imaginings of those who spread the legend by reporting an attack of unworldly beings, you could help at least to discomfort them.'

Far from being unwilling, they relished the thought of being instrumental in unnerving their masters without danger to themselves. He then asked that four long, slender branches with armfuls of twigs and leaves be gathered from deep within the woods. When collected he instructed that all their own weapons be retrieved, and those of the guards replaced in their scabbards, and each of the long branches to be sharpened with twigs and leaves still attached, then thrust deep into the wounds caused by the spears. Those bodies that had been downed by sword cuts had twigs and leaves pushed deep into those injuries. As far as possible, thick foliage was scattered all around and the grass brushed to hide ruts left by chariot wheels. While all this was being done a captive, who was broad and muscular with long bright yellow hair, approached Egen asking that the iron rings be removed from his wrists; he struggled with the language and had a strange guttural accent. He said he was so grateful he would come and fight for them. Egen, conscious of the danger to an escapee's family, refused.

'But I have no family,' said the man.

'In that case it is doubly certain that I cannot do as you wish,' he replied. 'You must already understand that if you do not return the punishment will be meted out on one of your companions and his family. I am sure you would not wish that.'

The man did not persist but grudgingly returned to the road. Some of the slaves who had been within earshot of the conversation expressed their thanks to Egen and confirmed that what he had said was indeed true. There would be no question of his being allowed to jeopardise the masquerade; fourteen to one was a sufficient guarantee of that.

Bidding farewell to the workers, they returned home by the same route. Some wished to stay and watch from a discreet distance, but that was ruled out for the simple reason that if unintentionally seen their efforts to sow fear and confusion among the superstitious Romans would come to nought. Berrim managed to persuade them that it would be better to rely on the acting abilities of the prisoners.

Two things had happened that day which made it different from previous forays. First and most importantly, the entire guard force had been eliminated which, if it had been appropriate would have allowed them to release the prisoners, and, arising from that, a slave had requested to be freed from his iron rings, but it had been thought unwise for the sake of the others.

'In any case,' opined Berrim, 'I am not at all sure I would have trusted that yellow haired one. He was a surly brute. He didn't appear to care much for the fate of his fellows or their families, and you may have noticed that he stayed apart from them.'

Having reported the results of the expedition to a more satisfied council of elders, Egen later related them to Josin. Not since their departure from their former home had he seen her so genuinely happy as she was then – an understandably sad and savage form of pleasure.

From that large rectangular building in the centre of the village the quiet murmur of voices grew gradually stronger as more and more people gathered. The old druid had let it be known that he wished to address everyone informally that evening. When all were there he strode to the centre of the assembly and stood for a short while looking around and leaning on his staff. The elders mingled loosely with the congregation, and Egen and Josin found themselves alongside Cadeyrn when Athan began to speak.

'Friends, I thank you for coming,' he said. 'It is with mixed feelings that I speak to you tonight. The movement to which I have given my life has summoned me back to our isle in the far west, the holy centre of our brotherhood. It would seem that it will soon be under severe pressure from our alien oppressors. They are gathering a large force and moving towards our island in a determined attempt to annihilate us. For many seasons I have arrived and departed at irregular intervals, but this time I do not know when, or even whether, I shall be able to return. It shall of course be good to see and greet the brethren once more, yet at the same time I have learnt to love this part of our land and its peoples whom I endeavour to serve. The evil that we all fight, regardless of whatsoever my own fate should be, must continue to be resisted; it is your duty to defend that which the gods have given you. It will surely be very many summers and winters before these lands see the departure of these ignorant savages. Let it be known among you that druidical history tells us that even before the arrival of today's self-proclaimed superior beings, there have been others. There was Caesar, the predecessor of the current invaders, but he was persuaded to leave. Before him were ambitious marauders known as Belgae, and many before that time who envied our fertile soil. It is a continuing struggle and it may well be that the struggle will continue beyond our own lives and those of our children also, and possibly longer, but depart they will, as surely as the lord sun will rise again tomorrow. I do not doubt that even then there will be more.

'At some time in the distant future their stone temples, villas and roads will be nought but crumbling ruins, reminding men of the arrogance and cruelty of Rome. These invaders, it must be said, brought with them a few things which are to be admired, which seduce some of our tribes to adopt their ways and succumb to their rule, but at a terrible cost to our own civilisation and heritage. Their skills in mosaics and statuary are undoubted, but our own skills in jewellery and metal working are far superior. They are unaware that long before Rome was founded we were trading amicably with sea-going merchants from the south. Our true mathematics we were teaching to all, and the relationships between our lord sun, stars and mistress moon and much of what they now use, originated in our land and northern Gaul. They are not originators, but destroyers. Most of their materials and wealth are stolen from other lands which used to be our trading partners. Because they do not understand all these things and our ways they accuse us of being barbarians. We teach by rote but they record with cuts in stone and marks in wax, and because of that we are barbarians. In those cuts and marks already they lie and distort the true nature of facts, and themselves, and us also. They record that we, as barbarians, are not fit to be, that they are great and invincible and the centre of all things; Caesar and the Belgae and others thought likewise. Many from that vast territory beyond the waves covet our misty islands, and would slaughter all in their way to gain them – but we are the barbarians. They do not like our simple roundhouses and communities and use any excuse to slash and burn them out of existence, as they did to the homes of our two new friends – but we are the barbarians. They worship gods that they themselves have made from wood, plaster and stone, and make great stone temples for them. They do not see the living gods all about us in the sun and sky, in the wind, rivers and seas – but we are the barbarians. They do not like the way we execute transgressors of our laws, but they hang their own and their enemies on crossed trees, then torture them and leave them to die in the utmost agony – but we are the barbarians. In enclosed theatres, for entertainment, they throw men to be torn to pieces by wild animals, and set man against man to the death – but we are the barbarians. They elect a man to be their emperor and declare him to be a god – but we are the barbarians.'

He paused and a young man queried, 'Much of what you say sounds like prophesy, as were many of your utterances on previous visits, all of which have since proven to be true. Would it not be possible to make clear the future of these things you now speak of, and see also your own fate in the west?'

'My son,' replied Athan, 'prophesy is something which must be attended with great care; there are many false prophets who use man's gullibility for their own purposes. True prophesy is really just the intelligent application of history and past experience to today's facts to see the way that lies ahead. It may well be, but only rarely, that the gods will help guide the words to inspire that application even further ahead, but they do not manipulate the course of events. It is easy to see that what has gone before, and what is now, will be repeated again from time to time. Those who would today subjugate this land came under the insignia of polished eagles. Whether it be more eagles, or gilded lilies, or broken crosses, or circled stars, to be free we must prevail against them. All are false prophets and revere only power over others. For those reasons true prophesies must always contain some obscurities. Most men, including your respected elders, are too busy attending to today's needs to study the past and what will be. For the brethren it is part of the reason for them to exist, as well as to calculate, measure, teach and preach. The true value of prophesy is to sharpen minds in the short term to help prevent bad decisions today; after all, what profit is there in knowing, or believing one knows, those things that will not happen until long after one's own death?

'But now I do not prophesy or preach but bring information to you about today. Information about matters of which I was aware, but have been confirmed to me by the same source that has summoned me back to Mona. Should any of you be persuaded to seek new homes far from here, as did a young family from this hamlet before the coming of Egen and Josin, then know this: those Britons to the south nearer the shore have many among their number who actively aid the invaders, and they would without hesitation betray those of us who would be free. To the north the king of the Iceni is dead, and his Queen Boudicca expects to inherit his titles and much of his lands. However, it is also believed that Roman power, in accordance with its own traditions, will not tolerate a woman leader, even over her own tribe, as we in this island have always accepted. To the west, in the hills which I must cross, Queen Cartimandua has yet again ousted her husband and king, and in order to ingratiate herself with Rome has taken a low-born man as her consort. King Caractacus, who suffered badly in battle against the imperial army, fled to her for sanctuary, but was chained and surrendered to Rome. All these things you should know to be safe.'

At this point Berrim eased his way to Egen's side and asked to be allowed to talk to him when Athan had finished speaking. They then heard the druid raise his voice to wish a general farewell to all.

Turning to Cadeyrn, Egen asked, 'Should we not give him escort when he leaves to see him safe as far as possible?'

'There is no need,' was the reply. 'He who travels alone is less easily seen, unless he wishes to be. This is especially true for a man as experienced as Athan. With that long staff he is better armed than most carrying a fine sword.' Seeing Egen's frown of doubt he continued, 'Many sunrises ago I was walking with him a great distance from here. We were actually surveying the surrounding territories for any sign of change or new danger to our community. The only thing that concerned us was a new villa under construction, though even that was in a valley in the far distance, way beyond our intended limit of exploration. But as we emerged from the wooded hillside, to our right were two cavalry horses tethered to the trees, and striding towards us came their riders brandishing the longer blades issued to some imperial guards. They were annoyed at being seen, or perhaps just thought to have some easy sport against two old men; either way, blood was to be shed. I hesitated but Athan planted his feet firmly on mother earth, and when almost within reach of their swords he had disembowelled one with the thinner end of his stave and cracked the skull of the second with the thicker part. Both lay at my feet breathing their last before my own weapon had cleared its scabbard. So rapid had been his strikes that I scarce saw him move. It is said by some that it is his hands that taught the bees to move their wings.'

'That,' said Egen, 'would explain your confidence for his safety, but to satisfy our curiosity please finish the story. What happened next?'

Cadeyrn went on, 'We then cut wide the clothing and allowed the bodies to lie where they had fallen. The horses, however, would be a valuable prize of battle and useful to the commune. We went to retrieve them and found them heavily laden with bags of roman coins. Thieves or travelling paymasters – we could not know, but we suspected the former. Coinage is, of course, of no practical use to us. It does not even melt down to a useful metal, and we have sufficient clasps, brooches and such like. We knew this treasure would be lusted after by the military or citizens and we did not wish them to profit from our actions. We therefore dropped the coins into a convenient hole at our feet and covered them with clay and turf. As far as I know or care, they remain there still. I then found that if there is one thing Athan does not know it is how to ride well. He sits like a man whose bones in his nether regions are far too close to his skin, and those horses are the same aged ones you can see today in the pasture.'

The subject of this conversation had begun moving around to make individual and more personal goodbyes. As he clasped hands with this imposing old man Egen was surprised to feel a pang of emotion. After all the brutality he had witnessed, the slaughter and destruction in his home village, his pursuit and punishment of the perpetrators, and attacks on road builders from this commune, he felt he should have been inured to normal human feelings and compassion; he was somehow relieved to find that he was not.

He then moved to one of the long benches below the eaves to hear whatever it was that Berrim wished to communicate.

'Early today,' Berrim said, 'I could not resist the urge to return to the site of yesterday's action. Nothing has been moved, all is as we left it; the bodies still lie transfixed with branches, only the workers have disappeared; even the guard we slew lies undisturbed, other than by hordes of buzzing blue flies. I would have liked to venture further on along the road but was too conscious of tonight's summons. Tomorrow therefore

I intend to return once again and if all is still the same I will this time travel farther to discover whatever is going on at the garrison. I cannot believe that without overriding necessity the commanders would allow this event to go un-investigated. I ask not only for your agreement but also that you accompany me.'

Since the announcement of his older friend's impending departure, a strange feeling of melancholy had overcome Egen. He felt languid and suddenly distant from his own previous resolve, quite lost. He reasoned that it was probably due to the fact that he and Josin were to lose the last human link with their early lives – it would be completely severed. This new home, new friends and companions, could not ease the ache he felt for his former life and family. Although agreeing that Berrim should do as he had suggested, he declined the request to go with him, shrugging off an added feeling of guilt as he did so. For the time being, and against his own logic, he felt only the desire to cling to Josin and their shared memories. He reckoned that with a little rest he could shake himself free of this feeling of apathy. He felt relieved, even better, when it transpired that she also harboured similar emotions. For two days they kept themselves to themselves.

At one stage she vehemently declared, 'In future, whatever you do, I do also, wherever you go, I go too.'

He was alarmed at this and replied that it could, almost certainly would, be dangerous. Above all, he wished her to be as safe and secure as he could possibly ensure.

'What is the point of either of us being safe without the other,' she answered. 'Kind and generous as these people are, it will be a very long time before we are of their community.'

The logic of this he could fully understand and finally, but reluctantly, agreed. That understanding in itself helped him to emerge from his torpor and start to worry about Berrim who had yet to return. Later that evening, however, he did return with news and explanations to offer to Egen and the elders.

'I circled back to the road-works,' he said, 'but nothing other than an increase in the stench, and an obvious interference by foxes, had changed. I then moved quickly towards their base and kept well hidden to watch. There was a great deal of activity, centurions and soldiers of all ranks arriving and leaving throughout the day, until eventually at sunset a group of slaves emerged, watched over by two guards only, and came towards the small copse from where I was watching. I thought at first that I might be discovered, but at about eighty paces from the fort they started gathering wood for fuel. They neared the trees but the two soldiers held back, more interested in the flasks they carried than the duty they were on. This made it easy for me to approach the captives unseen, some of whom I recognised as having been at the road-site when we attacked, including that surly, yellow-haired brute. Quietly and in turn, so as not to be noticed, they described the consequences of our onslaught. Apparently, the ruse worked well: the workers enjoyed behaving as though almost out of their minds with terror. The relief guards looked on the scene and could not move fast enough to get themselves and their prisoners back to the safety of the fort. That same day, however, the local governor had ordered all work on the road be temporarily stopped; he needed to comply with directives from higher authority to muster every fighting man that could be spared for the campaign in the west, that same area for which Athan was bound by a different route to oppose them. Just now the road has become less important to them than the campaign.

'All those relieved from construction duty are being transferred to the river and from there by ship upstream to Londinium. Fresh troops arrive to man the garrison until more reinforcements follow them from Gaul, and they in turn are transhipped; and so the process goes on, much as the adder makes progress over the land. The march to the west is gaining momentum and power; it would appear that the enemy's biggest problem is lack of capacity in their vessels. The continuous change of personnel and their exchange of news and views ensure that the mysterious events and legends attributed to this area are spread and magnified. It is fortunate that slaves are regarded as mere property and conversations take place around them without thought that information gleaned may actually be used against the speakers. Thus we now know, for the time being at least, that the fight is being taken out of our range, that there will be less danger to us when we move about but, unfortunately, we will not be in a position to harass or eliminate them.'

'Not necessarily,' retorted Egan, 'unless we just sit and ignore the situation. Should we travel directly north it does not take long to reach the great river.'

'But what good is that?' queried Jodoc. 'We have no ships or sailors to put up against theirs.'

'Do we need either?' replied Egen. 'We do not know just what we need until we see and assess the problem with our own eyes. After all, Athan was the only one who really travelled; he it was who supplied us with information and we cannot ask him now. I suggest that a small band of volunteers goes to the river to explore the possibilities, and I further suggest that it be soon. I for one do not feel inclined to wait around while the enemy builds up resources to destroy friends and brethren in Mona.'

He realised that the melancholia previously felt was finally leaving him; the urge to resume the fight was now flooding back.

'If we are to do this I feel we should wait no longer than two days, which should give us time to choose and prepare those who are to take part before setting out.'

'I agree that we cannot just ignore what may or may not be going on around us,' said Jodoc. 'That would be to live like Brock, staying hidden and only coming out at night hoping that the world will pass us by. But also I cannot help feeling hesitant; it will leave our hamlet short of young fighting men for its defence if the need arises. So far, to the best of our knowledge, outsiders know nought of our whereabouts, and we should not need to worry. Until now I did not realise just how much we relied on Athan for information and advice; now we must seek that for ourselves. Our raids on the construction site, although useful, have been only as an insect bite to an ox. I do not intend to sound negative; I am merely thinking aloud. With this cavalcade to Mona we need, and owe it to Athan, to do much more. The risks and danger will be great, but the need for information is paramount, and since there appears to be no viable alternative I agree, but please take all due care and do not unnecessarily risk lives. I will call for volunteers immediately.'

It had been accepted without question that Egen would lead the venture. Later, he related the details to Josin who listened attentively, then said, 'I am going with you to be your driver.' She spoke in such a determined way that he knew any argument would be a waste of time and breath.

5

Josin's Ordeal and Imperial Loss

For two days a sense of urgency and frantic activity pervaded the village: the unmistakable sound of blades being ground to a keen edge, harnesses being checked and conversations held in hushed but animated tones – and nearly everyone appeared to go out of their way to smile at him. This suppressed excitement unsettled Egen; he thought he knew what was happening, and he broadcast the message that he wished to speak to the volunteers in the village square. To his amazement, at the appointed time every man and woman without a small child, from the youngest to the oldest, who was capable of carrying a weapon, had assembled there. This was not exactly what he had intended when he first put forward his ideas, but not wishing to demoralise anyone he made his plans, such as they were, clearer.

'I am pleased and proud,' he said, 'to see such courage and determination to serve our peoples. I should, however, have been more explicit about this mission and its requirements. It is essentially as a fast moving scouting foray into occupied territory where few, if any of us, have been and of which we know little. We need to discover new and more effective ways to provoke and weaken the invader, ways to make him wish that he were back whence he came. As far as possible on this occasion we must avoid a direct confrontation in order to be able to bring back whatever information we gather. Should a battle prove necessary, of course, we shall not flinch from it. With this in mind I can take only charioteers, each accompanied by a fighting escort, and in every case those roles must be completely interchangeable.' A sigh of disappointment rose from many but he continued. 'While we are away, and I do not know how many moons that will be, our homes and families must be protected. As you are aware,' he said, with his hand on Josin's shoulder, 'we were absent from our former home when it was razed to the ground by imperial savages. It is something we wish never to experience again. Those who stay are as important to the mission as those I take with me, which will be eighteen warriors only. Will those that are to travel with me now please eat and rest? We need to start before daybreak.'

He was pleased to note that two sets of brothers had not only attached spears to their vehicles but bows also. They were the only men in the community who were considered proficient with such weapons, and it would be interesting to see what part they could play in differing circumstances. Several times he had asked to be allowed to try his hand with them, and although he seemed to have a natural ability he regarded the bow as a device for distant warfare only, not the close skirmishes and hand to hand conflicts they had so far been involved in. He was also of the opinion that, as yet, it needed further development and refinement. The Romans used bows and arrows (and they had captured some of these weapons) but not extensively. The personnel from within those sections which were so equipped all seemed to come from a province farther to the east, and their weapons were made of diverse materials affixed together, materials that were not readily available in this land. They were also distinctive in appearance, having a very exaggerated curvature. The native equivalent consisted of one long stave only and, although very effective, had only a limited life, which in his opinion meant that it required replacement too often. But that was something which could be overcome in time. He often wished he had experimented with it in his earlier days when he was concerned primarily with hunting for food, but at that time he had known of no one who used such a weapon, or could advise on its use.

Earlier even than Egen had intended they were woken by the sound of many half-hushed voices outside their hut. Assembled there were not only the chosen drivers and escorts but also their families and friends to wish them good fortune. Someone passed him and Josin a breakfast of bread, dried meat and milk. Quickly swallowing this, they then set off. On reaching the edge of the woodland he reminded his force that once across the vale and in the far woods any conversation was to be in low tones only. Going north from there they would be diverging slightly from the route by which Athan had initially brought them. Consequently, they would soon be in less familiar country and would not know for sure what they might encounter.

They crossed wooded hills and valleys interspersed with a few flat meadows heavy with dew, which sparkled green and gold in the early light of the rising sun.

From time to time it was necessary to stop according to the demands of nature. For the men it was quick and easy, but for Josin and her need of privacy it required a greater distance from her companions and a longer delay. On one of these occasions, having waited for what seemed to him to be a great deal longer than should have been necessary, Egen called softly to her but there was no reply. Again he called but somewhat louder; again there was no reply. He was now more than a little perturbed and shouting loudly he launched himself in the direction he had last seen her heading, followed by several of the group who had picked up on his anxiety. Soon they arrived at the thinning of the trees which marked the edge of the woodland. A vast grass plain sloped down and away to the west, obviously heavily grazed by sheep as the grass was well cropped. Egen's heart leaped violently: there, far across the open ground, they could see two figures, one of which was recognisably Josin, bound at the wrists and being dragged along by an extension of that same binding, the end of which was looped around the hand of a burly shaven-headed man. She was struggling but made no sound; it looked as if she was gagged. Even at that distance it could be seen that her captor wore the simple robe and large badge of a chief servant or steward of a Romanised household, one who would have been trusted by the owner; much further across the shallow valley could be seen a red-roofed villa.

Unbeknown to the group, the owner of this dwelling was a semi-retired successful merchant who he had been called away to assist with the provisioning and organising of the great march west. His major-domo, suddenly free from irksome daily duties, had given instructions and new responsibilities to the other servants in order to keep them occupied, then ventured out to find new diversions for himself. To his surprise just inside the forest edge he saw a young woman engrossed in adjusting her attire, which plainly indicated that she was a non-Romanised Briton; he also saw that she was completely unaware of his presence behind her. His immediate thought was that she was physically very attractive and would fetch a fine price in the slave market set aside for domestic workers, a fate which was normal for captured non-citizens who could not prove they were not anti-empire. As warily as he could manage he crept forward and with a small rock knocked her senseless. It was part of his usual mode of dress to wear a braided rope wound twice about his waist then over his right shoulder, the loose ends left hanging level with the hem of his robe. He was of the opinion that it gave him a superior and authoritative appearance, and it was this rope that he used to bind her wrists and form the lead before she regained consciousness. He had gained his stewardship not because of his intellect, but through his ability to bully his fellow servants and his fawning demeanour to his master. He never gave thought to how she came to be alone, or whether in fact she was alone; his only consideration was to profit from an unexpected opportunity.

Egen had had the forethought to grab a spear from the chariot before jumping down and charging through the wood to find Josin; his sword swung from his belt as a matter of course. Now his first instinct on seeing the situation was to rush forward, destroy the savage and release her. He realised immediately that such a course of action might prove more hazardous to her than a less precipitous move. He did not know what weapons, if any, the man might be carrying, or what actions he might be panicked into which could result in harm to his captive.

Accordingly, he quietly beckoned to Othris who was acknowledged to be the most skilled of the archers and asked, 'Do you think you can make a strike at that range?'

'Of itself the range is no problem,' the bowman replied, 'but an effective hit will be difficult and I certainly could not guarantee to bring him down. However, Josin, by virtue of that long lead, is far enough from him not to be in any danger.'

'Then please try,' said Egen, 'and ignore whatever I may do.'

He then stood to one side grasping the javelin he carried with him and carefully gauged the range. He judged it to be many paces farther than he had ever thrown before and hoped that Othris would excel in accuracy. He waited and watched closely as the bow's string was drawn slowly back; when he judged it was about to be released he leaped forward with a speed that even he did not know he possessed. The arrow whirred past him and he let out a hideous scream and raised the spear. By this time he had reduced the distance between himself and his intended victim by an incredible amount, and he hurled the projectile high into the air. Never before had he attempted a throw at such a distance and with such determination; at the same time he imbued the missile with as much accuracy and venom as he could muster. It arced gracefully towards its target, higher than the preceding arrow but in the same direction. The big house-servant had not noticed them. He had half turned towards his struggling and jerking prisoner, but hearing the unexpected scream he let fall the rope and straightened up, turning towards the source of the sound. Had he not done so the arrow would have passed harmlessly over his shoulder. His movement instead put him directly in its path. He received it in his larynx and, even as his arms flailed upwards to the source of this sudden and excruciating pain, the second projectile tore into his torso with such force that it threw him several steps backwards; he was dead before his body hit the ground. Having let fly the spear Egen swerved towards Josin without slackening his pace. Nothing could now be achieved by continuing towards the fated man; he had seen the trajectory of both missiles and knew that either alone would have fulfilled its purpose.

Josin, still dazed and confused and suffering from the blow to her head, did not immediately realise that she was no longer being tugged along. She was still trying to understand exactly what had happened, how she could have been so lacking in care as to be trapped in that way. It was then that Egen caught up with her and with palpable relief she fell against him. Steadying her with one arm, he cut away her bonds. She did not cry; he had not seen her cry since that bloody massacre and murder of her father in their former village, but she did cling to him desperately. He then saw the congealed blood in her hair and voiced his concern, but she responded that yes the skin was broken, she knew she had a swelling where she had been struck and also suffered a raging headache, but no more serious hurt, nothing broken, all would go in time with a little rest.

But now was not the time to rest. The mission had been delayed more than enough because of her lack of vigilance. He insisted however on gently binding her wound with a strip of cloth torn from his own clothing.

Berrim, who had never been more than three paces behind throughout the rescue, interrupted with a query. 'What shall we do with the body – and these?' He held up a curious curved wooden-handled knife and a purse of Roman coins taken from the corpse while retrieving Josin's sword and knife.

'The knife please offer to Othris, should he require it,' instructed Egen, 'otherwise to any comrade who may need one.' Then, remembering Athan's example, he went on, 'The body must be completely stripped and left to lie face up where it now is. Roman coins are of no use to any of us, and souvenirs are for those things we wish to remember; kept for any other purpose they are merely useless baggage to weigh one down, better they be thrust deep into his open mouth so that even in death he may choke on his own greed and his chosen master's image. To meekly submit to laws and directives of a foreign dictator from an alien culture is the basest betrayal of one's own self and one's own kind. It is better to die defending your own heritage, kith and kin than to suffer such humiliation. I doubt he will soon be found; we are too far from any habitation. Should he be discovered by man rather than beast it would do our cause no great harm; better still if we remove the arrow and spear and replace them with branches from the nearest trees.'

After all had been arranged as he had suggested, they returned to those waiting with the animals and chariots, and resumed their journey as gently as possible, mindful of Josin's injury, for all within the group admired her greatly. Egen would not allow her to drive but, for the time being, kept control of the team to himself. Meanwhile, he was mentally re-appraising the benefits of the bow: this incident had opened his mind to possibilities that he had not previously considered. From now on he determined to study the capabilities of every weapon known, from the simple sling and stone to the massive Roman ballista.

As evening approached they found themselves on a wooded hillside, having followed the easiest and most secluded path on the western flank. After the unexpected earlier incident they were surprised that they had travelled so far without further problems. They had seen few people and there had been convenient cover nearly all the way. Reaching the highest point of the hill they saw laid out before them a type of landscape with which Egen was familiar. The ground was less wooded and sloped away before them, reaching down to the great river which curled away to the north-west. Land and water met at the base of a large bow formed by the river following its natural course and its banks looked distinctly marshy. Clumps of trees were scattered here and there close to the water's edge, as though on little islands of higher and firmer ground in the sodden soil. By studying the varying shades of green between their viewpoint and the largest clump, which was also that nearest to the water, he calculated an intermittent way down to its cover which should be possible on foot without sinking too deeply into the cloying mud. It was late in the day now and the sun was low, a great scarlet orb, the reflection of which danced from the wavelets in rapidly flickering darts of red light contrasted with long dark shadows. It would have been difficult for a watcher to observe movement from any direction.

Moored on the far side of the river on the upstream arm of the bow, nestling in the reeds and mud, was an ungainly looking galley; further downstream, but on the near bank on the complementary arm of that bow and hidden by it from the first ship, was a sleeker vessel, unmistakably a Roman fighting ship with a long, pointed ram at the prow. Leaving the two oldest and most experienced men in a tree lined hollow to tend the animals and vehicles, they slipped, slithered and picked their way down to that largest clump of trees, only occasionally having to help pull an unfortunate colleague from the adjacent sucking, swampy ground. Now much closer, they could see why the galley across the river looked so ungainly. It was a fat-bellied mercantile craft to which extra side decks had been added, supported by struts from low down on the hull sides. This had apparently been done to allow a much greater number of fighting men to be urgently transported, but it would have done nothing for its stability or handling. It was of the type which under normal circumstances required two steering boards, one on each side. Even so, it would still have been tricky to manoeuvre, especially with the additional human cargo it had been adapted to carry.

On his fishing expeditions with Elred, Egen had not only learned to swim moderately well, but had also learned a fair amount about tides, currents, eddies and inlets which contained still water where fish gathered. Nevertheless, he was not a mariner, and did not at first understand why the two vessels should have moored up so relatively near to their destination. He watched and noted that it was slack water between tides and assumed they had come up river with the flow, and if they had continued they would have been caught by the ebb before getting much further. To work that heavy overloaded ship against the current would have been hazardous as well as laborious. He was unaware that the fighting ship, which would have been much faster, especially under oars, was a ceremonial escort, the commander of which had arranged that at a signal from his own horn blower the improvised troop carrier would head out into mid-stream on a rising tide. The escort would then round the bend, passing on the port side, and together they would sail in line into Londinium. There was no pressing need for an escort but arriving that way would be more impressive and, to Rome, ceremony and show was everything. It occurred to Egen that should the merchant ship not be able to make sufficient way to be effectively steered it might well drift close to where they were watching from the seclusion of the trees, but that depended on its happening before the returning waters gathered enough energy to force it further up river. There was little to suggest, other than its obvious ungainliness, that of itself it would actually have insufficient steerage, but the vague thought that its master would wish to get under way as soon as the flow became evident, and take advantage of the breeze that normally came with the tide suggested that it might happen. While he pondered the possibility of this unlikely conjunction of events he wondered whether it could be made to happen; if so, they would be in a position to rain missiles upon it with little danger to themselves. The whole possibility hinged on the ship's suspect steering ability. These thoughts nagged at him until he was persuaded that he had to try, no matter how improbable the chances of success. Inactivity and trusting in providence were not part of his nature.

To make it happen he would need to cross the river to examine the ship close to. Advising the others of his thoughts and intentions he started to prepare. Josin, feeling the need to reverse and repay what she considered the ignominy of the events earlier in the day, insisted on accompanying him. Scouting around he found a large bough floating nearby which seemed by its appearance to have fallen under its own weight, or been pulled down from the parent trunk complete with smaller branches and foliage attached. Having instructed the others to make as many of the rough spears as possible of the type that he had used in his hunting days, he crawled onto the bough and lay flat to be as inconspicuous as possible; Josin did the same behind him. The water was cold but not numbingly so. She was not a swimmer and therefore afraid, but also determined. Very slowly they paddled this uncomfortable conveyance slightly upstream and across what little current there was to allow it to drift looking as natural as possible to the forward mooring line of the wallowing vessel. Assuring himself that they had not been detected, he climbed gently and quietly up one of the newly acquired deck struts to peer cautiously over the top strake. Auxiliaries and crew lay packed closely together, with the ubiquitous wine flasks very much in evidence. Sailors apart, they all knew that on the morrow they would be re-joining strict military discipline under new commanders for the westward march. This evening therefore they were going to relax entirely, and that meant lazing about in the still warm air and falling into an alcohol induced stupor. After all, there was nothing to fear here – no danger, no threat. In keeping with the general feeling of lethargy, the steering boards had not been unshipped but allowed to hang limply in the water. Close to the deck edge lay a coil of strong rope which Egen was able to lift silently and pass to Josin. While she fastened one end to the nearest steering board he swam with the rest under the keel to loop it around the other. Then, having pulled it tight, he firmly knotted it. Bringing the remainder back again under the keel, he fastened it to one of the side deck supporting struts. Effectively, neither board could be moved, other than as far as taking up the tiny amount of slack between the lashings, nor could the rope be seen as it was hidden by the overhang of the added decks.

Very slowly and quietly they worked their bough back across the river, allowing it to turn a complete circle as though drifting in the eddying currents. Having dried themselves, they sat wrapped in the rough blankets that she now insisted he carried whenever there was a risk of not returning before nightfall. It was a lesson well learned from their first night away from home with Athan, and Egen gave thanks for her acumen. There was now nothing anyone could do but sit, wait, watch and conjecture. In his thoughts Egen re-appraised the circumstances that had led them to be here. There were now, for the time being at least, no enemy road builders to harass; there was no prospect of further advice or information being brought in from outside the hamlet. If they were going to continue the fight against Rome information was something they would have to gain for themselves, and Berrim had started this by his lonely foray into the Roman garrison. It was this expedition's purpose to build on the knowledge he had acquired. So far today they had experienced a brush with the occupation, or rather a collaborator with it, and now, if all went well, they were going to make an opportunist attack on the invader. In one day they were experiencing much, but what they were learning was not as yet absolutely clear.

Waiting was the hardest part. They waited for the tide to ebb fully, they waited for the slack water to change to flow, and then waited for the flow to grow. In the early hours a rasping wail of sound followed by two short bursts of the same noise rent the air from the direction of the war galley, recognisable as the same sound Egen had heard as a boy while watching the ceremonial parade from his hiding place in the woods, and emanating from long circular horns wrapped around the torsos of some of the marching men. Almost immediately, urgent activity was seen aboard the vessel opposite. Still affected by the intake of wine the previous evening, crew and passengers went about their business silently in the manner of automatons, except for the occasional curse as someone or something got in the way of another. The military personnel donned plate armour and helmets, and secured their heavily studded sandals or fighting boots firmly. Three sailors struggled with the rigging and sail while two, having released the mooring lines, used long poles to shove the bows off and away from the muddy bank, then rushed aft to attend to the steering as soon as it should be required. The breeze, as expected, came in with the tide but was so light that it billowed the sail hardly at all. The mist, which hung low over the river, was similarly almost undisturbed. Six men applied themselves vigorously to the oars to pull away from the shore. When far enough away to be taken by the current the two helmsmen leaned into their task, one pulling hard the other merely holding steady as his board was already where it should be. Nothing happened; neither board moved. Totally perplexed, the first leaned back and pulled with all his strength; again nothing moved. His opposite number left his own station to assist with the starboard helm but, inexplicably, it appeared to be locked solid. The master, who in normal circumstances could rely totally on these two most experienced of men, started to scream orders to the oarsmen and cursed the pair struggling at the stern. He did not understand their actions nor their problem, but only saw his prized vessel turning broadside on to the stream; unless corrective measures were soon taken it would not only turn away from its intended course, but find itself backing and drawn to the far bank. By now the fully armed militia packed the main and additional side decks, making it difficult for the working sailors to move efficiently. As each soldier tried to make room for a frantic crew member, he would invariably bring his metal studded sole down onto the toes of his closest neighbour. The shouting and cursing and disorder seemed to be self-generating and caused pandemonium all around. Even the non-sailing military men could not be blind to the fact that something very much out of the ordinary was happening, that control had been lost, and the ship was in trouble; they started to panic. Now that it was across the central stream the swirling currents from the ragged shoreline caught hold, causing it to gyrate slowly and drift towards the muddy south bank.

The warship was out of sight of the merchantman and captained by a man desperate to prove just how smartly his crew could pass the converted trader. It came sweeping around the bend of the river positioned to pass it on the port side as arranged. He was so intent on keeping close to the shoreline and urging his crew to greater efforts, that at first he did not notice that the other vessel was in trouble and much nearer to the south bank than it should have been. In fact, there was insufficient room to make a successful pass. Furthermore, having built up to maximum speed while rounding the bend it was going to be impossible to avoid a collision, even if the speed could have been reduced dramatically. He therefore ordered the helm to be pushed right over in a desperate attempt to pass under the stern of the ship ahead. Had his been another type of galley he might have succeeded, but the vicious ram of a fighting ship projected much too far forward from the hull to allow for that in this situation, and it tore into the planking of the lead vessel just where an added side deck strut had been attached.

They were now effectively locked together, water gushing into the crippled ship and the man-of-war stern on to the muddy bank. A galley such as this was designed to use its ram on open water, allowing it to back off under oars after striking its quarry, but here and now that was impossible. Confusion and chaos broke out on both vessels. Ironically, the shuddering impact broke the rope that had been looped and fastened to that strut. The sudden release caused the steering boards to swing violently, which in turn threw the two helmsmen back in an involuntary somersault over the side rails. That same strut having been wrenched away allowed the improvised side deck to pivot on its forward fixing well away from the hull and out over the swirling brown water; under the weight of the armoured men it cracked and sagged steeply downwards. Once again the inadequacy of footwear designed for firm ground or stone roads showed its drawbacks under these different conditions: the hard soles with metal studs could gain no purchase on the damp and slippery wooden planking, and man after man hurtled down into the curling watery sludge below. Each struggled to remain upright or afloat under the weight of his accoutrements. The first few may just have managed to do so, had it not been that they were struck down by successive comrades falling from that crazily swinging platform. Within moments those few were buried deeply under a massive heap of screaming humanity, thrashing helplessly in a futile attempt to extricate themselves from the sucking mud and their fellows.

Two cormorants that until now had been resting on a small log at the water's edge, disturbed and alarmed by the sudden uproar, rose high and erratically into the mist hanging low over this imperial marine disaster. As they circled uncertainly a flight of iron tipped spears arched gracefully over just below them, and cascaded on to the hapless auxiliaries who were panicking on the central and far side deck, followed almost immediately by a second flight of freshly fashioned spears with sharp, fire-hardened tips, mingling with a number of smaller arrows. These heroes of Rome were so closely packed that few could escape this onslaught from the air. Almost every flying weapon found a human target; any victim who had momentarily glanced upwards, schooled in the superstitions of Roman soldiery, could have translated what he had actually seen into almost anything other than what it actually was – avenging dragons, deities or demons, inhuman beings all bent on destroying them with all too solid and javelin-like branches.

No sooner had that attack subsided than another began on the occupants of the fighting ship. This time it consisted almost entirely of the makeshift spears. At this shorter range they were no less lethal, unleashed from the heart of the group of trees from which they had been crafted. A few more arrows joined the barrage and these were more accurate and deadly, taking out a victim every time.

The hastily improvised transporter, having now taken on huge quantities of water, began to settle heavily in the mud and, being inextricably locked into its would-be escort was now no more than a hulk. Together it would be extremely unlikely they would ever move from this spot again. The men on board both vessels, whether injured or not, had somehow to escape both the assault and the wrecks. The missiles, although diminishing in number were still killing and maiming many. Of those who jumped into the water many found, yet again, that the soft oozing mud trapped their sandalled feet. The shoreline and shallows, along with the wrecks, were littered with the dead, dying and injured. Even those who had somehow escaped injury were having great difficulty reaching safety on firm ground.

Egen stepped forward from the cover of the trees. It was all over. The noise, screams, shouts and curses continued, but the last of the shafts had been launched and the last arrow had flown its course. Any further action against these particular invaders would have been a waste of effort and weaponry, so he raised his arm to signal an end to the attack. Alongside the agonised screams the flowing and growing waves swished their passing. The tortured timbers of both wrecks screeched, groaned and cracked as they resisted the increasing tidal pressure and sank deeper into the ooze, the rigging and sails adding to the cacophony as they slapped about uselessly in the breeze.

The young villagers gazed in awe at the dramatic result of their improvised ambush, varying emotions churning within them. What had begun as a simple opportunist attack to discomfort an unwary enemy had ended with the destruction of two very valuable vessels and numerous Roman casualties. It represented a very serious loss to the occupying power. There had been no loss to themselves, not that they had expected any, as there had been no battle as such. Under Egen's direction they had, from a safe position, taken advantage of a situation that had presented itself. As far as they could see no more than six reluctant voyagers had been able to reach reasonably firm ground, and they were totally exhausted, their legs barely able to support them. It was inevitable that when these survivors came to report their experiences, not only would their reports differ one from the other, but they would be treated with contempt as either cowards or demented deserters, very similar to the treatment received by the lone survivor from the attack on Egen and Josin's village. There are never harsher critics than those who have not seen or experienced the event. Those ravings, nevertheless, would reinforce the tales of green men, dancing trees and flying demons in the susceptible minds of men newly posted to a distant, mist-shrouded island. Regardless of what those critics might say, there could be no denying the similarities between this reported incident and at least two previous happenings.

Returning his gaze to the area nearer to where he stood Egen beheld a scene of total carnage. The dead and dying lay everywhere, none of whom could have been reached, even had he wished to do so; the soft sucking mud was ready to swallow anything that weighed upon it. Yet, as he looked, all that he saw was the picture of his mother and father lying slaughtered in the village square. While that picture was still fresh in his mind, as it would probably always be, he could feel no remorse.

Forcing his thoughts back to the present, he ordered any equipment that could be salvaged to be collected for future use. He was thankful that he had left his father's finer javelins with the chariots, as he valued them and did not wish to lose them. The younger men were still unable to contain their feelings; the excitement of action would not subside easily. They stumbled back across the quagmire; they whooped and shouted and often slipped from the firmer ground. This is not what Egen would have wished for and he determined to instruct them later. His instincts as a hunter rendered him more aware and experienced than these companions. Even now he was certain that at some time in the future they were going to have to engage an enemy not only larger in numbers than themselves but better equipped and trained, and not necessarily at a time and place of their choosing. As a consequence, he intended to teach them self-control and form them into an attacking force which could appear unexpectedly, cause havoc, and then melt quietly back into the shadows, a combination of what they had been doing previously and the ambush they had carried out today, but more organised and disciplined.

They climbed back to where the men with the ponies were waiting, and the whooping and shouting died away, for the climb back was steeper than it had appeared on the way down and their breath was needed to cope with the ascent. Without exception, all were near exhausted from the day's events and Josin in particular was suffering from the added stress of her head wound and the cold and wet of her trip across the river. Egen did all he could to help her until they got back to the hollow and she had a chance to rest. He insisted that everybody ate at least a little before they dozed or relaxed for a short while. Although they had had an action packed day, he was conscious that the main purpose of the trek had not yet been achieved. Athan had advised them of the numerical superiority of the militia and the size and strength of their settlements, but until he was able to see for himself such things were not easy to imagine clearly. Burdened with the responsibility of the expedition, his thoughts were racing in all directions; he could not rest easily.

After a reasonable time had elapsed he woke Berrim and asked him to take charge, but to allow the men to rest for as long as possible to get over their varied emotions, yet also to post sentries and ensure that they were alert. Finally, and perhaps most importantly, he urged him to watch over Josin. Taking with him the two men who had stayed with the ponies during the action, Sild and Ragnan, who were more mature and less excitable, he intended to reconnoitre further up the river; should none of the three return before the moon was high, Berrim was to lead the group back to their homes.

All three made their way west, parallel to the river, keeping to the higher ground and the cover of trees and shadows. As always when travelling in unfamiliar territory, he kept looking back to memorise features in order to make the return route that much easier to find. Just as the old druid had promised, the landscape flattened out and the woodlands thinned. Also, as described, here and there they saw small huts badly constructed of varying materials, obviously used as homes but none looking as roomy, warm and comfortable as their own roundhouses. They observed only a few isolated people from a distance, apparently foraging for edible plants and berries. Going in opposition to the flow, they saw that the great river turned gently to the right, then straightened out, and there on its banks much more activity was evident.

To avoid being seen they crossed a well trodden track to move to the top of a small hill where they lay prone to watch. On the far side of that hill was another track coming from a more westerly direction which merged with the first to run on to a point on the river bank where a landing stage had been erected. Several small boats moored at the stage tossed gently on the grey wavelets. On the far bank a similar landing site marked the beginning of a settlement stretching far to the north and well to each side. The town was bisected by a fine stone road which ran north-east and, by repute, directly to Camulodunum.

To Egen, who had lived his life in secluded hamlets, the whole thing appeared vast. He had not really been able to visualise such a town from previous descriptions and began to appreciate the enormity of his ambition when he remembered that this was supposed to be merely a port en route to the Roman capital and small by comparison with it. He saw an arched stone gateway astride the road just beyond the landing stage; stone buildings divided up into small houses and shops ran in long continuous blocks on either side of the road and narrow streets were formed between the blocks. To one side three larger, more imposing buildings surrounded by wider streets on three sides and with a large open square on the fourth were obviously a barracks and administration centre. Either side of the river substantial wooden posts had been driven into the banks and well braced. These he knew were the beginnings of a substantial bridge which was intended to connect the southern tracks to the northern road. An earlier, more flimsy construction had been swept away by a freak storm. Moving about the streets and harbour were many people, some in military garb and others wearing simple smock-like clothes.

Reality having been given to his previous imaginings, he motioned his companions to withdraw with him. While returning cautiously and silently they surrounded a terrified forager, a middle-aged man, to question him about activities in the town. It transpired that two vessels transporting reinforcements from the coast and expected early that morning had not as yet arrived.

'Did you not see,' he enquired, 'beneath the gateway arch a squad of military musicians, accompanied by several centurions of high rank?

They were waiting as a reception and to take command of those being brought in on those ships. They are puzzled and unhappy at the delay.'

He further told them that many fighting men were being called back from Camulodunum and smaller posts in the north-east to gather in Londinium to supplement the great march west. That march was itself being constantly harassed by elements of local tribes. It was generally opined that the capital was being dangerously denuded of protective forces, but the governor and most commanders were convinced that destroying the druidical organisation was a major priority; unreasoning fear and hatred of druids obsessed their thinking. Each evening a Roman official would mount a rostrum near the gateway to harangue the citizens. Without evidence or knowledge, and with great exaggeration, he would attribute all evil to supernatural powers supposedly possessed by the Celtic priests. He would then display artefacts, also supposedly captured from the brotherhood – robes, sickles, mistletoe, staves and spears – and burn them in what was referred to as 'the cleansing fire' outside their temple.

'In truth,' the man told them, 'if all they burn belonged to Celtic priests, there would have to be more priests than the entire population of the land. But perhaps that is part of their magical powers: as one is killed two appear, in which case it would be a pointless task to try to eradicate them.'

'How do you know all this?' asked Sild.

'Because I am a ferryman,' he replied. 'I own one of those small boats moored at the stage, which, while I am away, my son watches over. Romans talk loudly and freely among themselves while being carried across the water; we are, after all, merely a part of the boat to them. It will be a sad day when they complete that bridge; our living will probably dry up completely.'

'Why not burn it before then?' queried Ragnan.

'It is obvious that you live in remote seclusion,' said the man 'They would crucify many, guilty or not; one does not needlessly anger the army.'

At this comment Egen's mind flickered back to Athan's 'but we are the barbarians' speech.

But the man continued, 'It is well for you to remember, you who live hidden but free and stamp hard on the earth on which to build your round houses, that Rome stamps hard on mankind to build foundations for its empire and is not discriminatory in its choosing. Romans do not like roundhouses, they are not of their style; they regard them as a form of independence from Rome. That is why we do not build them here. They would be destroyed as soon as erected – or before.'

With a friendly word, for that is all they had, they left him to continue his foraging and, slipping into the cover of the trees, arrived back with the group a little before sunset. They were all rested but Josin still suffered a bad headache. However, they were also all eager to make their way back to the village, as each had a tale to tell his family and friends, but Egen made them wait for complete darkness.

The sun was at its zenith by the time they crossed the low lush valley which in Egen's mind formed the boundary between home and the outside world – the place where Athan had first indicated the approach of the new Roman road, the construction of which had been temporarily suspended. Nevertheless, he had a feeling of foreboding as they advanced towards their homes. The northern woodlands from which they had just emerged were as usual full of the sounds of nature, the snuffle and rustle of small mammals and the calls of birds. By contrast, the southern woods which they were just about to enter were unnaturally quiet, the only sounds being the breeze in the trees and the occasional lazy, disinterested caw of a crow perched high in the quietly rustling foliage. All sensed the unusual silence and hurried forward in a hushed but urgent manner with their hands on their swords.

Suddenly, a squeal from one of the village women startled them as she rushed out from the cover of trees to their fore. Sobbing hysterically, she explained that they had been attacked in their homes.

'Thanks be to the gods that you are returned,' she sobbed.

Within moments others appeared, sharing her distress and confirming her story. At this point Berrim took charge and tried to quiet them, he demanded that a full account be given as calmly as possible. They explained that with only a hurried warning shout from a young look-out, quickly suppressed, a large group of armed men, comprising a few Roman militia and a larger number of Atrebates, had rushed into their midst killing all within reach and destroying their houses. Fortunately, the majority of older inhabitants and children had managed to flee and hide, while the younger men, taken by surprise, attempted to fight back, but with the lack of time to take up appropriate weapons they were driven back on to a narrow path entering the palisade which defined the village perimeter. Caderyn, who was the only villager permanently to wear a sword (more a badge of office for his guardianship of the armoury than anything else) despite his advancing years leaped forward, took command and ordered the younger men to retreat into the woods to guard the women and children while he himself held back the attackers.

'The last I saw of him when I looked back,' said one of the younger men, 'he was fighting like a demon, leaping and slashing from side to side more in the manner of one half his age. Even if he had actually been that he would not have been able to overcome those odds. He deliberately gave his own life to save ours.'

'How did they manage to get past your lookouts?' asked Berrim.

'As you know,' answered another, 'on the south side of our enclave there is a break in the palisade where each end terminates on a projecting ledge, below which the ground cuts back and drops sharply, then recovers much further down into a large meadow, for the most part bounded by trees with a small river on the far side. It has always been a bone of contention whether it was worth keeping a sentinel there at all, owing to the impossible climb from that direction. The night before last, because of the shortage of experienced fighting men, we stationed a young lad at that point. The climb must be less difficult than we thought, although it could only have been achieved by one or two persons at a time, building up gradually to a larger force. Whether the lad dozed or not while they gathered we cannot be certain, and as he is now dead, struck down from behind even as he shouted his warning, we shall never know, but it was his shouts which gave us the first alarm.'

'To give less care to any approach, whatever the reason and however improbable, is a mistake,' interjected Egen. 'But that sort of error is understandable, and one that will no doubt be repeated in other circumstances and at other times. It should be an integral part of our thinking that where one man can stand, sit or stay, another can also gain that space, the only question being how.'

Josin, remembering the circumstances of her own survival in the attack on her former home, urged them to hurry to inspect this atrocity as some could still be alive and needing help. As they approached the hamlet Egen's anger rose: bodies were strewn about, battered and bloodied. It was all too reminiscent of the scene which had confronted him, seemingly many moons ago, when he had returned from that hunting trip. This time there was no burning but every building had been pulled down by hand, and he surmised that the raiders had not wanted attention to be drawn to their activities from afar. His anger reached new heights when he saw the body of Caderyn sprawled on the ground, face down, still clutching his distinctive weapon, the blade of which was buried deep in the torso of one of the invaders lying close by. From the relative positions of the bodies it would seem that the old man had managed a successful thrust but, almost simultaneously, had been struck down from behind.

'How did they know where to find us?' queried Egen aloud of almost anyone.

'I think I know the answer to that,' said Berrim, 'and it is unlike you not to notice the unusual. That fellow digesting Caderyn's sword point – do you not see that he is yellow haired? The same man who was at the road site as a slave when we attacked under your leadership, and again present when I went alone to the Roman post and talked to the slaves. On both occasions he was wearing the iron rings of bondage which he asked you to remove; he is not wearing them now. I would guess that he followed me at least part of the way on my return, made an intelligent calculation of the remainder and sold that information to his masters in exchange for his freedom. He would have gained little, for he would have had nowhere to go that would have welcomed him. He would have become merely a camp follower, no longer even fed a slave's rations and having to beg for scraps and leftovers. They would have used him in the raid to ensure they were in the right area. Having little to lose, he would have joined in the assault on our homes. In effect, he would, without the iron bangles, and with less to eat and drink, be working for the same masters.'

'I must confess that in harbouring so much anger I had not noticed the traitor's yellow hair,' said Egen. 'But it does not seem so unusual to me, for somewhere at some time I have seen his like before. I cannot now remember where or when, but it will return to mind one day. Where now are his masters, the victorious masters of the universe?' he asked bitterly.

'If you refer to those who perpetrated this savagery,' said one of the young warriors who had been present during the assault, 'I have scouted about and you will find them camped in that field far below the ridge, the Romans to one side and the Atrebates to the other. They slaughter together but will not mix or eat together. It is evident they do not believe that any of us would remain here, and especially not that we would be joined by returning comrades.'

'Then as quietly and unobtrusively as possible,' ordered Egen, 'cover our dead while we consider our reprisal. Do not on any account cover the remains of the enemy. Remove any armour they may be wearing and cut open the clothing. How many are they?' he asked, as the germ of an idea came into his head.

'Two Roman militia, four Atrebates and one ex-slave of indeterminate origin,' was the reply.

'Then take all seven and, without being seen from below, lay them close to that ledge over the meadow whence they entered our village.'

While this was being done he spoke to each person or family in turn and a course of action was agreed. All, without exception, wished to return the savagery visited upon them. Some of the younger men wished not to waste time as they saw it, but to repay the violence immediately. He reminded them that since he had led them not one casualty had been inflicted upon them, other than a sprained shoulder by one who had hefted his spear too high and too hard against the enemy warship. It was a record that surely could not be kept but he would not break it unnecessarily. It was also true that villagers had died, but not as a result of an action he had planned and initiated. This compared favourably with the rush and slash tactics employed previously, which usually ended with at least one death and deep wounds for many.

'It is now nearly dark,' he said, 'and who knows what mishap may occur. A planned action has more chance of succeeding in the light; if we stay with an agreed plan we may all manage to emerge alive. Rush and slash can be of use, but only where the opponent is at a distinct territorial disadvantage or unaware of your presence nearby – preferably both.'

If successful, they could then move on; their lives here had been destroyed and would have to be resumed elsewhere. Following the hoped for destruction of the foe below the ridge, a few of those young men without families expressed the desire to join those bands already harassing the westward march.

'That is your choice,' he said, 'and I would not wish to interfere with it, but please be careful. We have lost too many friends already. Remember that until all the tribes of this land unite, develop discipline, train and agree on a common cause we stand little chance of freedom. Your joining them may speed that unification process. Our limited successes here without injury are because we have used ambush as our main weapon; in the open field against Roman tactics we would be annihilated. It is my duty to get the main part of the community, from the eldest to the youngest, to unite with the Iceni as they now wish. They have been made well aware of the troubles there, but the Iceni are a tribe of large family groups all working and fighting as one.'

Now the plans had been formulated and decisions made, twelve charioteers were chosen to prepare six vehicles. Axles were freshly lubricated, wheel rims and hooves heavily padded in soft materials and ponies lightly muzzled. When ready, they moved apart, three in either direction, moving in two wide arcs away from the site and down into the woods on either side of the vale. Once there they waited, hidden and silent, for dawn and a prearranged signal from the ledge.

The early light eased its way above the far horizon and a solitary Roman guard stood by the central fire leaning heavily on the thick shaft of his pilum. He glanced enviously at those sleeping deeply and noisily on either side; his own eyes were very heavy and it was difficult to keep them open, a condition not improved by the surfeit of wine consumed the previous evening. He turned his back to the fire, drew his cloak closer about him and gazed at the higher ground and shadowy ridge. Suddenly, he was startled into wakefulness by a screeching horn coupled with a scream, followed by the blurred vision of a body, similar to that of a bright haired camp follower who had been with them a day or two before, hurtling outwards and down from that same high point to hit the ground at the edge of the field with a sickening thud. In the shadowy semi-darkness he could not see that it had actually been thrown over by two of the strongest from the hamlet. Moments later he was confronted by comrades and allies asking questions for which he had no answers and accusing him of being asleep on duty. Three of the tribesmen, shaken into foolhardiness and convinced that not more than one or two escapees from the attack on the village would have the temerity to return and retaliate, rushed directly to climb that difficult way upwards with swords swinging loosely from their waists. As they scrabbled higher, foot- and hand-holds diminished in such a way that they were forced into single file, one almost directly behind the other. Slowly another body, this time of a fellow Atrebate, rolled gently over the crest and struck the highest man, sweeping him down into the following pair. All four flailing bodies slid, rolled and bounced downwards, swords snapping and bones breaking, to come to rest near to the spot where the first flying corpse lay.

When it became obvious at the start of their climb what the three were attempting to do, the men below had gravitated into a tight group near the fire to watch. Only one of the climbers, partly cushioned by the other two and the corpse, was able to crawl away with a broken ankle, and a spine that felt as if it should have been. Whatever else might happen subsequently he would be in no condition to react. The group by the fire, while trying to ascertain the cause of the climber's misfortune, next saw a dark cloud that could have been a swarm of starlings, ascend slightly above the ridge and swoop down towards them. It was a heartbeat or two before they recognised that, far from being anything to do with birds, it was actually a close packed flight of spears and arrows descending on them, given extra impetus by the height of their launch.

Pandemonium erupted as the watchers attempted to flee in different directions. Other than those on the outer edge of the gathering, no one managed to move more than a step or two without being impeded or tripped by his neighbour. Consequently, most were wounded, either fatally or seriously. Those who had escaped injury flew in all directions, searching for shields or protection of any kind. Responding to a signal from the launch site, three chariots burst from the trees on each side, cutting down the running men, wheeling and racing to ensure that few got away.

'Like hay before the sickle,' chortled one of the elders watching from above as he helped to manhandle the remaining bodies over the edge of that drop.

Only one Roman found a hiding place in the woods, while two Atrebates managed to reach and cross the river. As instructed, the charioteers did not attempt to pursue them further; if plans were to reach fruition there was insufficient time for a chase. They then made certain that any foe who still breathed did so no longer; by the time those from above had made their way down the work was complete. It now only remained to claim anything from the site that might be of use on the trek. This included three light wagons, complete with six ponies and three Roman cavalry horses, all of which were straining terrified on long grazing tethers.

Josin and others collected enemy weaponry and threw it into an agreed spot in the river. In answer to a query from a young boy she replied, 'No, they are not intended as an offering to the gods, although I do know that is a practice adopted by some. Should the gods have use of them, they are welcome to have them. However, to be of true worth an offering should be something of one's own which the giver would otherwise desire to retain. In this instance, once our friends have recovered spears and arrows that they value, we have more than sufficient equipment of our own loaded into the baggage wagons, and there is little point in unnecessarily burdening ourselves for the journey. We cast these things into the deepest part of the river overshadowed by the tall reeds on either bank, in order to put them out of sight and reach of itinerant rogues or murderers who may pass this way and do not wish us well.'

She ushered the boy back to his family while Egen took another look at the corpse with the yellow hair and shook his head; although it mattered little, he wished he could recall where he had seen another who looked similar.

6
The Trek North

In the past Egen might have thought he had had some difficult tasks to perform, but now he was experiencing one of the most frustrating yet: not fighting, not hunting but simply trying to get this grieving confused community moving, to put as much distance as possible between it and this scene of carnage and despair as soon as possible. It was now late morning and all had previously agreed that it would be foolish to remain. Their location was now known to outsiders, their homes had been destroyed, and sooner or later allies of the attackers would come looking for them when they did not return. It was conflicting emotions that created the problem. He reasoned, pleaded, cajoled and used harsh words, but was unable to get some of them to move more than a short distance away without rushing back again. The case for speed was obvious, but to wrench themselves away from wrecked homes, memories and the remains of relatives and friends whom they had so recently lost was almost too much for many.

Eventually, he managed to persuade the majority to move on, calculating that those who remained, feeling their utter isolation, would catch up with the main group of their own accord. In this he was proved right, but he also arranged for constant checks to be made to ensure that none were separated or lost; he remembered well the anxiety he had felt when Josin disappeared on their mission only two days ago. He also arranged that the most infirm and aged without their own carts or wagons were given the opportunity to be carried on others' vehicles or horse litters as much as possible. He had no certain knowledge of the route, but knew they must travel in an enormous half circle to avoid Romanised settlements and to meet with tribes and families massing with Boudicca's Iceni. He constantly searched his memory for scraps of information gleaned from Athan's travel stories to help lead him in the right direction.

Very soon they reached that shallow valley between the north and south woodlands and crossed it for the last time. He wondered whether the lone crow croaking mockingly behind them was the same one that had greeted them on their return the previous day. When all were safely across he again directed them in a westerly direction towards unfamiliar country. He allowed them to separate a little to ease progress through the trees, but made sure he kept runners in contact with them all. Mentally he gave thanks that none of the experienced and skilled wheelwrights had been harmed; they travelled alongside and carried the tools of their trade with them, from which none would have been parted until death overtook them. Some of those tools also made excellent defensive weapons. On such a journey over rough and difficult terrain, their skills would almost certainly be required often.

At about midday the four would-be 'great march harriers' stated their intention of leaving to search ahead, in the hope of joining those fighters already harrying the enemy. Despite feeling apprehensive, Egen could see no reason to detain them further. The only words he could use to aid them were, 'See others before they see you, approach all unknown with caution, and may the gods go with you.' They then loped ahead, obviously excited and with light hearts. Although it might seem harsh, he insisted on continuing the trek by the main group in the same direction for another handspan of the sun's movement before allowing a short rest to consume those meagre rations they had been able to salvage from their ruined homes. None had really needed the advice offered by Josin to also salvage at least one woollen blanket each. He then turned the march north, deliberately creating a zig-zag route in order to confuse possible followers.

They had not travelled much further before the forest thinned and ended in a small plain grazed by a multitude of sheep. These animals appeared to be without any sort of shepherd and ranged uncontrolled across the entire grassland. It was noticeable, however, that much of the plain, which sloped upwards to the right where the woodlands started, had been deliberately cleared for grazing. Where the terrain was lower it was also considerably more level and a Roman style villa had been built there. It was white-walled, red-roofed, inward facing and constructed around an immense courtyard. Voicing his thoughts aloud, Egen had the impression that although he had not been here before it somehow appeared familiar. Berrim assured him that indeed he had seen it before but from afar, from the top of that hill on the day that they had rescued Josin from the white robed thug. He had probably been too concerned then to visually memorise the surroundings, now they were much nearer and had come upon it from a different angle.

A rough picket fence completely surrounded the buildings. The wild grass and vegetation outside that fence, which the sheep had avoided, was very tall, but within it was fairly close cropped. A walled garden was contained within the complex, but of more immediate interest was the wisp of smoke curling up from beyond the courtyard walls; otherwise, there were no visible signs of life. Berrim and two others volunteered to investigate the interior while the rest of the assemblage remained hidden within the forest, from where they could observe their progress. Using the wandering sheep and then the long grass for cover, they reached the fence apparently undetected, lightly hopped over it and disappeared into the shadows on the longest side, towards the doors which had to be situated at the far end. As time elapsed Egen began to wonder whether he should send in a rescue party, but just as he was about to do so the three volunteers appeared leading a fourth unknown individual. When closer to the company, which had started to emerge more confidently from their cover, that fourth person was seen to be a very pale, very undernourished youth dressed in what could only be described as rags.

'The doors were unbarred and slightly ajar; this was the only occupant,' explained Berrim. 'We found him cooking a piece of meat over a small fire. We have questioned him closely and searched the building thoroughly. He says his name is Orin, and that he lives with his parents in a hovel far beyond that wooded rise to the west. He claims they are too feeble to move as a result of a strange illness contracted a long time ago. The villa has many painted rooms with tessellated floors, and at the far end are store rooms packed with foodstuffs: preserved meats and fish, olives, grain, oil, wine and other things, enough to feed a small army – or an entire hamlet – for many days.'

'It probably will yet, very soon,' said Egen.

Berrim continued, 'In the outbuildings, apart from stables and agricultural equipment, is yet more food being prepared for preservation. This lad's story is that, about a lunar cycle back, his master, the owner and retired merchant, was called out of retirement to help with the logistics of the great march west. He set out with his family in the direction of Camulodunum. Judging by the amount of food available here they must be a very fat family. The hated major-domo who ruled the other servants with a rod of iron, had taken the opportunity to wander and amuse himself in the wider surrounding area. After he failed to return a couple of nights ago, a search was instigated by the junior slaves who found his body stripped and pierced in two places by slender branches and leaves. This discovery created panic, for when the merchant should return he will be certain to accuse them of the deed; consequently, taking small easily carried items of value, they fled. This poor wretch used to arrive at dawn to clean and set the fires that heat the building, tend the garden and small animals and help with the horses. He would stay until sunset, all in exchange for a few scraps of unwanted food for his parents and himself. Each morning since the departure of the household servants he has returned to continue to feed himself and his parents though taking only a minimal amount.'

'Do we have reason to doubt his words?' asked Egen.

'His appearance supports all he says. I have no difficulty in believing him,' replied Berrim.

Egen turned to the boy. 'You will stay here with us tonight,' he said.

He then instructed the entire gathering to enter the villa. Never before had the building accommodated so many, but room was found for all.

'In the meantime,' he said to the youth, 'find some suitable clothes or material to cover yourself with to keep warm, also some sandals that fit – there must be many stored here and you should know better than us where to look. On the morrow you will take all the food you can carry to your home, after which do not return for by then this iniquitous place will not exist.' He then enquired, 'In which direction did your master go, and how would he have crossed the great river?'

The youngster answered, 'Anyone who wishes to cross the river without the use of boats must go north-west from here, over those two hills yonder and meet the waters between two bows of the river. At that point the stream is young before the many tributaries join it to make it great. It is not so deep and a bed of stones has been deliberately laid there, making it possible to cross with wagons. However, on the far side is built a small wooden fort, a Roman checkpoint manned by some twenty or more auxiliaries with a centurion visiting often; they control all movements over the crossing.'

Ragnan, who had been standing quietly listening. was incredulous at the amount of detailed information offered and asked, 'How do you know all this, boy? Have you travelled there? Have you seen all with your own eyes?'

'Never,' replied Orin, 'but my master speaks to his guests and companions with a voice that is as loud as he is fat, and to him I am nought but dung upon the grass, to be noticed only to be avoided lest I should soil his sandal. I rarely speak, but overhear much; my memory is filled with pictures and information from the words of others spoken to others. Those pictures I retain in my mind and allow them to occupy my thoughts instead of conversation. Some day I may have a chance to leave here and see the outside world. Should you wish to cross the river at that point, there is little chance of meeting with him as he planned to go thence to Londinium, from where he will re-cross by boat in order to return here. I heard him planning the route with a representative of the army. His timetable will be subject to the requirements of the military. However, you will still have that check-point to contend with.'

Using the food available in the store-rooms, the company ate well that night, and, although crowded, they rested warm and sheltered under a solid roof. The following morning they bade farewell to Orin and Egen gave him his own hunting knife as a farewell gift, at the same time urging him not to reveal their whereabouts to anyone. Not being accustomed to being spoken to kindly, not even by the lowliest servant, Orin was overwhelmed.

'I would rather die first,' he said, 'but I doubt that I shall even see another, my status is so low that neither the master nor his servants will suspect me. They will not even bother to look for me.'

Then, laden down with meat and grain, and fingering his gift, he stumbled happily home to his anxious parents.

Once the whole group had breakfasted they removed all the remaining provisions and items of use and the order to destroy the building was given. But they did not burn it, being fearful of distant observers. Ropes were passed through the window shutters from the outside, then lashed around logs inside that were longer than the width of the window apertures. When attached to the horses and ponies, these devices enabled them to pull the walls outwards and bring the roofs crashing into the rooms and courtyard.

Somewhat reluctantly after a warm and comfortable night and with their appetites sated, the villagers resumed their journey towards those two distant hills. Egen estimated it would take an entire day to get his followers over the first and into the wooded valley beyond, provided that nothing untoward arose to impede their progress. It was pleasantly warm and dry which made the going reasonably easy.

He had exchanged his place in the chariot for an acquired Roman horse; this enabled him to move about the group more easily and quickly and to oversee that progress. It also gave him time while jogging along dreamily to allow his mind to flicker back to thoughts of the slain yellow-haired ex-slave; it was not important, but he found it irritating that he could recall nothing that would fill the blank in his experience. At midday they stopped to eat in a wild meadow. When all were seated the high grass provided a satisfactory degree of concealment. To some it was all too soon before they were being asked to resume the march. By late evening they had entered the woods in the valley between the two hills.

Once it was established that here they would spend the night, they demonstrated skills and abilities Egen never knew they possessed. They immediately set themselves to building simple temporary shelters. He and Josin watched with interest as a young family set about their task. Two long branches forked at their upper ends were chosen and pressed into the ground; a further long stout branch was bound into the crutch-like fork ends, making a crossbar at about shoulder height. A number of much longer more slender branches were then laid against the crossbar, ensuring that the sloping side thus formed would face into the breeze which filtered its way through the trees. They then sealed these sloping limbs to the ground with a mud and moss ridge; cut turves would have been preferred but not being close to the forest edge they were not easily available. This sloping side was then overlaid with twigs supporting a great deal of foliage which in turn was covered with a thick layer of bracken and a further thickness of twigs with ample leaves. This whole sandwich was then lashed securely to the underlying supports with long stems of ivy which grew everywhere. As Elred had done decades earlier, they then drew in loose undergrowth to close the triangular openings formed at each end. Once the uneven ground beneath had been levelled and cushioned with more bracken the occupants were quite snug and warm when rolled in their blankets. The whole operation had taken very little time. It was explained that over the years it had become more or less traditional in the commune to pass on these skills to successive generations to help cope in emergencies such as this; and it was assumed that the same applied elsewhere.

It did not take long for Egen and Josin to copy and build their own; they also scooped a hollow in the soil to the front of the shelter, surrounded it with stones and kindled a low glowing fire, which of course would have to be tended from time to time during the night. Having settled comfortably beside Josin, he watched carelessly as a father and two sons crouched behind their construction adjusting some of the sloping members which were not to their satisfaction. Just then some debris gusted into the fire causing it to flare up momentarily. The sudden leap of flame illuminated the hair of the three he was watching, making it appear much lighter and more yellow in colour than it actually was. The image sparked a complementary flicker in his memory and instantly the connection was made, the blank had been filled. He remembered not only where he had seen similar hair similarly fashioned to that of the turncoat slave, but also the entire day when he and Elred had achieved nothing that they had intended, and he related it to Josin.

He had been little more than a boy when, on a very hot and sultry day, Elred took him over the ridge behind the village towards the great river estuary; the intention being to make a big catch while the boy would practise his swimming skills, each of course helping the other. As they rounded the last of the greenery before the foreshore Elred suddenly grabbed Egen and pushed him down firmly behind a large bush, at the same time indicating with his fingers over his lips that not a sound must be made. When Egen peered through the foliage he saw what his companion had espied before him. Pulled up on the beach was a small ship with a high prow and stern, constructed along similar lines to that of normal Roman vessels, but somehow lower and sleeker and not so wide in the beam. It had about twelve oars on each side hanging from the top strakes, some of which helped to hold the boat upright. It had a small mast and spar from which hung a loosely furled, brightly coloured sail. Three men crouched at the base of an oar trying to adjust its position, their hair varying shades of light straw-yellow reflecting the sunlight.

Leaning against the sides of the ship were several strange short swords and large axes. As they watched a shout went up and about twenty or more men of similar dress and appearance ran from the trees. Then, from much further down the river, a large troop of Roman cavalry appeared galloping towards them, and the men at the vessel moved towards the weapons as if to resist; those who had emerged from the trees shouted words which were unintelligible to the watchers, but the gesticulations clearly indicated that the ship should be pushed back into the water. The reason soon became obvious as a second troop of horsemen rounded the trees; together they greatly outnumbered the seafarers. They all heaved at the ship which slid very easily into the river, jumping in as it did so. Those in first grabbed at the oars and heaved mightily while others quickly dropped the sail to take advantage of an offshore breeze. A spear was thrown by one of the leading cavalrymen but it was no more than a futile gesture for the receding vessel, aided by the wind, was out of range and the missile fell short and was lost in the waves. Waiting until the ship was no more than a speck on the horizon, the two groups of riders cantered back from where they had come but left one man from each troop to keep watch. It was some considerable time before the two troopers considered it safe to return and join their comrades.

By this time both Egen and Elred were cramped and very hungry and thirsty; they decided to return to the hamlet. On the way back Egen asked, 'Who were those strangers and where did they come from?'

'I do not really know,' was the reply, 'but I have heard there are marauders who live soley by plunder, somewhat like the pirates who come from Hibernia and raid the far western side of our land near Mona. Perhaps you noticed those strange blades resting against the hull. They are a partial confirmation that they are related to those marauders who come across the wild sea which this river runs into, and whom I had not seen before, if indeed they be the same. But an example of those swords I have seen previously, in the hands of an auxiliary before we were driven from our first homes. He boasted that he had taken it from a fair-haired savage he had killed in the land of the Belgae before being transferred here; he said it was called a seaxe. Some say the only good thing to come from our subjection is that the Romans regard our soil as their own, and while they are here they repel other invaders. Should we at length be able to eject them, or for some other reason they leave our shores, we will have troubles with those invaders. Now, youngster, you have cleaned from my mind all knowledge or suspicions about those people as thoroughly as you gut and fillet a fish. I know no more.'

Thanks to the great gluttony of the villa owner, at daybreak they were all able to have a satisfying breakfast. Well fed and rested, they dismantled their shelters in such a way that their sojourn had little effect on the woodlands and happily resumed the march. As they ascended the succeeding hill the trees became less widespread and finally stopped. Once over the brow they were able to look down on the river far below. The two bows described by Orin were clearly visible, but the water as it tumbled and sparkled through them indicated a high degree of turbulence, whereas the stretch connecting the two was much wider and shallower. This was clearly the crossing point as several rough tracks ran towards it from the near side, while on the far side a single metalled road rose from it, and at a short distance further on sat the small wooden guard post. It was clear that no one would be able to approach the ford without being observed by the garrison stationed there.

Egen was now faced with a new problem: somehow they had to face trained and disciplined soldiers on open ground; no ambush tactics could be employed here. He had sometimes contemplated such a situation and theorised on solutions, and as he recalled those imagined solutions he realised that he might just be able to combine two of them successfully. It would be dangerous and require the exposure of the most skilled and daring of his charioteers, but he also knew there would be no shortage of volunteers.

Deliberately, he advanced the assembly into the clear view of the guards on the far bank. Out of sight behind the gathering he had had six vehicles specially prepared. Two were made parallel axle to axle, a horizontal post was lashed to the one on the left side and made to protude over the other, a strong rope of calculated length was then attached to the shaft of the first chariot, looped very loosely many times over the added horizontal post and the other end tied firmly to the shaft of the second. As the travellers moved closer to the river a lone horseman burst from the building and galloped into the far distance. The guards were now thoroughly confused and alarmed. They were used to dealing with no more than two carts or several people wishing to trade at the nearest settlement; now they were faced with a comparative horde of people obviously intent on crossing but with no indication of purpose. Disciplined as they were, they formed themselves into a force of seven archers and spearmen on the roof and two ranks of six armed only with swords straddling the road. Being so rarely required, they had not given thought to bringing their long oval shields and javelins from within, and in any case those approaching appeared to be of widely varying ages and only lightly armed.

As the first line of the horde reached the water it suddenly parted in the middle and the two prepared chariots charged through carrying four riders crouched very low. Keeping their hubs no more than two hand-spans apart, they made at great speed straight towards the centre of the guards' lines. The men on the extreme ends of those lines instinctively hastened to bolster the central defenders against the threatening charge. When almost upon the foremost line the charioteers suddenly veered apart to pass through the spaces vacated by the men from each extremity. In so doing the rope was very rapidly pulled hopping and jumping from its supporting post, loop by loop, until fully extended tight between the two vehicles at about waist height. Not being able to see the rope until the moment that the chariots moved apart, the soldiers were caught unaware and swept off their feet in a mass of flailing arms and legs; some of those whose accoutrements had tangled with the rope were dragged bouncing and screaming a considerable distance along the road. For men who wore armour or chain mail over their torsos, but covered their lower bodies only in linen skirts or woollen shorts overlaid with metal studded hanging straps, and wore open toed boots or sandals on their feet, it was a painful and bloody experience. The rope burn alone, where it sawed across bare flesh or even through skirt material, was sufficient to incapacitate most men. Those on the fort roof were so amazed at what they were witnessing that only one was able to summon sufficient control to loose an arrow. Whether it was luck or skill will never be known, but it found its mark in the back of the nearest driver. By this time the other four prepared vehicles were galloping in line astern towards the check post; the first three of these each towed an enormous bundle of brushwood, and the second, third and fourth also carried a blazing torch. The first deftly and accurately cut loose its burden to lay it against the farthest corner of the wooden fortification, then continued past the suffering militiamen to join those who had initiated the attack. The second just as skilfully planted its bundle against the gates but drove straight on to thrust its torch into the heart of the first to be dropped, then turned to confront the guards who were still trying to regain their feet while nursing wounds they never expected to receive. The third repeated the procedure, targeting the nearest corner with its brushwood bundle and going on to set ablaze the one lying against the gates before wheeling around to line up with the second crew. It now only remained for the fourth to fire the bundle deposited by his predecessor and then join it to face the discomforted auxiliaries. These Romans were in no condition to oppose the six carriages and eleven riders which collectively bore down on them. Had it all been a demonstration of practised skills before an invited audience, without the pressures of real action and its dangers, it could not have been executed with more panache.

Those within the post were now too busy trying to escape the flames which had taken hold of the main structure to continue defensive manoeuvres. Some descended to try to open the gates but were driven back by the flames and heat; returning to the roof they joined those attempting to climb or jump down at the rear away from the conflagration. The advancing villagers were by this time waiting for them, and they suffered a moderately less painful death than would have been the case had they waited for the flames to engulf them.

The grieving family of the fatally wounded driver took his body to be covered in the nearby woodland. There was no need to hurry; the horseman seen rushing away before they crossed the river would need at least the remaining daylight hours to report the threat and collect reinforcements, then most of the following day to return with them. There was enough time for them all to show their respects to the deceased and his family. There would also be time to tidy their ranks and their persons before continuing with the march. Egen felt an unreasoning guilt and melancholy; this had indeed been a victory in dangerous circumstances, but for the first time they had suffered a fatal casualty under his leadership and he felt it keenly. Such was his frame of mind that once all had been done that needed to be done, regardless of the fact that there was no need to hurry, he urged them to resume travelling as soon as they were ready; he needed to leave this place and the thought of that loss far behind.

They kept to the high ground well to the right of the road, but from where they could see and follow it guiding them towards the land of the Iceni. Down this road contingents of soldiers would be travelling to join the march to Mona, and scouts were kept ahead to ensure that they did not tangle with them. He was constantly conscious that he was leading many old and very young people as well as those of fighting age. Eventually, the surrounding countryside became more open and although no one was seen, other than the occasional worker in meadows far away, they all experienced a feeling of being watched. For three sunrises they kept the road in sight, using rarely found copses to shelter in at night.

At dawn on the fourth day two scouts advised him that several warriors, non-Romanised natives of that area, had approached wishing to speak with him. Accompanied by Jodoc, Berrim and Sild he went to meet them. They were still astride horses which had clearly been rescued from Roman stock; all insignia had been removed, but recognisable and useful riding paraphernalia, such as reins and halters, retained.

Addressing the nearest man, who seemed to be their spokesman, he said, 'I am Egen, by common consent leader of these people while on route to join the Iceni gathering, if they will accept us. What is it you wish to speak of?'

The spokesman still astride his mount replied, 'I am named Aaric. The one thing we did not know about you was your name, and now you have informed us of that. You will of course be welcomed by the Iceni and massed tribes. Your reputation has preceded you, your exploits are already known to us.'

'How is that?' queried Egen. 'Neither I nor any of my fellows have been near here before today.'

Aaric replied, 'When trees can dance where demons fly, the passing wind can speak of all it sees.'

This was an enigmatic response but Egen did not consider it of sufficient importance to press for further explanation.

Aaric continued, 'We have come to advise and help you. Walk for one more day, then cross to the north side of the road, leaving it behind you. You will see a low blue hill in the far distance. March directly towards it over the flat lands that lie before it. You will be met and welcomed. Until then do not worry. That horseman who raced from the garrison at the river crossing did not reach his destination, nor will he return; this is his mount.' He patted his horse's neck, then gave a form of salute and galloped away with his companions.

Trusting in the genuiness of those messengers, Egen led his followers according to the directions given. The blue hill referred to was eventually seen, but so far away in the hazy distance it could easily have been missed. The wild flat fields stretched on, seemingly endless, to that same misty horizon, with the tall grasses and bright, mottled flowers swaying in gentle waves driven by a light breeze into obscurity. Only some indistinct shadows in the middle ground broke the continuity of the scene. As they came nearer, those shadows became distinguishable as a much extended settlement wherein people moved about. When nearer still, young children ran towards them laughing and playing excitedly; they tried to drag them by their hands towards the many adults who had followed them out. Never before had any of the weary travellers seen so many people.

The settlement consisted of every type of dwelling or shelter imaginable, from the simple type they had made for themselves on their journey to various sizes and quality of roundhouses. They stretched out in all directions, covering a huge area of ground. From the varying styles of dress and accents it was obvious that many different tribes had assembled there, and to the newcomers it seemed that the entire native population of the land was concentrated before them. They had without doubt been expected and were immediately overwhelmed with kindness. They were led, almost thrust, towards and into suitable shelters to rest, and were fed unstintingly.

Egen and Josin were shown to a small roundhouse, sparsely furnished but well provisioned. It was, as they learned later, to be their home for only two nights. A little later Aaric sought them out to welcome them and advise them that Queen Boudicca would see them tomorrow when they were fresh and rested. That evening, before lying down for the night, they searched out their travelling companions to be sure that none were in need of anything. For the first time for many a night Egen was able to relax completely, feeling that the major part of his task had been accomplished.

The next morning they had barely finished eating when Jodoc and Berrim arrived to accompany them to to the Iceni queen. They were directed to one of the larger houses which, apart from its size, was little different from any other and ushered in by Aaric who had been waiting outside. Boudicca was a tall handsome woman with careworn features; two young, apprehensive girls followed her about, never more than an arm's length distant as she bustled about normal household chores. Her hair was deep chestnut red and hung in very long, slightly wavey tresses. Her plain woollen cloak hung right down to sandaled feet, and although simply dressed she carried an unmistakable air of authority. She sat down on a wooden stool by the fire and invited them to do likewise opposite her. There followed a conversation concerning their travels and experiences, although apparently she already knew much about it. Egen tried to interest her in his ideas about training and discipline to reduce losses to her subjects, in effect turning Roman methods against the Romans; he also wished to form an ambushing force to harass the enemy with little or no loss to themselves by employing planned actions instead of uncontrolled attacks. Had he not thought it out beforehand, their crossing of the river would almost certainly, as in previous exploits, have been carried out as a wild attack and fight resulting in far more casualties to themselves. She, however, held up her hand and declared, 'In other circumstances and given more time you would be right, but I am forced to see things from another perspective. The Roman military are unrestrained mercenaries from many lands, unhindered for the most part by ties of family or personal responsibility. Few, other than senior commanders motivated by ambition, actually come from Rome or have even seen it; they may be trained at any time that is convenient to their superiors. Look out there!' She waved towards the entrance. 'We have very many fighting men but most are burdened with family commitments. We have Iceni, Cornovii, Trinovantes, Brigantes, Corieltauvi and even a few Cantiaci such as yourselves who joined us many seasons ago. It is difficult enough to combine disparate tribes into one fighting force with a common aim, but to try to impose strict discipline and training as you advise, though advantageous, would take the time we do not have. The timetable is dictated by the movements and activities of our enemy. I reason that such is their fondness for fine stone buildings erected in large towns, for warming their buttocks on fire-heated floors and gorging themselves on food and grains stolen from other lands, all of which depends on the suffering and subservient work of slaves, and because those towns house all the administrators serving imperial Rome, it is to our advantage to destroy those towns, thus crippling their morale and administrative abilities. At the moment the bulk of their army is either in, or travelling to, the far west. We must move against those towns while they are away. Rush and slash as you term it has been the traditional fighting method of our people for generations; we do not have the time to change that now, so that is what we must continue to rely on. Even if they turn back unexpectedly we would use our sheer weight of numbers to overcome them. You wear a fine and beautiful sword. I am sure it would give a good account of itself in any situation, rush and slash or otherwise. Let me assure you that I am aware you wish only to restrict our losses. Given enough time I would agree to your suggestions, but on the way back to your shelter look around and you will see the signs of urgent preparation. We move against Camulodunum tomorrow. After the barbaric treatment meted out to my two young daughters, from which I sometimes wonder if they will ever fully recover, and because of which they may never be able to trust a man again; after the vicious treatment visited upon myself and the oppression of my people, I have no intention of waiting longer. I could not hold these people back even if I wished to. If you intend killing Romans, and I am sure you do, you are welcome to fight alongside us using whatever tactics you wish. I will look for you on my left flank.'

There was nothing Egen or his companions could have said that would have changed the situation or Boudicca's decision. They therefore returned to prepare themselves for whatever was to come, and Egen felt a sense of relief that he did not now have the responsibility of leading, but would on this occasion be a follower. It did not take a great deal of looking and listening to see and hear once again the sights and sounds of preparation for battle: the slow rasping screech of steel being sharpened, the thump of shields being tested for tautness, the creaking groans of straps and trappings being tightened and adjusted. Above it all was an atmosphere of expectancy charged with excitement. Something they noticed that was not entirely expected and slightly disconcerting was an apparent new relationship growing between the villagers that had travelled with them and their council and elders. Previously that group had lived as an almost indivisible community, but now they had not only very quickly made new friends but almost become an indistinguishable part of the new society. It was comparable to yeast being added to fresh dough, separating and spreading but becoming an integral part of a new entity. Yet it had happened so speedily. From now on the group, while remaining respectful and friendly, would never again be so reliant on their previous advisers.

While getting ready for tomorrow's events Egen and Josin discussed the position they found themselves in. They had experienced living in two distinct communities, but here it was not really a community but an avenging horde bent on retribution; not that they disagreed with the ferment, but the whole atmosphere was unsettling, to say the least. While admitting that he felt relieved that he no longer had responsibility for those he had led here, Egen still felt concern for their well being. They were now part of a much larger society, unprepared for battle with an experienced enemy. It was true, as Boudicca stated, that she had not time to prepare her people. Events after the unexpected death of her husband Prasutagus, including the inhuman outrage perpetrated on her daughters and her own flogging, added to the oppression of her tribe, had forced her hand. It was also true that reprisal while the greater part of the enemy was elsewhere would be more successful and produce fewer casualties. Even so, one way or another, there was going to be a great deal of bloodshed; he earnestly hoped that not too much of it would come from his friends and companions. It worried him that there appeared to be no firm plan of action, only a resolve to march against the town and react to whatever they found there; complete surprise was the one thing being relied upon.

There was little they needed to do in preparation, but both were restless for they did not know what the morning would bring. Josin dealt with this by bustling about tidying up. She explained that as they did not know whether they would be returning she wanted to leave the place clean and tidy. Egen decided that a walk in the night air might relax him a little and strode out in no particular direction. As he approached a small house near the edge of the settlement he noticed Aaric talking vehemently to someone in the shadows. When a little closer he was able to see that the other person was short, slight, but very wiry and held the bridle of a fine looking pony. Then, with a wave to Aaric and a glance in Egen's direction, he mounted and galloped away. Egen was curious, though it was not really any of his business.

Nevertheless, he asked Aaric, 'Was that a friend you bade farewell to just now?'

'You have not seen him before?' queried Aaric.

'Never,' replied Egen. 'Should I have done?'

'I would have thought that you would have seen either him or one of his fellows at some time, but as you have not I feel it is timely you should know. You may need to be aware of them some time soon. He is a member of a small band of volunteer messengers organised by the brethren your friend Athan belongs to. Their purpose is to transmit information between certain members or elders of our habitations. They are chosen because of their resourcefulness and ability to travel far and fast alone, unseen and without getting lost. They are also instructed, because of the importance of the information they carry, not to get into physical conflict with the enemy unless it is absolutely unavoidable. Should they be captured by Rome and recognised for what they are they would face the most rigorous questioning and suffer the most agonising of deaths. It is a sparse and fragile web but gives us much needed information. It allows us to know what is going on elsewhere very quickly, sometimes almost as soon as it happens. They are totally trustworthy and brave and have nearly as much stamina as their ponies; they never even offer their names but we refer to them collectively as 'the passing wind'.

When he discussed the incident later with Josin, she remarked that she had wondered how Athan had received the summons to return to Mona.

'It must have been secretly by one of these galloping phantoms,' she said. 'The vast amount of knowledge he possessed about events throughout the land, he could not have gained travelling as he did, alone and on foot.'

7

Blood, Fire and Revenge

The early morning light began to filter through the eaves and Egen's senses hesitantly hovered between sleep and wakefulness. Soothed by a continuous swishing sound as of shallow waves over loose pebbles he would have been content to lie for much longer, but the gradual realisation that within earshot was nowhere with moving water – not stream, nor river nor sea – shocked him into full awareness of his surroundings.

Josin was standing by the entrance, half turned towards him, saying, 'I was just about to wake you. Come and see.'

Immediately he was at her shoulder looking out. That which his sleep befuddled mind had interpreted as slurping water was the sound of hundreds of sandaled and soft-shod feet moving over rough tufted ground. There was no visible urgency but all the marchers moved closely and purposefully together. Few spoke, but the voices of those who did were thin and noticeably of a higher pitch than normal. The majority wore stern expressions and were absorbed with their own inner thoughts.

'It has started,' he said. 'Be quick!'

Never before had the couple breakfasted so speedily, neither wishing to be thought of as tardy. Each grabbed a few slices of cold dried meat which they ate as they moved about, and washed it down with a few mouthfuls of the thin, nettle-flavoured beer favoured in this area. They were harnessing the ponies when Boudicca appeared, surrounded by some fierce looking foot guards.

'Good morning. I was hoping to see you soon,' she said. 'Can we talk inside for a short while?' Without bothering to sit she explained, 'I have to lead and be with those you see advancing outside. If we succeed in destroying the town as we fully intend, it would be to our benefit if news of it is not allowed to reach other centres until we are ready to deal with them also. The last thing we need is for formations of legionaries to rush back from the west, or anywhere else, until they have nothing to rush back to. On the far side of the city is an unfinished road leading to the coast which matters not, as I say it is unfinished and they do not as yet have a port there. It does, however, have a junction turning south towards Londinium and Verulamium which we must guard to prevent news reaching those places. It has been well noted that you and your followers are fast and skilled in the use of wheeled vehicles; I would ask that you and two others, together with a trusted guide whom I shall appoint, circle the far perimeter of the town without being seen and approach from there. Should any person or messenger leave by that route before the town is subdued from this side, you must endeavour to prevent such an escape. That would then leave only the problem of the lesser road to Lindum.'

There was no question but that they would accept the proposal. It would be good to have a definite role to play rather than to accept whatever presentd itself. Egen was emboldened to ask what the problem was concerning the Lindum road.

'As you may be aware,' the queen said, 'Lindum is a considerable distance away in the opposite direction, well to the north-west, but last evening we received information that the Roman commander, Quintus Cerialis, is already assembling a combined force of cavalry and infantry to march on Camulodunum. It is almost certainly because of complaints from its citizens that it has been left under protected owing to the requirement to raise large numbers to fight in the west; it is unlikely that he has heard of our impending attack. In normal circumstances it would take him, with unmounted men, about three to four days to get here; that would give us two days to complete our task, then march on Londinium.'

Egen was again concerned and asked, 'Would that not make us more vulnerable? We would just about be facing Suetonius's defenders when

Cerialis came upon our backs.'

'That is a very good point,' she conceded. 'We may have to eliminate him and his auxiliaries before turning on Londinium. We will see the outcome of our action here before committing ourselves either way.'

There was no more time for discussion; to get into position before the main body fell on the town necessitated their moving with all due speed. Their guide turned out to be a young man of the queen's own guard named Garvin. Not only was he well acquainted with the geography of the area, but knew exactly what would be required of him, and although they had to take a very circuitous route in the almost treeless terrain, they arrived unseen in a hill gulley overlooking the eastern side of the town. They had been there only a short time before the first shouts and screams were heard, soon after which smoke began to billow up in the far distance. He pointed out that the long building in front of them with walled extensions on either side and gates to the fore, was a stables and training compound for the garrison. Even as he spoke the gates swung open and two riders hurtled down the road with Egen's companions in close pursuit. Josin, holding the reins, was eager to follow, but Garvin held her back saying, 'That road goes nowhere. Wait a while and let the others deal with them.'

No sooner had he spoken than another rider cautiously emerged, looked around, saw nothing and galloped off in the opposite direction while the gates were closed by unseen hands.

'Now!' screamed Garvin to Josin. 'After him!'

With practised skill she drove the team out of the hollow, down the hill and after the fleeing horseman. He then heard and saw his pursuers, gave his mount its head and pressed it on to maximum speed. With the drag of a heavy load her ponies could not make up ground on their quarry. On and on she drove, almost mercilessly, but the larger horse was fresh and strong and drew away remorselessly.

'Keep going, keep going!' shouted Egen unnecessarily. 'You never know what may happen.'

Almost as though fate had picked up on his words the flying mare stumbled; it did not fall but slowed to a hobbling gait unable to continue apace. Its rider realised the futility of trying to urge it onwards and without dismounting turned to face the chariot, at the same time unsheathing his gladius. It drew alongside him, and once again the inadequacy of a short stabbing weapon for a mounted man proved itself. Desperately he thrust at them but could not reach; on the other hand, Egen's much longer sword, glittering as it whistled and swept through the air, sliced effortlessly through the upper armour and straps to flesh and bone beneath. The body tumbled from the saddle as the animal reared and limped away.

Garvin could only stare in disbelief. 'I do not know from what metal your blade is made,' he gasped, 'but apart from blood it is unmarked along its edge. Such a weapon could only have been forged by the gods.'

Egen did not wish to answer for he did not wish to admit that he did not know its origin, so he merely replied, 'Yes, it spares me much time at the whetstone.'

He stepped down, removed the harness from the horse and examined its fetlock. Had it not been injured he would have availed himself of it, but although the injury was slight and would soon cure itself, at this time it would have been a hindrance rather than a gain. He left it to graze peacefully and to be a fortunate find for a lucky local farmer. He asked Josin to return as quickly as possible without distressing the ponies. Nearing the point where the chase began they found the others waiting, having expeditiously dealt with the decoy pair; Boudicca's concerns had been well founded. To ascertain the progress of her attack, Garvin made his way back to the far side of the city while all the others waited and watched for anything untoward. He returned after what to them seemed an excessively long time and advised them that many citizens had been captured and dealt with before they could gain the safety of the city complex. Others had barricaded themselves within the numerous and closely packed buildings. Since then the attacks and retaliation had evolved into a sort of missile war, oil-soaked burning bundles being used as the main weapon. He also brought back instructions that they remain here until relieved; prising out the justifiably terrified inhabitants from their refuges was proving extremely difficult.

The majority of fighting men previously stationed here had been sent to strengthen the force driving towards Mona; only about two hundred trained and fit men remained in the city. These were supplemented by a combination of several hundred retired militia and very many Romanised inhabitants who had fully adopted the Roman way of life and its traditions. It was ironic that the administration had for years extracted excessive taxes from this civil population to support the retired military who in turn denigrated civilians, yet both were now obliged to defend the town as equals. Slowly, the defenders were driven from the buildings on the perimeter to others nearer to the heart of the town. In most cases this meant an opportunistic and calculated dash across open ground with many dying in the attempt. For others it involved moving through little known interconnected cellars and passageways. It was truly an untidy and vicious conflict, Boudicca's followers using their traditional tactics – the uncontrolled rush with wild slashing and stabbing at any and every target which presented itself.

Meanwhile, she positioned herself beneath the great victory arch which served as a gateway to a city devoid of the usual city walls. In recent circumstances this had been where travellers and tradesmen had been taxed before they were permitted to enter the town. Now she had arranged for prisoners in military garb to be brought there, hoping to recognise any who had been involved in the outrage committed on her daughters, Camorra and Tasca, and her own flogging. The only difference between those recognised and others was the manner of their deaths. With only one ranking officer left in command the defenders were devoid of unity and their famed discipline evaporated; consequently, the resistance was erratic and fragmentary. The sudden collapse of a burning building with an ear-splitting crash, billowing dust and smoke, gave the hard pressed and scattered inhabitants a chance to seek refuge in the most capacious and impregnable building within reach, the great temple of Claudius. Even then some could not get within its doors before they were pulled shut and barred from the inside. For two days the siege of the edifice continued until they resorted to burning it to the ground with all inside. This marked the end of the battle; there remained no enemy to oppose them. There were, however, other things to attract the attention of the victors: provisions were stocked in homes and store-rooms which would not now be required by those who had placed them there. Symbols of the despised occupation, buildings, temples and statues were razed to the ground. Egen and his group had been relieved some time earlier and he and Josin had been asked to meet again with Boudicca. On their way to the meeting they passed the still burning great temple They did not enjoy the sight, but compassion was not yet a known concept in this subjugated land.

'We now have the problem we spoke of earlier,' Boudicca said to him. 'I have been advised that Cerialis has been made aware of our activities here and has quickened his pace; his mounted men are pushing his foot soldiers to greater efforts. You were right and somehow we must dispose of that threat before turning our attention to other towns. The question is: which method is for the best?'

Egen assumed he was being asked to propose a course of action and replied with another question. 'How far away are they now, and what is the surrounding area like along the Lindum road?'

Garvin, who was also present, answered for her. 'It is estimated that he is two full days away. He was initially delayed a short while gathering reinforcements from small posts on the way. The road for the most part is less wide than that to Londinium and runs across undulating ground, not widely forested but comparatively soft and uneven either side. The only distraction of note is a small farming community which straddles the road about one half day's march from here, with a small copse on one side and a few farm buildings on the other with hedgerows marking out the fields – and they brew good ale at the main house.'

Turning to Boudicca Egen said, 'As I see it there are several alternatives. We could wait here for him to arrive and set upon us; by sheer numbers we would prevail but suffer many casualties. I do not believe that would happen, however; he would see, or more probably hear, before he got here, that the city is no more and I am sure he would not try to defend something that no longer exists. That would be an illogical waste of his own men's lives. Only a desire for unreasoning revenge would inspire such an act. The other actions he could take would include a return to Lindum but that would reflect badly on his reputation, and he still could not be sure that we would not follow and harry him. He could perhaps turn onto the road I am told runs directly from Lindum to Isca Dumnoniorum to join the western gathering, or turn south to warn and aid Suetonius in Londinium. None of that really matters should we decide for him by setting up an ambush before he knows the true situation.'

'What do you suggest?' she asked.

'Really something quite simple,' he replied. 'I will explain, and as Garvin knows the country well he can correct me if I am not right. I propose that we take at least twenty chariots in two groups of ten, one group led by myself and the other by Berrim, and that each vehicle carries four men. It will not be comfortable but would enable at least eighty warriors to get to that steading well before Cerialis with enough time to secrete ourselves, allowing him to pass but not return, provided we start very soon.'

'It needs no further explanation,' she answered. 'It is a good plan and I allow it, although time is short. Choose your men while I rouse our people.'

Having seen the mindless celebrations and looting throughout the ruins, he knew that would be much easier said than done.

Cerialis, occasionally cantering ahead or dropping back a little to check their progress, tried to chivvy his foot soldiers onwards, aided by his cavalry nudging them from the rear. Sometime before they had plodded through a rain storm without stopping; they were cold, wet and miserable.

'Keep going, men!' he cried. 'The city needs us, it is under threat.'

He pretended to not hear the muttered responses suggesting that Camulodunum, its occupants and commanders could all go hang. More than one of the company informed his companion alongside that he would exchange the whole of that place and all it contained for dry feet and breeches – add to that a warm, comfortable bed and a good meal and he would part with the whole damned province.

One man deliberately raised his voice and said, 'Yes, it is days since we have had a good hot meal, and I will wager that the next time our bellies are filled it will be with hard cold steel.'

Cerialis, however, was not listening; he had seen the farming complex ahead and was trying to remember how far it was from their goal. He was so concerned about reaching that goal before it was too late that it never registered with him that, apart from a few cows lowing miserably in need of milking and the occasional bleat of grazing sheep, not a living thing was abroad: no sound of work, no smoke from household fires, no dogs barking. only the rustle of leaves blown about by the breeze, the sort of ambience that would have alerted a hunter. He looked ahead along the road they were travelling and noted a low line of threatening cloud stretching wide and hiding the far horizon. He was not happy; they would have to march into its shadow. He then turned to concentrate on pressing his men onward again.

The grating thud of studded footwear, followed by the less rhythmic clatter of hooves, passed through the straddling farm area when two scouts he had sent ahead returned at a gallop and halted the march. They informed him that nothing remained of the capital but smouldering ruins; that Boudicca had massed thousands of followers to destroy his unit and were not far away. Looking beyond the scouts, he realised that the dark cloud was indeed threatening, but it was not cloud; now getting remorselessly closer, he saw it for what it was – a horde of tribal warriors and their families, thousands of them, armed to the teeth and advancing with determination. Dismayed, he knew it was pointless to go on; he turned to look back from where they had come, and his heart sank even further. Behind the complex they had just passed through were more Celtic warriors emerging in chariots from behind hedgerows and buildings, while more on foot were climbing out of ditches and hollows. He did not know how relatively few they were but he was effectively surrounded, and even if he had known it mattered little, for to try to fight through them would only have delayed him sufficiently for the advancing horde to be on his back. There was nothing else he could do but form up his infantry on the road with the cavalry protecting their flanks as best they could; that in itself would be difficult as the ground on either side was uneven and soft, churned from years of trampling by cattle and made worse by recent rain. He felt he would be like a lone pebble on a beach trying to stem the rush of the incoming tide. That feeling had also impressed itself on his men; it was clear that few, if any, would survive this encounter, especially those on foot, and it was unlikely that the mounted men would fare much better.

He had never seen such a thing before, but when the enemy was nearly upon them the infantry broke and ran in all directions. They were hacked to pieces as they ran; riders, although slashing at everything within reach, were pulled from their mounts. Cerialis and three other mounted men were whirling around in a defensive circle when he saw his moment. A rough timber bridge thrown over a deep ditch and on which several Celts were standing had one end kicked away by a prancing horse; it fell into the ditch together with the men standing on it. This left a small gap in the lines and he charged his steed at it, jumped the ditch and, stumbling and slithering on the far side, regained control and made off. Two of his colleagues managed to emulate his feat but the third, unable to control his horse on landing, slid with it into the same ditch. The animal was saved but its rider and the remaining military were annihilated.

When the three felt it safe to stop and confer they planned their next steps. A story was concocted about their being left for dead, which they hoped would maintain their honour and reputations, and Cerialis with one companion travelled on to join those in Isca Dumnoniorum, while the third man turned south to warn Suetonius in Londinium. The parting of the ways was close to another small copse some distance on, and there was no one to observe it other than the passing wind as it slipped quietly through the trees, gently swaying the foliage as it went.

Boudicca, relying on the new-found confidence of her people and their desire to punish Rome, let it be known that they would now be expected to follow her in a march against Londinium. It was late in the year and only those families with very young children or infirm dependents would be excused and allowed home with honour.

The journey south was not fast. Moving chariots and horses had to mingle with the footsloggers, and as Josin juggled with the reins Egen looked about him. They were near to the front of the horde, but looking behind or to either side it was not easy to see where the disordered ranks began or ended, and this despite the fact that a quarter of their number had taken the offer to return home for the sake of young families. No matter how big or strong Londinium proved to be it would be totally swamped by this mass of moving humanity. When it became obvious that they were nearing the outskirts of the town Boudicca ordered them to set camp for the night. She wanted her followers to be fresh and rested when they attacked the following morning. This time it proved an unnecessary and costly precaution; a battle as such there would not be.

Suetonius Paulinus, whose responsibility it was to defend the city, had abandoned it that same afternoon. Hearing that a threat might arise, he had rushed back to organise the defence, but had then been informed of the destruction of Camulodunum, the annihilation of the ninth legion out of Lindum, and now the vastness of the numbers advancing towards him. He decided that he commanded insufficient men for the task and did not wish to suffer the same fate as the capital or the ninth legion. Had the queen of the Iceni but realised it, and had she not delayed to rest her people and continued straight into the city and a battle with Paulinus, it could have changed the whole outcome of the conflict between Rome and Britain. The whole course of British history would have been changed. He totally ignored the entreaties of the citizens, who by this time had submitted fully to the Roman way of life, to stay to defend the city or to take them with him. To do so would have resulted in an exodus of refugees. He simply continued to make his retinue ready; when the pleadings could not be ignored he screamed that he was a soldier of Rome not a wet nurse.

'If you need to protect your assets or yourselves,' he shouted, 'you will need to do it for yourselves. My allegiance is to the Roman army, not you.'

When he actually departed he ordered that a double time step be used so that any following citizens could not stay with them. He was only hours ahead on the road to Verulamium, and there is little doubt that had Boudicca entered the settlement on arrival she would certainly have trapped his little army in the narrow streets and obliterated it. As it was, they rampaged through the alleyways and byways burning and looting as they went. Most inhabitants tried to flee, but the problem for them was where to go. North of the river no roads, other than difficult track ways, led east, and it was little better in the opposite direction; they felt they would constantly be trying to keep ahead of their pursuers. The most logical step was to try to get south of the river but there were few boats. The ferrymen were demanding gold and silver for the passage and their families and friends were squirreling it away in hidey-holes somewhere on the south bank. They would take no Roman coinage unless it was in huge quantities; they expressed doubts as to its having value after the uprising had been settled one way or another. Baggage and huge piles of discarded belongings lined the riverside, behind which terrified and screaming crowds tried to push their way to the boats. Many a pathetic bundle was seen floating downstream on the outgoing tide. One or two people, abandoning everything, tried to swim across, while others in desperate efforts to escape clung to anything that would float. This activity ceased when the first insurgents broke clear of the lanes and buildings close to the quay and started to butcher anyone wearing Roman dress. Panic and confusion were everywhere; anything that would burn was burned, from boats drawn up on the shoreline for repair to the landing stage and the incomplete bridge. The boatmen had pulled away and were now reasonably secure on the far bank. The only inhabitants who escaped the slaughter on the north bank were those who found a secure hiding place and stayed there. Stone statues, idols, arches and monuments of all kinds were dragged down and cast into the water where the jetties had stood, it would be a long time before it could again be used as a port. Egen could not help but wonder about the safety of the ferryman whom they had questioned when they had first spied on the town from the far bank; he hoped that somehow he was still on that side away from the massacre.

Although it was not a town of great military significance Boudicca had a deep desire to punish Verulamium. Consequently, she issued a command stating that she did not care how they used their time beforehand, all had to be ready to march at dawn to follow in the footsteps of Suetonius Paulinus. He was now well ahead but if they could somehow make up ground on him so much the better. The town was not a great distance and they soon came upon it. It proved to be a rather rambling settlement with few brick or stone structures, but many of wood and wattle and daub. Her desire to humble it emanated from the honours granted the town by the Roman administration, as it was one of the earliest Celtic townships to submit completely to Roman culture and authority. Many neighbouring tribal rulers resented such easy subservience, including the queen of the Iceni, despite the fact that after putting up an initial resistance, for the sake of peace they had co-operated with the invaders in a sort of joint governance, a situation the Romans were pleased to refer to as client kingdoms, a term which meant little to most but made them feel that all the tribes were completely subservient.

They fell upon the town and their fever for revenge was unabated. If anything, it had increased and Boudicca was not going to waste that raging anger of her people. However, she did not wish to allow Suetonius to get further ahead; after all, much of his force was on foot and therefore not much faster than her own; nor did she wish to bypass Verulamium leaving it unmolested, yet to delay the march just to give the town a quick thrashing, seemed an unsatisfactory option. She called Egen and Garvin together to get their views. She had come to trust Egen as one of her close advisers without demanding that he stay near, his talents being of best value when he was able to wander freely and observe. While Garvin was of the opinion that as the sack had started it might be as well to allow it to continue to its conclusion, and catching up their quarry was not going to be easy, Egen felt that it was important to prevent Suetonius from joining the main force in the west. He would have preferred to gather every chariot driver together with a fighting companion to overtake the Romans, and if they could not defeat them at least to harry and delay them until her main body could catch up and eliminate them. In the event that they beat the army Verulamium could be dealt with on their return. Considering the options, Boudicca decided that to try to stop the rampage and turn it in another direction would be impossible.

'Let them have their heads,' she said. 'We will continue tomorrow, even if it means marching to the western seas to catch up with them.'

She was not to know it, but the decision not to pursue Suetonius more vigorously would be costly to the insurrection – a second chance lost to change the course of British history forever. She was completely convinced that when the final great battle came, wherever and whenever that should be, he would be decisively overcome. It seemed that no great rush was necessary; it would be perhaps more advantageous to proceed against the enemy with unhurried deliberation. It was not known for certain where the imperial army was gathering and waiting, if indeed it was waiting, but it would not be difficult to follow Paulinus' tracks as he raced to rejoin it.

That night, as they lay together, Egen and Josin earnestly discussed the day's events and anything that had attracted their attention. This was not unusual, but owing to the events of the past few days and the almost continual activity, and despite being tired in the extreme, they found it difficult to sleep. They talked animatedly about many things, but mostly about how they both intensely disliked the amount of bloodshed they had become involved in. They agreed, however, that if these islands were ever to be free from oppression it was necessary and justified, and neither could forget the fate of their parents. Somehow, sometime, these lands *must* be freed from tyrants, the people united, strengthened and free to govern themselves in all things, with complete and unadulterated sovereignty. An apparently minor thing that kept imposing on his thoughts was the Roman soldier's preference for using the short gladius when mounted, rather than the more effective long sword, which he knew they all possessed. Josin had also noted this peculiarity and had remarked on it to Garvin. His knowledge of their military procedures seemed unlimited, and he had informed her that regulations demanded that they be armed at all times; in this territory they would never know whether the next stranger they met would be friend or foe. The longer weapon, whether hung from waist or saddle, was not particularly comfortable while riding; consequently, although it was frowned on by higher authority they chose to carry the short sword which was easier to accommodate, though as shown by the incident outside Camulodunum, they sometimes suffered for it. Despite their vast numbers, the fact that many of the queen's people were poorly armed could not be ignored. Some had weapons obviously taken from their adversaries, while many appeared to be ready to do battle with little better than farming implements, building tools and clubs. Garvin explained that, after the shaming of Boudicca and her daughters, the Iceni had been totally disarmed by the local governor. Before further conversation could take place Josin realised that Egen had collapsed into an exhausted sleep.

An early start the following day saw them moving in an untidy massed formation towards Venonae, an abandoned hamlet but through which their prey had left traces. This was to many a mystical area, not far from a high point which long long ago had been geometrically calculated as the very centre of the land. It emitted an aura of quiet mystery which to those susceptible to atmosphere was unsettling. It had been a day free from conflict but devoted to covering as much distance as possible, although keeping the mass moving in a controlled manner was difficult and tiring. As they settled beneath their improvised shelter they picked up on their conversation from the previous evening, but now in a more relaxed manner. The extraordinary peace and quiet somehow encouraged them to speak more of the teachings and pronouncements of Athan, and of things which meant much to them. Egen could not help but express his antipathy towards constantly having to fight the invader, which prevented them from living a more rewarding existence. Josin reminded him that Athan, who was equally committed to resistance, had taught them that it would always be so. He had told them, 'These islands are for the greater part surrounded by a land mass of enormous size, supporting large, unrelated tribal groupings with ever-changing territorial boundaries. Owing to an aggressive desire and need to acquire more fertile soil, they frequently set forth to find new land and take it for their own. Our island hangs before them like a ripe and succulent fruit, protected only by narrow, twinkling mist-laden seas. From times beyond counting, adventurers from those alien shores have arrived and tried to settle and take control. Fighting has been inevitable, although on occasion, but usually to the south and west, honest merchants from other less well-known places have arrived for genuine and peaceful trade. They offer fair exchanges for copper, tin and grain. Rome is only the most recent and powerful of aggressors, aggressors who have an arrogant pride in their own existence; they build in stone ever larger buildings and statues to provide a legacy for their supposedly superior lives. These structures are meant to last forever. Some may well do so, but it is a totally wasted ambition; to enjoy any experience it is necessary to be there and witness it. What does it benefit any man to gain a fame that he will never see? Our little round homes provide all we need while we need it – there is no requirement for more. Even after they have departed it is certain that we, or our successors, will have to repel others.' All this was true and could not be argued against.

Egen then told her he was thankful for the latest order from Boudicca: because of the great distance covered that day, and the suspected proximity of the enemy as reported by the scouts, he would be expected, with the help of Aaric and Garvin, to form her followers into a more disciplined and closer formation, making for a slower, but more determined and irresistible, advance. Despite the scouts' reports of sighting militia resting and not being urged in any particular direction, there could be no certainty that operations against the druids on Mona were complete. It would indeed be fortuitous if the brotherhood was still holding out; she would then be able to fall on the attackers from the rear. Nor could she know how informed Suetonious was of her own recent actions and present position.

Much rested and full of confidence, on a pre-arranged signal the entire assemblage moved as one, not strictly disciplined but with an unhurried gait. The mounted scouts rode confidently, well to the fore, followed by a mixed formation of foot-fighters and charioteers. This formation stretched back in a seemingly endless procession until eventually followed up by families and ox-drawn pack wagons struggling to keep pace. It was known that at a place called Manduessuedum, which lay not far ahead, not long ago a Roman staging post or fort had been built. What was not known was whether in these fast moving days it would be manned or abandoned. Suddenly, the leading lines were halted by the foremost riders and the following ranks caught up and stopped with them. Jostling for position they looked down on a narrow shallow valley, three sides of which were bounded by forest on the upper slopes. The arriving warriors stood massed on the high ridge of the open end. The track continued for a short distance and curved around the expected new fort until hidden by the trees, but the moor adjacent to that was covered by hundreds of flag bedecked military tents; the confrontation on Mona was obviously over and Paulinus was on his way back.

Egen and Josin stood looking down into the valley. As they did so the unmistakable wail of one of those great body-wrapping horns he had first heard as a young boy assailed their ears, and armed men in uniform began to appear below from all directions onto the valley floor. They emerged from tents, forest and fort, and scrambled urgently to the top of the slope at the closed end of the cup formed by the woodland. Boudicca, with Aaric beside her mounted on his Roman horse, drew level with them.

'What do you see?' she asked.

Before either could answer Aaric shouted excitedly, 'They see what we all see: Romans fleeing even before we have arrived. They have seen our strength and are afraid.'

'My friend,' said Egen, 'that is not what I see. If you observe more carefully you will note that they all carry a full complement of arms including the required amount of pili. None go beyond the line of the trees at the top of the rise, and even as we speak they form themselves into ranks for battle. The only difference from their usual practice is that, owing to the narrowness of the open ground between the trees and the crest of the vale on either side, they are unable to deploy their cavalry in the normal way to protect their flanks. Instead it is sited more to the rear, impeding its ability to support the forward lines. No, they may be afraid but they are not fleeing. They are choosing the ground on which to fight. They will soon be assembled in such a way that they have the tactical advantage. If we attack now they will be able to remain static or advance easily downhill towards us, either way forcing our men to push and strain uphill to get to them.'

'What then would you do'? asked Boudicca.

'If it were mine to command,' he replied, 'I would just stand; just stand and wait. We have our supplies to hand behind us. It would not be difficult to cut off the approach to the fort where they have almost certainly stored their provisions. We could with ease strengthen our position there with added bowmen and lances. Even the imperial army cannot stand the entire day and night without access to food and drink. Eventually, of dire necessity they would attack. That would then reverse the advantage of the high ground.'

'It is a good plan,' she answered, 'well observed and well thought out. It is good to have someone nearby who thinks a little as well as fights; our people are brave but inclined to be hot-headed. Like Aaric here, they are impatient and would attack at once.'

Aaric, chastened a little, said, 'But look at our numbers. We stand covering more than twice the area of ground that they do.'

Josin interjected, 'You are counting the numbers only and in that you are correct, but you are not calculating and allowing for the differences. In the force we are facing every man is of fighting age, fit, fully trained, well armed and, above all, disciplined. Our peoples are untrained and without military discipline; they range from young boys, barely able to lift a sword let alone swing one effectively, to old men, too proud and angry to remain at home. Were we to take only those men of our company who are comparable with the enemy in age and fitness, it might well be that we would be far fewer than they – and, as has been said, the Romans are fully armed. Only a minority of our people have weapons as such; many are equipped only with scythes and sickles, some only with flails which they normally use to separate the chaff from grain, but now aspire to separate limb from limb.'

'I too am impatient,' said Boudicca, 'and desire to throw our weight against those overdressed savages immediately, but that puts me into a dilemma: for myself I care not – I have been too deeply scarred and humiliated by those barbarians – but to cause the blood of my tribe to be spilled in larger quantity than is necessary without good reason would be unjust. Also, I care greatly for my daughters here. Give me a little time to consider.'

Unfortunately for all, the decision was made for her. Her extreme right flank was composed of a large group of young men attracted together by nearness of age and disposition, an unthinking desire for adventure, excitement and fame; too young, too foolish, too inexperienced and without care for authority and discipline. Wishing to demonstrate their prowess to each other as well as all around, and without waiting for any sort of command or signal, they charged down to commence the attack. Visibly slowing after having crossed the uncontested field, they climbed towards the enemy. Those nearest them when they started their rush were confused by the unbidden charge, but most assumed they had not heard a significant order and followed after them. It was a disastrous error. Group after group swept down the slope in their wake. Boudicca tried desperately to redeem the situation by screaming for all to follow her and careered headlong towards the fray. As previously arranged, Josin veered and sped towards the left flank, and as they looked back the attacking groups gave the appearance of peeling smoothly from the hill down into the valley, rather like an ebbing wave on a rising sandy beach followed by an obedient diminishing curve.

With the increased speed of battle-heightened senses they were able to appreciate the success of Roman training and obedience to orders. On the serrated front rows of the square formation every man at the base of the saw-like indentation, when that part of the row was confronted by an attacker, would step away from his adjacent comrade, thus leaving an inviting gap for the assailants to rush into. The unsuspecting tribesmen, using their traditional rush and slash methods, duly obliged. The gap would then close around them and they would be cut to pieces. They saw Sild and Ragnan with their new found friends disappear into such a trap. Egen had often tried to propound his idea of what he called a harvesting approach. He would say that when facing a Roman formation it was best to approach it as would a farmer and his family reaping a field of wheat – not to rush into the centre scything as one went, but to take it layer by layer from the outside edges – and as Josin and he flew towards their position she shouted that this was the tactic she would try to use. He shouted back that as they were probably going to die anyway, they might as well test the theory for themselves. Choosing a point near the extreme end of the opposing ranks, she turned and drove directly at the advancing auxiliaries. The expected void opened up but at the last possible moment she pulled on her ponies to swing sharply to the left, and skidded the chariot along the front of the leading soldiers. She and Egen had practised this move endlessly, and he was able by leaning over the side to take out four of them with ease with his long glittering blade. A further consequence of this surprise move was that the hail of pili launched from within the lines arched harmlessly over in entirely the wrong direction. Continuing the turn away, she ran for the open ground in front of the stamping, shield banging platoon, then turned to face them again and repeated the manoeuvre exactly as before. The Roman forces, unable in the heat of the moment to adjust mentally to a changed situation or resist the force of rigid training, ritualistically presented the gap to her. Again the opening was refused, again she swung away at the last second; this time the javelins rained down much closer to them but without causing damage, and another three men were eliminated. Knowing that each centurion in the back-up ranks carried two of these missiles, Egen calculated that all within striking distance would now be exhausted. He adjusted his footholds to stand a little higher which would enable him to reach somewhat further into the throng and perhaps inflict extra damage on the enemy. The charge, the proffered void and the skidding turn were all repeated, four men were fatally downed and at least two seriously maimed. As they raced for the open field ahead a pilum from somewhere behind the leading line of infantry, strongly heaved and accurately directed, flew after them. Egen's gasp of shock and pain as it bit deep into his left shoulder from behind caused Josin not to turn but instead to race for the grassy slope before them. Had they not been speeding in the same direction as the flying weapon the slender metal fore-shaft would have pierced him completely through, but instead it inflicted a deep wound.

As he began to sink to his knees desperately clutching the wicker side, she was able to put her arm around him below the wound and hang on tightly, using her other hand to control the ponies. Fortunately, the weight of the long clumsy shaft was supported by the woven side to which he clung, thus preventing the thin metal fore-piece from bending as it had been designed to do. She held on to him ever tighter as she urged the animals on over the rough rising ground. Seeing a flat area at the top of the climb, not far from where they had entered the valley, she made straight for it. There they stopped. They were far enough from the fighting and she needed to attend to his injury urgently. With great care she eased him out onto the grass, making sure that the still embedded shaft was not likely to cause further damage, and that it did not bend, which would make it more difficult to remove. Just then, however, she heard the drumming of distant hooves, and looking up saw a cavalryman approaching fast. He had been at the rear of the action but had observed their movements and retreat. With an instilled hatred for the indigenous population he was determined not to allow any to escape the carnage. Unable to get through the fighting formations below, he had circled the high edge of the vale close to the tree line and now galloped towards them. With no further time to attend to Egen, she leaped into the chariot, took hold of the reins in one hand and grabbed the longest of the inherited spears which always travelled with them in the other. She had no plan in mind, merely a determination to defeat this new threat and protect her man. The horseman drew near and raised his sword, while Josin steered her team at speed straight towards him. Almost at the point of collision the ponies swerved to the left of their own accord, and the horse reared wildly in panic. The man, trying to remain mounted, dropped his weapon and threw himself forward to grasp the animal's neck; simultaneously, Josin raised the tip of the spear while butting the rear end into a lower corner of the vehicle's frame behind her. The weight of the rider, increased by the momentum of his having thrown himself forward, added to the impetus derived from the opposing force of the speeding chariot, drove the lance entirely through him for more than half of its length. Her mind in turmoil and body shaking as a result of this violent and unexpected encounter, she again dismounted, calmed the fretting horse and disentangled its reins which had somehow trapped themselves in the rider's sword belt, then hitched them loosely to the rear of the chariot. Not knowing what the next situation might be, she judged that defensive equipment would not go amiss, so picked up the man's sword and hung it from his saddle. By now she had herself under control and calmly put her foot into the back of the corpse, grasped the spearhead with both hands and pulled it completely through and out. Of necessity she wiped it clean with the unsullied part of the man's own cloak. It was not until later that she realised she had killed this man in a manner very similar to that in which Egan had killed his first man. Before leaving the spot she cut long strips from that cloak to use for binding and tying, then hurried back to Egen and carefully removing the javelin, dressed his wound with pads torn from her shift. By this time he was semi-conscious, and almost unable to help as she struggled to lift and drag him onto the base of the chariot. The effort nearly took the last of her strength. Nevertheless, she managed to tie him at the waist and feet in such a way that there was little possibility of his sliding out.

She took a final look at the fighting. It was continuing ferociously, but she was disconcerted to see that far fewer bodies wearing glittering armour appeared to be lying motionless than those dressed in the more sombre colours of native fighters. Boudicca, however, was still standing there in her chariot, fighting like a demon, a Celtic sword in her right hand and a long lance in the other, slashing with one and stabbing with the other, her ferocity and speed of movement undiminished, her long hair now plastered to her body with the blood of her victims. Even her horses, prevented from moving forward by the piles of bodies before them, appeared to be in tune with her state of mind, kicking and lashing out in all directions. No one could get near them from the front; to have attempted to do so would have been akin to grain launching itself into the quern. With her two daughters crouched at her feet she presented a spectacle both hopeless and magnificent.

Josin's gaze rose from the conflict and she saw, but did not recognise, a small group of mounted men watching from a narrow opening between the baggage lines, where the families waited, and the fort and trees on the far side. They wore a strange mixture of dress and arms and made no attempt to get involved, at least not while she watched. As she stared hard one looked back towards her but made no move. Quietly she returned to the waiting animals and led them off into the nearest part of the forest, filled with guilt and indecision. At that moment she had a double duty: to look after Egen, and to continue the battle. To save Egen if possible was to her paramount, yet she could not help but feel that she should not leave the place where many friends were still fighting and dying. Had it not been for Egen, she would unhesitatingly have rushed back to fight alongside the queen to the death, but to do so now would have meant sacrificing both of them. She eased her mental conflict with the determination to ensure his survival and, between them, rebuild a movement to continue opposition to the invaders.

8

Mother Berringa

Once she judged they were out of sight and out of danger, she stepped back in beside Egen, now barely conscious and muttering incoherently into the blanket, and increased the pace. The rapidly setting sun flickered erratically through the trees. It would be necessary soon to find somewhere to rest, if only for a short while. When she reached a clearing she stopped and stepped down once more. As she did so she realised just how hungry she felt; neither of them had eaten since early morning. She was well experienced in foraging for suitable food, and the newly acquired mount carried a flask of fresh water at its saddle. She tethered the horses at roughly equal intervals around the site, knowing that their whinnying of fear, should anyone or anything approach, could be as useful as a dog's bark or a goose's screech. All of a sudden the world seemed very large and very empty, and she had no idea of where to go or what to do for the best. A full moon began to rise, making everything almost as clear as day. Never before had she felt so alone and helpless. The chirruping of some birds, encouraged by the bright moonlight to think it was dawn again, served only to magnify her sense of isolation. The events of that day seemed somehow long ago. After having eaten a little of the roots and vegetables she had gathered, she dripped some water into Egen's mouth and made him swallow, but he could not accept any solid food. Relying on the highly sensitive hearing of the tethered animals for protection, she dozed fitfully for a long period. In the early hours she ate a little more and persuaded Egen, even in his torpor, to swallow more water, then continued her journey into nowhere. Somehow, somewhere she had to find help for him. He was certainly no better, and fresh blood was oozing through the dressings. It was now only a question of choosing a direction to take and hoping fortune would be on her side. Not knowing what lay ahead, or even where she might be, she decided to go south, turning west when the forest thinned; there was more chance of seeing someone or something outside the darkness of the trees. Without knowledge of the area, one direction was as good as another, and the only thing to do was to trust in luck and have the determination to proceed. But, with no one to talk to, loneliness crowded in on her.

A further day's journey, with only a short stop to forage and water the horses at a stream, saw her no better off, and Egen looking decidedly paler and weaker. He no longer muttered, but neither did his eyes flicker open. By late evening she not only needed rest but was near to desperation. Nothing arose to buoy her up; the only noticeable change was that the surrounding countryside was hillier and the forest less dense. It started to rain lightly, and she decided it would be more comfortable to continue travelling than to stand without adequate shelter and wait for it to stop. With a blanket over her head she straddled Egen, trying to keep the water off him. By sunrise she was on the verge of collapse and finally halted; the rain had stopped and she pulled together a rudimentary shelter from fallen branches and bracken, stretching a similar arrangement over the chariot and, although cold and wet, she slept until the sun was high.

Weary and shivering, she rose and with difficulty forced a little more water into Egen's mouth; he now had a fever. She could not herself eat anything, but she had somehow to carry on. Slipping and sliding down a treeless slope, she headed towards a hill visually higher than others in the vicinity with a small copse on its summit, which would provide a useful vantage point from where she would be able to view all around, to see or find something, anything which would give her hope. As she crossed the intervening space, from high behind her a falcon swooped down into the vale ahead of her. It did not, as might have been expected, fall upon some unsuspecting prey, but instead flapped its wings gently to rise high again to drop and disappear into the copse ahead. She watched and thought she saw a wisp of smoke rise lazily out of trees exactly where the bird had disappeared. Her stomach twitched. Where there is smoke there is usually a human presence; a little nearer and a second wisp confirmed her first sighting. Tense and alert, she urged her tired horses to greater effort, and at the same time loosed her sword from its scabbard. She reasoned that where there is one person or more there is almost certainly shelter and warmth and possibly food, even if one has to fight for it. Right now she was more than ready to fight the whole world if necessary just for a chance to dry out, a meal and somewhere warm to rest.

Rounding a rocky, moss-covered outcrop, she saw, only a short distance before her, a tallish figure covered from head to foot in a voluminous black woollen cloak. Once within hailing distance a cracked but recognisably female voice called out and pointed to the weapon.

'You can put that away. I come to help, not to harm. I have been waiting for you.'

Josin, a little bewildered, thrust the sword away but kept her hand near it. She allowed the old woman to come nearer and then to circle them, noting that if age had not bent her she would have been noticeably taller. Her very lined face could possibly, a long time ago, have been attractive, but now it was sunken and careworn.

'My name is Berringa,' she went on. Looking at Egen, she added, 'Your man is desperately ill.' Then, pointing to the small roundhouse now visible within the trees, and from which the thin plume of smoke rose erratically she said, 'Help me to get him inside where he can be cared for. You are also in need. Put your animals in the shelter behind the house where there is hay, straw and water. The boy will care for them properly when he returns.'

Argument was pointless; she was being offered everything she could at this time have wished for, and the crone seemed sincere. Together they heaved Egen into the house near to the central fire and laid him face down before it. She then returned outside and unhitched the horses to tether them loosely inside the lean-to outhouse. When she got back Berringa had removed the bloodsoaked dressings and was cleaning the septic wound, which actions confirmed her good intentions towards them. Josin's relief was palpable, and even without the fire some warmth returned within her just by now having someone to talk to. With the relief her almost overwhelming tiredness returned, but she forced herself to remain alert to be of help to her new found friend. As they worked a noise outside startled Josin but Berringa calmly said, 'Fear not, it is only the boy.'

Nevertheless, she was not entirely relaxed and watched cautiously as the entrance cover was pulled aside. Her astonishment was complete as the youth who stepped in carefully clutching the handle of a hunting knife proved to be Orin. He was noticeably sturdier, better fed and more confident than when she had last seen him. He was equally amazed and rushed to embrace her, but was filled with concern when he saw the prostrate Egen and the dire condition he was in. He wanted to ask questions but was silenced by Berringa who said they could all talk tomorrow, just now Egen's survival was the more urgent matter, and if Josin was not allowed to sleep soon she also would collapse.

'Pass that container to me,' she ordered, pointing to a skin-covered vessel. Unsealing it, she scooped out some dark green mud-like substance with her fingers.

'Mother Berringa,' gasped Orin, 'It smells foul – like a centurion's latrine.'

She smoothed the mess over the wound saying, 'The smell may be bad but its powers are as near to magic as you will ever be privileged to witness. If the odour is so offensive to you go rub down and settle those horses, make sure they are comfortable and well fed. They too have had a long hard day.'

Obediently, he did as requested. When Orin returned he found the injury had been covered, and the two women were trying to get Egen to swallow a little thinned stew which had been simmering over the fire. He was still not aware of things around him and much of the food dribbled onto the straw beneath his chin. Some was consumed but it was a relief to all when they decided that trying further would be a waste of effort. The green unction may have smelt repellent but the aroma of the stew was almost irresistible. After the patient had been made as comfortable as possible Berringa shared it among them; Josin was sure she had never tasted better.

When dawn broke she awoke to find that the old woman had been up and about for some time, preparing more food and a soft fruit drink of her own concoction, which was not only different but quite luxurious and made a refreshing change from goat's milk, water or thin ale. Astonishingly, Egen was slumbering almost contentedly, and soon Orin entered from voluntarily checking the horses. Now no longer desperate for sleep, Josin was able to take a closer interest in his story, and remark how big a change had come over him – not only his appearance in better clothing and the way he had filled out and was stronger, but also in his readiness and joy in being able to converse with them confidently. Naturally, this resulted in a tendency for him to babble a little too profusely. His concern for the still sleeping Egen was real, even though that sleep was now peaceful, and he rushed to help when they tried, only partially successfully, to get a little more food into him.

For his own part it transpired that within two days of leaving the merchant's house his parents had died, literally within hours of each other. He had buried them, as they had wished, in a pretty part of the wood near to the hovel they had called home. Then, having nothing or no one to care for, he had gathered whatever few possessions he had, including some much better clothing he had acquired from the servants' quarters in the merchant's home, and set forth he knew not where. What he did know was that the resistance to Rome, which he had always secretly wished to join, was continuing in the north and west; and for no better reason than it was the direction he was facing he decided to seek it out in the west. Without having dependent old folk to think about any longer, he could live on his wits without worry as he travelled, although travel on foot was slow and arduous, especially when he avoided roads which might be used by the military. A few days ago he had come across Berringa – or maybe it was the other way around – and she had been good enough to shelter him and provide him with the best food he had ever eaten. Despite this, he had determined to pursue his quest in a few days' time, but he would not now leave until he was certain of Egen's recovery.

All this he related to Josin as Berringa busied herself replenishing the stew pot, with one ear cocked to the conversation. She confirmed that it would be perfectly in order for him to stay longer if he wished; she enjoyed having him around, but reminded him that she was very old and probably not long for this world, so it would be more advantageous for him to go on and start a new and independent life as soon as he could. Concerned for her safety and to be sure she was aware of it, he advised Josin that a small imperial staging post was located in the valley on the far side of this hill, about two thousand paces away at the junction of two minor tracks. The permanent garrison was composed of only twelve auxiliaries; there was little to worry about as none came more than part way up the hill because of their great fear of Berringa. Typical of most Roman military, they were highly superstitious and firmly convinced that she was not entirely human and had the unearthly ability to change herself into whatever evil form she chose, most often an enormous carrion crow.

Berringa smiled thinly. 'Yes,' she said, 'I believe that when they first built that small fort it started as a joke among themselves, but with these people the suggestion of anything mysterious, especially if supposed to be supernatural, takes root very quickly in their imaginations. I used sometimes, and occasionally still do, deliberately allow myself to be seen at a distance while high on this hill, and then extend my arms beneath my cloak. Those Mediterranean heroes disappear with alarming speed.

This was all confirmed to me when I listened to their chattering without their knowledge. From time to time I am in need of certain things – salt, cereal or oil and suchlike; they have more than enough of each in their store-rooms and, fortunately for me, a Roman guard is almost a contradiction in terms. At night I can find my way in and out without leaving a trace, except of course for a slight diminution of their stocks. It has sometimes been necessary when inside to hide myself in a store room and I overhear their conversation when so concealed. Their talk is always boastful but usually informative, and often highly amusing in its inanity. My supposed ability to change form was firmly fixed in their minds by an incident of their own making many moons ago. A couple with two young children peacefully traversing the hillside below here, were set upon by two Roman savages who, purely to amuse themselves, cut them to pieces. The family's purpose in passing here was to try to escape the advance of Rome on their home and village in the east. Athan, on his way to those eastern villages, one of which may have been your own, unseen in the long summer grass, arrived too late to save the family, but with his staff and incredibly fast hands he disposed of those assassins on the spot.'

'Athan!' cried Josin. 'Do you know him'?

'If it is the same Athan of which we speak, I know him well, he is my son. He visits when passing on his journeys across the land. We took the family, or what was left of them, and covered them decently in that mound in the wood behind the house. Athan, as is his wont, stripped the assailants' bodies and let them lie, having discarded any weapons and helmets. The bodies were so covered with puncture wounds from his staff that they could easily have been mistaken for the probings of a giant beak. Natural processes removed the flesh speedily and the bones were soon scattered; the only remaining signs are a few decaying straps and buckles. A search party from the outpost had found their dead comrades early, but superstitious fear did not allow their friends to remove them. They are thoroughly convinced that it was the work of the legendary large black crow and will not come near my nest. They know nothing, however, of the foully murdered family.'

Josin turned to Berringa. 'When we met you yesterday you called out that you had been waiting for us. I do not understand how you knew we were coming. I only found your home by chance. How did you know about us?'

Berringa had learnt to enjoy being slightly mysterious and replied, 'Not a thing happens in this world that does not have a reaction in some way on whatever is near or passes close to it; there are also eyes that see in order that they themselves may not be seen. It is possible to read and understand these things, to put together many tiny facts, from the trail of the snail imported by Rome, to the flight of the finch or a sound on the passing wind, and then you know what is to come. You have yourself already told me that Aaric knew of your exploits before you ever met him and neither had been previously in each other's space. If you have from time to time been taught by Athan, I am sure he will have explained his theories of prophesy, and the longer I live the truer they prove to be.'

She then rose and told them she would be gone for a short while, and asked them to prepare the meal in her absence.

'I wonder where she goes to,' mused Josin.

'It is almost certain,' said Orin, 'that she will be checking her domain. She assures us of her security here but I know she does not take it for granted. I have been here for only a few days but have learnt that on occasion she patrols around with a caring eye on the fort. You may not have noticed that under that sombre cloak she carries a long pointed knife. The wildlife is very used to her and accepts her presence, especially a magpie, a crow and a family of foxes which she frequently feeds; by their behaviour she is warned if someone or something is near. I have also learnt, but only by pretending to be asleep, that her particular favourite is a hawk which hunts the vale whence you approached. It sweeps the vale and then drops onto her roof and she speaks to it. Whether they are sensible words or not I could not hear, but it seems to croak responses; I would not be surprised if they understood each other. Without any special protection, other than a tight fold in her cloak, she allows it to alight on her arm and feed very gently and carefully from her hand; I have never seen the like. I have not seen them, but am certain that a person or two may arrive in secret. I have noticed fresh dung and hoof prints not far from here at the far side of the trees. If these things are taken together, as her son Athan would do, there is less of mystery than she would have us suppose.'

Berringa returned sooner than expected, and while they talked and shared the meal Egen showed signs of waking with little grunts and a flickering of his eyelids.

'It is time to examine that shoulder,' she stated, and carefully removed the dressings.

The stench was even worse than when the mess had been applied. Now it was almost black, but as she wiped it away and cleaned the area the flesh beneath looked pink and clean with no blood or seepage, and the wound had started to heal satisfactorily.

She looked at Orin and said, 'I think you will agree that repulsive odour was well worth enduring.'

She carried on cleaning and smoothed a sweet-smelling, lavender-coloured fluid over the area before covering it again with pieces of clean cloth. He was by this time sufficiently awake to accept a little more food and drink, after which he relaxed into a new slumber. For the rest of the day, while he slept, they contented themselves with minor tasks and gaining a little more knowledge about each other. It appeared to Josin that Orin was restless but trying to hide it; she then remembered that he had seen even less of the outside world than she had herself. She hesitated to talk about any future moves, wishing Egen to be fully aware of any decisions which would affect him also. That night Josin awoke to find Berringa absent. However, she soon returned and resumed her rest, but her boots were noticeably very wet. The sun had not yet risen when she was again woken, but this time by Egen struggling to get to his feet; he was fully alert and studying all about him. Though disoriented and confused, he had recognised Orin and was as amazed as she had been when she had first seen him in this place. Quietly, being sure not to disturb the others, she related to him all that had gone before. He easily remembered their charging into the battle and recalled the agony when the javelin struck, but from there on things were a complete blank until waking up in this unfamiliar place.

'I have lost some days from my life,' he said.

'But you have retained life itself, thanks mainly to Berringa,' she replied.

There was now no doubt that he would recover, although it was also obvious that his left arm would never be the same again. Never again would he be able to raise it much above elbow height, and temporarily he would have to have it lightly strapped to his body. Orin, now satisfied that Egen was out of danger as far as the injury was concerned, expressed his desire to resume his travels the following day. Having quietly discussed it between them, Josin and Egen offered the Roman horse to him. It would ease his journey, but he would have to try to avoid being seen by Romans while astride a recognisably Roman mount. Never had he possessed anything of value before and he was overwhelmed.

'I have had from you my freedom, a fine knife and a horse, and from mother Berringa shelter, fine food and much kindness. Whatever else may happen to me in the future I shall never forget these things.'

He was up very early, preparing his newly acquired steed for the journey. His servile duties at the merchant's home had taught him all he needed to know to be able to care for the animal, but he had had very few chances to mount and ride. Even more rarely had he said farewell to anyone of whom he was fond, and now it turned out to be a very emotional experience; he was completely torn between the need to see what was happening in the world and his desire to stay. He embraced them all in turn, and then twice more he rushed back to repeat it all before being able to mount and ride unsteadily away, not daring to look back.

She could not be sure but Josin thought she had detected a tear on the old lady's lined face. Although having known him for only a very short time, she felt equally emotional, feeling it likely they would never see him again. Egen then made his way to the stable and chariot and removed a spear. Several times he lifted it in his right hand and made practise moves as if to launch it, but with the restricted movement in his left arm it was going to be necessary to develop a new technique, adapting to a new balance. In a similar manner he tried a few swings with his sword, and again balance was to prove a problem, he would need to practise daily with both weapons, and resolved to do so.

Berringa advised him not to travel for at least seven days in order for his wound to heal fully, and in the meantime they would have to take care not to be seen from below.

'That vehicle is not now the most suitable for your needs,' she said. 'You require one which is longer and has four wheels, which if necessary you could both lie within.'

They agreed, stating that it would be unlikely that with a damaged arm they would be able to do battle in that manner again; they would have to look for a replacement in due course. During the second night after Orin's departure Josin was woken by the rapid rattling cry of a disturbed magpie, followed by the lower caw of an angry crow. She lay and listened for a while, putting her hand closer to the hilt of her sword, but neither was repeated, so she felt no reason to be concerned and dropped back into sleep.

She would not have thought more of this had Berringa not wandered back into the house the following morning and announced, 'The gods have responded to your needs. Your chariot has been reformed into something nearer to your requirements. You must have done something outstanding to please them.'

Slightly bewildered, both Josin and Egen went out to view this phenomenon, and saw that where their two-wheeled vehicle had stood was now a four wheeled conveyance of longer proportions and a more enclosed appearance. Egen's keen eyes searched the surrounding terrain carefully, and with his experience and instincts as a hunter saw much that she did not.

'If indeed the gods reshaped our vehicle,' he whispered, 'they did it elsewhere, then hauled it through that gulley near that track and around the trees to its present position.'

The seven days soon passed and he had visibly grown a lot stronger. His arm, however, gained little more flexibility. For the past three days Berringa had noticed an increase in activity in and around the fort below and estimated that about ten new auxiliaries had arrived. Giving the appearance of searching for something, patrols of three men would ride out and circle the vicinity, but never came high on to the hill. She had discussed the possibility of her guests staying longer, but they had all agreed it would increase the risk to her security. Now for the first time in their relationship they were just a couple alone, needing to find somewhere to settle and put down roots. Egen wished for it to be somewhere far from Roman influence, where Josin could lead a more peaceful existence, but such places were few and far between. Nevertheless, should the chance come to harass the invaders they would not let it pass. To this end they had already planned a route away from Berringa's hilltop, down the more wooded eastern side of the hill through the gulley to the track, then west towards the staging post until arriving at a spot about five hundred paces before the junction and post, at which point they would turn left to circle around the fort to a place where the track ran south-west to whatever lay beyond.

On the chosen day of departure they made their farewells to Berringa with feelings of guilt for having to leave her alone once more. But this is how she had lived for a long time before their arrival and she appeared quite content.

Returning the stare of a fox that sat in the long grass some distance away watching them, she said, 'I am not alone. I have my friends.'

They reached the track as planned and quietly made their way west, but a little way before they had arrived at the turn off the sound of hooves reached their ears. They turned to see three mounted men in military garb racing to overtake them. One was well ahead of the others and moved so as to pass them on the left, and he clutched a short sword in his right hand. Josin drove the ponies to their limit as Egen twisted and firmed his body into the corner and braced his feet hard against the base, in such a way as to face the oncoming rider. He kept his sword low in his right hand, hidden beneath the side until the last moment. Then with a mighty swing that far outreached the short blade of their pursuer he cut him down. At the same time they heard a faint whirring sound and saw two arrows arc across from each side of the thinly wooded track to thud into the chests of the other two mounted men. The archers were well hidden in the greenery, but a voice called out and urged them to turn left and keep going. They were not about to argue. That had been their intention in any case and they drove on as directed. Quite soon, four horsemen in simple dress pulled out from the trees and crossed in front of them, causing them to slow and stop. She was not at all certain but Josin felt that she recognised the animal on which the leading man rode – perhaps a confused memory from the great battle or its aftermath. All the riders carried bows.

It seemed superfluous but Egen said, 'You must have been the ones who saved us back there.'

'We eased your travel, certainly,' said the leader, 'but it would appear you might have managed quite well on your own. I understand you have no place to stay overnight, or any other night from here on.'

Egen replied, 'From whom do you get that understanding?'

'It matters not,' was the answer. 'The wind travels from many directions.' These mysterious responses seemed the norm outside his home villages, and he assumed that in the wider world, where it was wise to be more cautious, such speech had been developed as a form of defence mechanism, so he did not press for clarification.

The man continued, 'If you would follow us we can solve the problem of your accommodation for tonight and then talk at length. You will be able to add to what we know of you already.'

It was now that Josin remembered the horse. It was the one she had seen standing between the trees and the baggage lines at the great battle, but before she could query it they were on the move again following the four strangers. It was well past midday when they turned into a narrow gorge and stopped beside a cave entrance well hidden by large boulders. The interior was much more spacious than the narrow entrance would have suggested.

Their leader then said, 'We have food in plenty. It will not take long to heat.'

'We do not yet know your names,' said Egen. 'I am Egen and this is Josin.'

Pointing to each in turn the leader said, 'Brennus, Morcant and Drustan, and I am called Venutius.'

Egen's eyebrows rose. 'Is that Venutius, king of the Brigantes?' he queried.

'It is one and the same,' he answered.

'As I understand it,' continued Egen, 'that is a very troubled territory.'

'Let us warm the food, then eat and talk in comfort,' responded Venutius. As they sat he pointed to a far corner of the cavern where there was a plentiful supply of straw and blankets. 'You and Josin may sleep there. Do not worry about watch duties. We four are well acquainted with each other's habits and share the guard duty equably. Now to expound on the troubled situation you spoke of. The union of my Queen Cartimandua and me was arranged for reasons of harmony between our families. There had always been bickering between them and factions with opposing views had arisen. As sometimes happens, instead of increased harmony the bickering got worse. Cartimandua and I are also constantly opposing each other within the factions, and power periodically swings from one to the other.' Noticing the puzzled frowns on the faces of his guests, he continued: 'To understand the reality that is Brigantia it is best to think of it as that mythological beast, the great red dragon born with two heads, each facing in a different direction, and each hating the other owing to its inability to have sole control of the body. The two are in constant strife, yet if one sleeps the other controls the talons. Because their other organs are shared, should one mortally wound the other both would die. The carcase would then be dissected and consumed by that Mediterranean scavenger, Imperial Rome. In the real world it is our duty to deny a permanent foothold to that bloated, self-indulgent monster. At this time my wife sits upon the throne with my former armour bearer as her consort. Had I had the foresight I would have had him spit-roasted and fed to the dogs. Meanwhile, the two are guarded by contingents of Roman militia, and I must fight Rome elsewhere while re-building a force capable of retaking my lands. But before that I have another duty to perform. Tomorrow, should you both agree, we have more to show you, another place to rest, and a proposition to put to you.'

Although being given a free choice, both Egen and Josin felt that, yet again, they were not going to be in control of their own fate. Up until their enforced stay on Berringa's hill, their lives had been controlled by the needs or actions of others, and now that situation seemed to be creeping up on them again. Only this morning, before the chase began, they had been planning to find somewhere to start again and put down roots, and Egen had hoped that that would be far from Roman influence where Josin could lead a more peaceful existence, but such places were few and far between. That chase with its thunder of hooves and swish of swords and arrows took their minds back to the battle and its highs and lows of emotion and sheer physical exhaustion. It made them realise that whatever one's choices they were always going to be affected by circumstances. As Venutius had reminded them when they first spoke, they had no particular plans in mind, and it would seem churlish not to agree, at least until the mysterious proposition was revealed; further acquiescence would depend on the nature of the proposal, and their guides seemed happy with that.

It was a long and arduous journey. After leaving the gorge they soon crossed a metalled Roman road but very quickly left it behind. From there on they travelled across a vast grassy moor surrounded by low hills. The ground was very uneven and littered with water-filled hollows. Had they still been using the chariot it would have been almost impossible to continue, but the fact that it had miraculously changed to a four-wheeled carriage made things a great deal easier. If one wheel sank the ponies were able to drag it forward on the other three. Even so, they would have preferred to be riding horses.

Towards evening they sighted a group of roundhouses in a large area of wetland. Smoke curled up from most of them and there was an irresistible aroma of cooking.

'I am famished,' said Venutius. 'Let us eat.'

And he entered the largest dwelling, followed by Egen and Josin, while the other three took charge of the horses.

9

A Queen Resettled

They entered as a group and, as Venutius stepped aside, Egen and Josin gasped in astonishment. Standing before them and stirring the contents of a cooking vessel was Boudicca with, as always, her two children keeping themselves near to her reach.

She looked up smiling. 'Welcome. It is ready; we can eat at once.'

She was very different from when they had last seen her. The blood had been cleansed from her skin and hair and she wore a new long woollen dress, but her face showed increased strain. Her daughters also looked different, wearing white cotton shifts and plaited hair. They all positioned themselves around the central fire to exchange experiences.

'I was rather busy at the time,' said Boudicca, 'but I did see Egen struck by that javelin. I thought he had been killed. It was not until Brennus conveyed the news that I learnt the truth.'

'From our position after that,' said Josin, 'I saw you totally surrounded and slashing and stabbing at the barbarians. I cannot understand how you survived.'

'Had it not been for Venutius and his friends I would not be here,' Boudicca replied. 'My animals could not go forward owing to the wall of fallen bodies, yet their flying hooves kept the foe at bay from the front. He and his small band arrived just before you had to depart. It would have been not only suicidal but futile for them to have wholeheartedly engaged in the battle, but for some reason they felt a need to rescue me. They charged in and somehow managed to reach the harness of my team, forced it around and steered it up to the baggage train; even then one of his men died – they began as five. My chariot being damaged and the horses exhausted, they transferred all three of us to their own mounts which we shared with them. Paulinus and his troops had not had it entirely their own way. Far more of them were slain than will ever be admitted to. Unfortunately, nearly all of our followers, including the women and children standing innocently with the baggage, were cruelly cut down. In the confusion I believe they did not see us escape. I am eternally grateful to these men, not for myself as I would have willingly fought to the death, but for my daughters. It is amazing, and I am sure you will have had a similar experience, that while stabbing, parrying, killing and exerting oneself to the limit, it is possible at the same time to think clearly and calmly, as with a separate corner of the mind, about other but related things. As I slashed and stabbed and pierced I was conscious of how unfair I was being to my children here; how I love them and should never have got them into this predicament. They have suffered in a way that no child ever should. I must somehow make it up to them – help them to recuperate, to learn what a real and natural life is all about.'

Venutius interjected, 'We could not let any of them die. We will have need of such people again one day. Now you know what it is that those Romans near Berringa's hill were searching for: it was Boudicca. They know not what happened to her. They had not found her body nor those of her children, and they are now for their own purpose disseminating the rumour that all three took poison. That now brings us to our proposition; you may not be aware that today we have completely crossed the lands of the Cornovii and are now in those of the Dobunii. This is as far as my companions and I can go. We need to return to organise the liberation of our own territories, Queen Boudicca and the princesses would be safer in the lands of the Dumnonii much further south, and if necessary even beyond in those small islands to which some travel to meet traders and barter their tin, but which it is not known the Romans visit. Whatever their final destination they require a reliable and trustworthy escort, and that, we hope, will be you.'

Egen for a while hesitated, then said, 'Are you sure of what you ask?

You are suggesting that a one-armed man and a young woman act as fighting escort for a queen and two princesses, travelling across a hostile environment.'

'That,' said Venutius, 'is a bit of an exaggeration. You still have two arms, though one has restricted movement owing to a shoulder wound. However, you have already proved that your right arm, your sword arm, is near unaffected. You can swing a sword and cast a spear, and, although it is not one of your preferred weapons, I would leave you with a bow and a plentiful supply of arrows which I hope you would practise with – Josin also. Because of the pain and difficulty of raising your left arm high, which in time may improve, your aim and stance would be different and awkward, but, provided you can loose an arrow, no one in a closed opposing group would be aware which of them was the intended target. We already know that in many ways Josin can fight as well or better than many men. That sword she wears is not just for show. She can swing it well and even use a small knife on a large assassin to good effect, not forgetting that Boudicca is herself a warrior without equal. All that is well and good for our purpose, but it is really secondary in our thinking. What is more important is that your queen needs a man who thinks as well as acts, a man who has the instincts, eyes and experience of a hunter and the ability to avoid trouble before it arrives. Those we believe are the required qualities, and you have them.'

To Egen it seemed that their hosts had thought it all out to their own satisfaction. There was little in their reasoning that he could argue with, and after much thought and discussion between himself and Josin they agreed; after all, they still had little planned on their own behalf and they would be only too glad to help Boudicca and the girls. After a large breakfast Venutius and his friends turned back, leaving Egen to lead the venture from there on.

In the same way that he and Josin had started the previous day they had no firm destination, merely a rough idea of a required direction in which to travel. He asked the children to ride behind Josin on the supplies and blankets in the wagon, while he and Boudicca followed on two riding ponies they had been given, which were a little taller and sturdier than their own, but every so often he would bound forward to scout the way ahead. He had earlier explained that he and Josin would not be exhibiting any outward respect, not because it was not due, but in order not to raise unwanted attention or curiosity from others they might meet – they wished to appear as a normal family. It was still early and he wanted them to be on their way before the few villagers were up and abroad. They continued to follow a south-westerly route and, having left the wetlands behind, they were soon in hillier, more rugged countryside. It was grey and misty with occasional rain squalls but they saw no sign of habitation whatsoever, and it remained that way into late evening. He was then conscious that he was looking for a place for all of them to settle, that Boudicca and the children were just as disinherited and lost as themselves; their one need was not to be traced.

That night was much as those they had spent during the initial march to join the Iceni. They erected simple shelters just inside the edge of a wood so sparse there were hardly enough trees to hide their presence. It was also noticeably colder than when they had done the same earlier in the year. After a less than comfortable night they pressed on until they arrived at a vast, rough moorland where they could just make out a thin column of smoke on the far side. He decided to head straight towards it. As they got nearer they could see that it was a small hamlet of about five or six homes on a natural mound but enclosed by a high, man-made earth bank. Outside the bank and distanced from it was a large roofed erection with many stout uprights but no walls, protecting a forge-like construction near its centre. Sheep, goats and dogs wandered freely both inside and outside the bank. A gated entrance through the bank was on the side nearest to their approach, and several men and women of widely varying ages came to stand beside the gate and wait. Egen indicated to his companions to hold back while he went forward to speak to the waiting group. He addressed the most aged looking man, assuming him to be the village elder.

'We are reluctant travellers,' he said, 'looking for somewhere to rest. Our homes have been destroyed by fighting with the Romans in the far north. We need somewhere to shelter for the night. Is there perhaps somewhere nearby that would suffice?'

A taller and much younger man whose proportions had obviously been formed by hard physical work stepped forward and replied, 'I am Tegrin, spokesman for these people. We have no accommodation within the earth wall, but if you are truly in need there is a hut the goatherd uses from time to time a little way beyond my forge. It is not in good repair but, once tidied up, it may it may serve your purpose for a night.'

Egen thanked him and called on the others to follow him to view the offer. It was just large enough, though there were gaps in the walls and roof. An old besom had been left lying around and the two women were soon sweeping and tidying, while he made temporary repairs with small amounts of wattle and bracken. After making a small fire they were reasonably warm and comfortable. While they were doing all this, Tegrin surprised them by appearing with a large container of hot stew, which he just indicated was for them before abruptly leaving.

Egen, having got accustomed to the inconvenience and intermittent pain from his shoulder, had regained his previous traits of being a light and alert sleeper. Although distant from the village, he was sure that in the very early hours he had heard the hurried arrival of a horse and rider, and its departure a short time later. He lay and listened for a while with his hand grasping his sword, but as no one attempted to disturb them he tended the fire to ensure that it would burn through the night and returned to his rest. At first light, as they were preparing some left over food, Tegrin reappeared at the entrance but this time looking uncertain.

'I regret that your welcome last evening was not so fulsome as it could have been,' he said, 'but in an isolated village such as this it pays to be very wary. I have since been made aware that you are all more than you would appear and that you deserve courtesy and assistance.'

'We require no more courtesy or respect than you would afford to any of your fellows,' replied Egen. 'We thank you for your tolerance thus far. We expect no further help, but should it be offered we would gratefully accept. I am also curious to know whence you received information about us.'

Tegrin responded, 'It was brought on the passing wind, accompanied by a dapple-grey mare.' He then hurried to add, 'If you would care to stay, my friends and I would be happy to erect another house within the compound, sufficiently large for your needs. Whatever skills you possess could be shared with us, and mayhap you will learn new things. It is not an easy life here, and the winter, which is due soon, can be very severe, but we are free.'

As he was speaking it occurred to Josin that the only dapple-grey mare she had seen in a long time was that ridden by Morcant – a fine animal and probably the fastest and strongest in that band. Then her attention was drawn back to Tegrin as he continued.

'It does not take long to construct a home if all help. As you undoubtedly know, the biggest delay is in waiting for the daub to dry, especially as it is now towards the end of the seasons. If you could see yourselves remaining in this hut for some days you could soon be installed in a suitable building, and the finishing off, including the last stage of drying which occurs on the outside, could be accomplished while you occupy it.'

They did not know how much information about themselves had been passed to him and the villagers, but in any case this was a very generous offer which it would have been very difficult to refuse, even if they had wanted to. The winters might be hard, but much more bearable here than if they had nowhere to go, and the apparent isolation would increase their chances of not being traced. The few children from the hamlet were happy and excited to meet new people, and once the decision had been made their parents were equally welcoming. The entire population of the village, such as it was, seemed eager to start building. The ground was cleared and the circle of uprights and roof supports installed within two days. Wattle walls were made and positioned and, together with the roof covering, fixed within another two. Egen was pleased to note that in this area they were very adept in constructing firmer and more solid doors and entrances; this was considered a necessity against the extreme weather in this part of the country. Soon after that, the daub was mixed, trodden and applied by all, including the very young; even Camorra and Tasca, who rarely spoke, began to leave their mother's side to join in; they also began to take an interest in the youngest children and started to play with them. This pleased Boudicca immensely but she said nothing. As soon as practicable. a small fire was lit within the new home to aid the drying process, and suitable locations chosen for sleeping, storage and other activities. It seemed no time at all before they were living as an integral part of the community with neighbours giving advice and help.

They learnt that it was not quite as isolated as they had first thought. Tegrin's furnace and forge were the central part of a network of operations, whereby a few small hamlets, thinly spread within a large radius, brought in tin and copper ore for smelting. It was a declining activity, but still a useful resource for the village. At this end of the season they concentrated on producing the charcoal that would be needed in the spring, as well as a surplus for domestic use. They also preserved and stored fish and meat, and stocked up on vegetables to see them through the coldest periods when they would almost certainly be locked in their homes by deep snow. The rivers would be frozen and inactive and they would rely mainly on milk for their drink, especially that of the goats. This last did not worry Egen, for ever since that last morning when he had set out to hunt from their first home, warmed goat's milk had been his favoured drink, although he still had a high regard for Berringa's fruit concoction.

It transpired that Tegrin also had a shared ownership in a boat kept on the river about half a day's walk away. It was not so large that it could not be easily handled by two persons, yet large enough to transport a fair amount of metal ingots, or passengers. It was used alongside others from local areas to carry those ingots to small islands well off the southern coast for barter with traders from a more distant land. It was a trading tradition he was convinced had existed since the start of time itself. They met at regular intervals on these islets to which the Romans were not known to go; indeed, it must be said that the waters approaching these islands would have proved hazardous to the more deep keeled Roman vessels. However, their ships could occasionally be seen plying the waters close to the mainland, and if it took their fancy they would not hesitate to attack and rob any other vessel. Roman ship masters did not regard themselves as part of the imperial militia, and once off shore they were a law unto themselves. Tegrin and his companion would, on rare occasions, use the boat for deep water fishing and even to visit other communities.

It was within a few days of moving into the new house that the snows arrived, light and flukey at first but then developing into an almost continuous fall which, for the first three days, marooned all but the hardiest inside their homes. Despite the wind they were snug and warm, protected by the impenetrable layers of snow. It was inevitable, but not pleasant, to be called upon to help search for lost animals buried under deep drifts, or to break the ice from the nearby river to melt for water when necessary. During this period Tegrin, who was not espoused and lived with his parents, voluntarily took on the responsibility of visiting each dwelling to ensure everyone's wellbeing. He appeared to enjoy spending time in the newcomers' home in deep discussions, learning as much as possible about other regions and tribes as well as Roman activities; and with a little knowledge of her past he gave special deference to Boudicca's views. He also seemed to wish to befriend her daughters, but their uncertainty with adult men was quite obvious. Josin also pointed out to Egen that he appeared to be fascinated by Boudicca's long red tresses, and had difficulty taking his eyes from them. As in his early years, Egen would risk the dangers to hunt for fresh meat to share with all, but now, because of the restrictions of his left arm, he would seek a young strong volunteer to accompany him and help carry the prize. Two together also reduced the danger a little in these treacherous conditions and rough terrain. He was pleased, however, when one morning he looked out to see water dripping fast from the eaves. The lying snow was less smooth, and sodden grey-black scrub showed through here and there. The little river was glistening brightly and attempting to move: the thaw had arrived.

The snow cleared and Egen threw himself into the life of the village; Josin however, did not seem to be so positive as was her usual nature. Whether or not it was the reaction to being cooped up for so long, or the comparative inactivity, he could not be sure, and she was not readily responding to his questions or concerns. It was several days more before she confided to him that she was with child, and that she was not at all certain that this is where she would wish to bring up that child. He was delighted with her news but also admitted that it raised one or two new problems. The first and most important was finding somewhere she would feel safe and happy. He felt that he still had an obligation to Boudicca and the girls, and the villagers had proved to be so generous in providing the house and other things, not to mention friendship. That evening Tegrin arrived for one of his discussions and they revealed to him and the others their news and concerns. To their surprise, no-one was put out by their desire to move on, although it was repeatedly expressed that when they found a new home they would be missed.

'Your child and a suitable place to raise it are your most important considerations,' said Boudicca. 'You have demonstrated your loyalty to me and risked your lives alongside mine, you owe me nothing. The obligation is all on our side.'

'In any case I will make myself responsible in your place,' interjected Tegrin. 'Provided she is happy to do so, Boudicca and her children can continue to live here, so the house is no issue. The only real problem is where to look to satisfy your needs and desires.'

Apart from the occupying power and its acolytes, the couple were agreed that none had shown ill will towards them, and wondered just how good a society could have been developed had it not been for the invasion. Naturally, there had always been internal brushes between tribes, but the Roman incursion had exaggerated that situation enormously. In claiming to be a great civilisation Rome had destroyed another that it did not know existed, and for the main part did not care about.

It was fully seven days before Tegrin spoke of the situation again, during which time the snow had cleared completely, and apart from other things Egen and Josin had regularly practised with the bow. She very quickly became quite skilled. Her condition was not so advanced as to affect the activity and, despite his difficulties in having to bend his head down almost to his arm, Egen learnt to send an arrow in roughly the right direction, though without any real degree of accuracy. The information imparted by Tegrin was to the effect that contacts had been made but generally things had become difficult.

'There remains only one settlement,' he said, 'which I believe would meet with your requirements, and at this time it has one dwelling vacant owing to the death of an aged and sickly couple who, despite much care from their friends and neighbours, did not survive the winter. The problem is that during our climate-enforced lock-down, which I am given to understand was not nearly so severe elsewhere, much has happened across the land. Since the sacking of the towns in the east and the great battle north of here, the Romans have been very busy, not only rebuilding but also cruelly enforcing the strict military administration. They have instituted frequent and large patrols from Isca Dumnoniorum to the coast near Dintagell, then south from there for some little distance where they have set a small fort-cum-staging post. Those patrols stop and question any persons at large. If they even suspect that they are not fully supportive of the empire, they do not hesitate to execute them on the spot. Whole families have been slain without compunction. The significant problem to us is that the home I refer to is in Dintagell, inland from that coastal staging post, which happily is considered by the occupier to be strategically unimportant and consequently seldom fully manned. The surrounding countryside is hillier and warmer than here with a rugged coastline. Probably higher but I believe in many ways comparable to your original home where you were raised. I have sent word to them and, if you so wish, I will guide you there soon, the problem being to avoid those evil patrols, and the best way to do that is to go the long way round by sea. Even then in concert with the land patrols their ships are now more frequently interfering with our trading excursions, but fortunately the number in these waters are few and we are mostly able to avoid them.'

Josin was anxious to explore the possibility. She was grateful to these people and liked them a great deal, but it was not the sort of place she wanted to settle in. It was almost another seven days before they were able to set off, but by then the travelling conditions had improved, although it was still very cold. They enlisted the aid of another young man who would return the horses and wagon, which would then become the property of Boudicca. Until that time it enabled them to transport themselves and their few belongings in comfort. Their farewells to her were emotional, and even the two girls had tears in their eyes and held Egen and Josin tight. The entire village came out, even though it was early in the day, to see them off and pay their respects.

The journey to the boat was uneventful; they saw nothing to cause concern. The boat lay tethered on the river with Tegrin's co-owner, Elissed, watching over it. It was a flat-bottomed craft with four thwarts, a single stepped mast and a square brown sail furled beneath a single spar. The moment they clambered aboard with their baggage Elissed pushed off. At first, the river was narrow and they did not use the sail but guided it by use of the steering board alone, allowing the current to carry them on. Quite suddenly, the river widened appreciably and Tegrin spread the sail to take advantage of a following wind. A small headland jutted out from the right bank and once past it they found themselves reaching out towards the open sea. It was not warm. Josin had heeded Tegrin's advice and was wearing her thickest woollen cloak. They veered north and, after a small adjustment to the sail, the wind continued to aid them, but also encouraged a dense mist sweeping in from the ocean to follow them. The two sailors appeared to know exactly where they were heading but never allowed themselves to lose sight of land. To Egen and Josin who were unused to travel by boat it seemed they were endlessly moving slowly forwards, up and down and rocking side to side, the waves alongside rolling into high and smoothly rounded crests and deep troughs. They soon got used to the perspective and realised they were travelling faster than it appeared against the backdrop of the far shore. Josin found it exhilarating to be able to see nothing ahead at one moment, other than a steep sloping wall of grey-green water, and the next to be sitting at the top of that wall watching those apparently solid smooth crests dashing themselves to pieces on the rocky shore far ahead.

They were all concentrating on the way ahead when their thoughts were interrupted by that now familiar screeching wail of a body-looped horn. Looking back, they saw emerging from the bank of cloud behind them the unmistakable shape of a Roman war galley, under full sail and straining oars. They watched as it turned more directly towards them and heard a repeat of that unearthly wail.

'They have seen us,' screamed Tegrin unnecessarily. 'Move to that thwart behind you. I will need room to adjust the sail and use the oars. Elissed will steer from aft.'

'Can we outrun them?' asked Egen.

'No,' replied Tegrin. 'We are much smaller and lighter, and we turn much more quickly, but with those oars they are much faster in a straight line. However, because of its weight that ship sits much lower in the water, while we more or less scud along the surface with only one set of oars and a small sail. It is going to be a trial of seamanship. Ellissed can manoeuvre a boat better than most. We are dead if they catch up with us; we must therefore do whatever we can to avoid them.'

Josin could not help but shudder at the thought of being thrown into that icy water in a race to get away, and involuntarily drew her cloak more tightly about her. They skipped along, alternately high on a crest then low in a trough. Their pursuers in the heavier craft, rowing frantically but strongly, were getting nearer, its high prow and long ram first rising above the wave and then digging deep as it dropped down into the trough. Tegrin and Elissed began to exchange hand signals and shouted into the wind before settling back to concentrate on their allotted tasks.

'What is happening?' screamed Josin.

Tegrin replied, 'You must trust us. We are attempting to trap them, it is our only chance. We are going to try to ride constantly on the top of this roller, surfing along with it, keeping our speed allied to it with steering board, oars and sail adjustments. If you look ahead at the top of that rolling wave about five ahead of us, in a few moments you will see two small spumes of white water erupt about half way down that wave little more apart than our boat is wide, and a faint creamy line joining the two. That indicates rocks at the deepest part of the trough just below the surface. Elissed knows those rocks and their exact position well; he does this often for sport. The vessel chasing us sits deeper in the water, and the master appears to be concentrating on overhauling us rather than watching the way ahead. I think you now understand. It is not going to be easy, but should anything go wrong hang on hard to Egen who I know can swim.'

She did not bother to remind him about Egen's weak arm, but looked once more at that icy water, clung to him and remained motionless. She felt the boat come to the top of the wave and watched as its crew worked furiously to keep it there. They successfully sped along without dropping low, and she kept her eyes on the spot where she expected to see the tell tale spumes appear, low down and behind the roller in front of them. Momentarily they were there and a heartbeat later they disappeared beneath them; she held her breath. Then they were past the point and suddenly dropped into the trough, turning broadside on as they did so and getting drenched in spray. They were still afloat – wet but afloat – and she turned her head to look back. She saw the high prow and ram of the following ship rise above its wave, then dip into the trough, and before it could rise once more come to a thunderous, jarring halt. The following wave lifted the whole ship once more and lurched it forward to smash down again with a loud crack, much louder than before, and the stern was lifted high on the following wave; its back was obviously broken. The ram broke away and pointed skywards, and the mast jerked forward as though to meet it when the supporting stays broke. Ropes, chains, shields, weapons, smashed and broken timbers, and smashed and broken bodies, were hurled into the whirling water and onto the rocks on which the wreckage was now stuck, reminiscent of, but much enlarged, the bucket of slops ejected overboard by a crew member not much earlier.

She and Egen watched this event almost in disbelief – it all seemed to happen in slow motion as they mentally recorded every detail. Conversely, the other two glimpsed only a small part of the drama as they were too busy controlling their own vessel, using oars and board to try to turn it away from the shoreline.

Elated, Tegrin shouted, 'I have never seen you shoot that jump better. Good work!'

'It took two of us,' replied Elissed, 'but it is good to have escaped their clutches.'

Gradually, pulling and working hard, they brought the boat around. Eventually, they were able to tack back onto their original course and reset the sail, after which they made steady progress. Josin could not help but wonder at her own conflict of emotions, whereas she had never relished the idea of going into battle with spear or sword she had never shrunk from it. Today, however, the prospect of being plunged into that vast grey-green ocean had terrified her. She rationalised that in the one situation it was with hot blood, but in the other she would have been entirely helpless and icy cold. Today she was also carrying a child and that in itself put her feelings and emotions at odds with each other.

Soon they headed for a very small bay with a sand and shingle beach under the protection of a rocky promontory. To the right of that projection, just above high water mark, was a cave from which four people emerged and came forward to help pull the boat aground. Once they were all ashore and unloaded Tegrin introduced them: Haerviu the chief of the elders, Genofeva his wife and Ninian and Seisyll their two teen-aged sons.

'We were not expecting to be met,' said Tegrin.

Haerviu replied, 'We knew you would be arriving today and kept vigil. When we saw a fighting ship on patrol we had hoped to signal a warning to you somehow.'

'We saw it and avoided it, thank you,' stated Tegrin. 'But as you are now here we will, with your permission, start the return journey immediately; the conditions are not in our favour and it will be long and difficult. We shall need to set a course towards the tin islands, and even then pull hard, and at some appropriate point tack back to our home river, but with more assistance from the wind.'

Josin was concerned and asked, 'Are you not worried about meeting another ship?'

'I told you that they have few vessels in this vicinity; now they have one less. We would be extremely unlucky to meet another.'

With that they pushed hard into the surf and rowed strongly into the waves.

Genofeva turned to Josin and said, 'We have cleaned and perfumed the house, should you decide to stay, and if any repairs are needed we shall help with those also.'

'I am sure that whatever you have done,' replied Josin, 'is far more than we deserve. My only concern is the proximity of the Roman post; now that I am carrying a child I have little desire to harm it by having to thrust a lance or swing a sword.'

Haerviu broke in, 'The fort you refer to is certainly much nearer to you now than is the house prepared for you. It actually surmounts the cliff directly above us, but do not be too concerned. Its regular garrison, if it can be called that, comprises only two legionnaires and four auxiliaries. It is there merely to maintain a presence; should any of them venture out for any reason it would leave the fort vulnerable. They therefore do not open its gates for any purpose other than to change the personnel every seventh day. The new guard arrives on foot, accompanied by twenty others. They then have a change-over ceremony. The old guard returns with them to their main camp, about five thousand paces distant; then, I am given to understand, they get thoroughly drunk. They know little or nothing about the vicinity or our village, and care even less. Provided we do nothing to disturb them, they reciprocate by not interfering with us or our hamlet. If it became necessary to swing a sword, it would more likely to be against pirate slave traders from Hibernia, and even they usually operate much further north. Our village is about one thousand paces inland from here, surrounded by woodland. Please come and see.'

They were guided along a narrow path up and over the cliffs away from the headland and sea into a thinly wooded area. They then traversed more difficult rocky ground towards thick forest, some distance into which was a clearing allowing for the small village. It was, as predicted by Tegrin, much like their first home but on higher ground composed of hard rock. They both felt immediately at home and memories of their former lives flooded back. They were shown to the vacant house and found that it was not only clean with sweet smelling new hay, straw and blankets, but also had several days' supply of provisions.

'If you would like to rest,' said Haerviu, 'we can talk tomorrow. You have had a long and eventful journey.'

Almost the entire following day was spent in discussion with him and his family, exchanging knowledge and experiences. He correctly assumed that Josin, who had always been present at Athan's gatherings, listening to his teachings and pronouncements, would have a great deal of stored knowledge of such. Now that the brotherhood had been severely savaged on Mona, and it was likely that few, if any, had survived, there would certainly be no further missions from that place. This left a great void of wisdom and friendship to be filled. She herself was amazed at how, with a little prompting, her memory of that teaching could be extracted like a continuous thread of hidden knowledge. Even more surprising was that she found that she could, simply by concentrating on a related word or phrase, recall information imparted by Athan which had been lying dormant in some inner recess of her memory. As Haerviu had perceived, Josin would be able to help fill that void.

Egen's long experience of hunting and his fighting abilities would certainly not be superfluous to the hamlet's requirements, where existing skills mainly centred about agriculture. Both of them would be welcome assets to the community, and both were eager to be accepted. To raise a child here would appear not only to be pleasant but no more dangerous than anywhere else in this occupied land. They gave the whole of the next day to settling in and getting to know their new neighbours, the nearest of which were Arthfael and Elvina with their young daughter Cara. The well built Arthfael was the village's metal worker, as had been Gwain, Josin's father, and because she was able to recognise and understand many of the processes used, a friendly rapport was immediately built up between them. It was agreed that on the following day, while Elvina would show Josin around the facilities available in the hamlet, Arthfael would take Egen beyond its boundaries to familiarise him with the surrounding terrain. Neither ponies nor horses were available at that time, so they would be gone for at least two days. Egen insisted that the first item on the agenda be to reconnoitre the fort; these days his wife and his future child were his main, if not his only, concern, and their security was uppermost in his thoughts.

Dawn saw both men on their way and, despite his heavy build, Arthfael proved to be surprisingly fast and agile, and the distance between home and the coast was covered in a very short space of time. From the cover of the trees, and on one occasion by climbing a tall oak, Egen studied and committed to memory the layout of the post. It was quite small, consisting of one single-storey L-shaped stone building with a pitched roof and a wide door at one end only. The shuttered apertures were high on the walls and smoke curled up from a short chimney emerging from one of those walls, indicating that the building was occupied though no other sign of life could be seen. He had already been told that they did not set a guard to patrol the walkway until sunset. The entire stronghold, including a small forecourt, was encircled by a comparatively high spiked wooden palisade with the walkway at the inside top, in such a way that it came within reach of the chimney wall. At the opposite end were two large gates held closed by a substantial oak beam dropped into iron hooks at each end. It would have taken at least two men to remove the beam. Satisfied, they returned, but skirted north of the village to a track on its far side, passing through the trees, after which they emerged into open ground sloping slowly away from them. Continuing on and down, they passed a meadow-like area bounded on three sides by very steep, rock-filled banks and, lower down. on the fourth alongside the track by a wicker fence and gate. In the meadow grazed two very old ponies and several goats. A hut stood to one side within the enclosure, rough but weather proof.

'These are our only transport at the moment,' said Arthfael, pointing to the ponies. 'Very old and only of use for the lightest tasks. The goats, however, are also communally owned and very useful. Young lads take it in turns each day to watch over them, using the hut for shelter, among other things. They are quite happy to do it. The villagers know it is a boring job so pamper them with good food and drink while here. The older boys actually vie with each other for the privilege as it gives them somewhere to be with a girl away from prying eyes.'

From the gate the path was less steep and petered out onto a scrub-covered moor. Here they rested to eat a little of the food they carried, then proceeded in a slightly more northerly direction. At one point they crossed a Roman road, turned and travelled parallel with it to the east, ensuring they were not seen by other travellers. Then, in the distance, they saw a fortification with a small town growing about it. On they went and skirted the complex but noticed that annexed to the south side of the fort was stabling for about twenty horses. Egen studied the area carefully and concluded that all the animal tracks travelled to and from the east. None went westwards, the direction from which they were approaching. From a few hundred paces behind the town, and then as far as the eye could see, the terrain developed into wetlands with clumps of varied vegetation and trees here and there on islands of firmer soil, but if access to any of them existed it was well hidden. Arthfael stated that although traversing those wetlands looked impossible, to those in the know it was perfectly possible at certain points, and many of the islets were joined by pathways. A system of secret markers had been developed and pointed the way across.

'I can certainly see no markers,' said Egen.

'That is because you are not meant to,' was the reply. 'I will explain them to you. Few people know how to espy and use them, certainly not Romans or their allies, and it must be kept that way. Look to your right and you will see a sapling with a different type of growth around it and slightly taller than its neighbours.'

'You mean that one without growth below about two thirds its height?' asked Egen.

'The same, and that lack of lower branches is not an accident of nature. Now look for another similar tree out in the marsh, but nearer to it than others and dressed in the same fashion; between the two will be a straight treadable path. At each change of direction of that path will be found another small tree similarly treated. By following that route most of the larger central refuges may be safely reached. Without this knowledge, anyone who sees those trees in those surroundings actually sees nothing and understands nothing. Those large central plots are for the greater part covered in high scrub and encircled by tall reeds. Thus it is possible for very many people, even a small army, to hide from pursuers for a long time. They would be quite safe, provided the secret of those paths was not revealed to their enemies; in any case, it takes practice to use the system with confidence. Those trees are kept that way, and the paths maintained in reasonable but unobtrusive condition by locals who are not town dwellers, and when seen by "townies" they give the impression that they are innocently coppicing. Now you know the secret I must swear you to keep it such. Groups of patriotic warriors hide in there and probably watch us at this moment. We have a blanket each and there is concealed cover. We can spend the night here and, should we meet with others, I can introduce and vouch for you.'

With Arthfael leading they entered the swampland and proceeded along a wandering track towards the central mounds of vegetation and firm ground. As they progressed Egen noted that the system of markers worked very well. From time to time when well into the morass they would be challenged by armed men, but Arthfael was always able to reassure them. This happily confirmed to Egen that the resistance was continuing. Having found a suitably isolated and sheltered spot they wrapped themselves in their blankets and waited for morning.

When the sun rose they ate and made their way back to where they had entered the swamp. Egen then suggested that they would get back much earlier with the help of horses. His companion immediately understood and grinned. Carefully and quietly they retraced their steps to the fort and town. Approaching from the south, they were relieved to note that outside the town perimeter no one was abroad at that hour, and were able to select a suitable spot from which to watch the stables. Soon three men in half armour only, yawning widely and without helmets, rode from a side street alongside the stables and loosely tethered their mounts. They each took another horse, attached bridles to them and walked them back into the side street.

'I believe some sort of training exercise is being readied in the town centre,' whispered Egen. 'Now, quickly and quietly!'

Silently they emerged from their hiding place, grasped the reins of the three saddled horses, led them back to their vantage point and mounted them, the third being hitched to Egen's saddle. Certain that they had not been seen, they turned again towards the wetlands; when almost there with no sign of pursuit, they changed direction again and took a large circulatory route across the moorland until facing north-east and home. On the journey back they regaled each other by imagining how those cavalrymen would explain to their commander how three horses, complete with all accoutrements, could have vanished into thin air. Whatever explanation was accepted or recorded, if any, it is almost certain that the distribution of wine would be seriously curtailed for some considerable time, and the amount of denarii credited to their pay packets reduced. Soon they were at the moor-land which sloped gently upwards towards the forest in which was home. At the gate to the pony and goat enclosure they whistled for the duty goatherd who came out of the hut silently but with an uncertain look on his face; they assumed he was upset at being disturbed, especially as a distinctly female foot and ankle was just discernible within the hut. Without explanation, but with instructions to care for them, they handed over the horses into his keeping and walked towards the village.

As they got near they somehow sensed that all was not well. The first to meet them, with a grave look on her face, was Josin. Curiously, she held Egen back while at the same time motioning Arthfael to continue home. All the villagers had congregated in small groups but turned to watch as he passed between them. Josin quickly and breathlessly explained to Egen an event which had happened while they were away which shocked, angered and disgusted him. Just after the two men had departed the previous day, young Cara began collecting sticks for the family fire but had become engrossed in the antics of a red squirrel darting about gathering food and innocently followed it about. She then realised that she had strayed far away from home and was completely lost. She tried to retrace her steps but in her panic moved in entirely the wrong direction, emerging from the trees to find herself very close to the staging post. Before she could escape she was scooped up and carried inside, where two soldiers then subjected her to physical abuse of the most savage and demeaning kind, while the others looked on and laughed. She was then thrust out and the gates shut and firmly barred. There she was found in a hysterical condition by the villagers who had been searching for her. While she had been relating this to Egen they had been walking towards Cara's home. They did not go in; instead they stood quietly outside, waiting. They did not wish to intrude at such a time but remained ready to help.

All was silent for a while, then came a howl of anguish and Arthfael rushed out with a sword in one hand and a large hammer in the other, his face so distorted with rage that he was hardly recognisable. Egen stepped in front of him, held him, and asked what it was he was going to do.

'To kill them of course, kill all of them.'

'If you go now,' said Egen, 'I will certainly go with you, but stay a moment to think. Should we actually get near to that stockade, which is unlikely, we still have to get in. They are stupid savage fools without humanity, but even they, after such a crime, would realise it would be unwise not to keep a watch day and night. Should we somehow, either by force or trickery, get within those gates, which is even more unlikely, the possibility of killing two or more before we ourselves are slain is also remote; that would only worsen the situation for both Elvina and Cara, not to mention Josin.'

'You are not suggesting that I let them live!' wailed Arthfael.

'No, my friend,' he answered, 'let us be certain to kill them all. Give me until this evening to devise a plan. Should I not be able to work out a scheme, all of us, few as we are, will attack in such force that they will not escape the consequences of their evil acts. Until then return inside and comfort your women. It will give you time to steady your sword arm to cut them down more effectively.'

Without realising it, he had taken command of any fighting potential available without objection from anyone. Arthfael, still striving to cope with his deep anguish and anger and unable to think clearly or decide what would be for the best, acquiesced and hesitantly retreated back to his family; the sounds of combined grief could be heard from within the dwelling.

Egen's thoughts had been racing ahead and he turned to Josin and said, 'I know from watching you practising that your skills with the bow have improved remarkably. Do you think that from a distance of about forty paces you could strike a target in moonlight about the size of my hand? What I am trying to say is that from the observations by people of this village the garrison divides the night into four equal parts, who take it in turn to patrol that high walkway, although they are not very diligent in doing so. While striding about only their heads and shoulders show above the parapet. The shoulders and chests are covered in armour and the heads shrouded by helmets, so the target area is small. We need to take one out as the others sleep, and we need him to die silently; you would have to aim for the throat. For them it is a long and lonely vigil and inevitably as they pace about they tend to stop and look out into the night. That is your opportunity. Success depends on the accuracy of your aim. You must kill him but, should he make noises of alarm, we will storm the wall regardless, it will take time for his colleagues to respond. I hope that in your condition this will be the last time we require a war-like action from you, at least for a very long time.'

'What you are asking will be very difficult,' she answered. 'I can only say that I will do my very best.'

He nodded, then sought out Haervieu. 'Is there a long ladder in the village, long enough to climb the palisade?'

'The way we build our homes and the modest height adopted does not require the use of such,' he responded, 'but if that is what you wish you shall have one by nightfall.'

'In that case,' said Egen, 'the only other requirement is several armed and brave young men as back up.'

He then went to explain the plan to Arthfael.

As the whole round moon rose into a cloudless night sky it caused grotesque and intense shadows to be cast from the trees and fortification. This enabled Josin, well hidden by those shadows, to get much closer than had at first been anticipated. It also meant that she would be aiming upwards, much nearer to the vertical. Egen and Arthfael waited unseen under the trees with the new scaling ladder balanced on their shoulders and an old blanket tucked under Egen's belt. The patrolling guard mentally granted himself a minute or two of stand down from duty – after all, who would see or challenge him – and with arms outstretched resting lightly on the sharpened posts of the palisade, stared out at the shiny reflecting horizon of the sea, bored and sleepy. At the precise moment that Josin loosed her arrow the waiting pair leaped forward and threw the ladder against the wooden wall. Her aim was perfect. The arrow pierced the man's under jaw and drove straight up into his brain; he was dead even before his legs stopped giving support to his body. Much later Egen was to remark, when recalling the incident, that had the arrow had only a little more force behind it it would have lifted the unfastened helmet clear of the man's head. Although the body fell and rolled off the unguarded footway to the courtyard, it made only a dull thud, insufficient to wake anyone sleeping in the building. Both men dashed up the ladder and threw themselves over the top of the sharpened timbers, and even at that moment of intense action Egen was able to reflect how he had been able to adjust to the restricted movement of his arm and how little it interfered with his actions. He threw the blanket to his companion and descended quickly and quietly to make sure the man really was dead, that Josin's shot had been as accurate as had appeared. The blanket was stuffed into the chimney to prevent any further escape of smoke before Arthfael leaped down to join him. One of the back-up team, a little bolder than the others, also climbed the ladder and watched from the walkway as both men hurried silently to the closed door and waited with Arthfael to the fore.

It was not long before they saw smoke curling out of one of the slatted shutters. A little later they heard intense coughing accompanied by shouted curses and choking gasps, followed by the crashing of furniture being overturned. The door flew open and two men stumbled forward pushing against each other in a desperate attempt to get out, choking and coughing through the smoke. Arthfael felled the first with a single thrust of his sword and smashed the skull of the second with a wide swing of his hammer. Two more in the same state of distress and unable to see what had happened to their comrades, also struggled through the opening and tripped over the bodies. The force of the swing of his hammer had pulled Arthfael well to one side, allowing Egen to step forward and annihilate both with a single swing of his blade. They stood at the entrance as they could hear a fifth man coughing uncontrollably. With his arm masking his face Arthfael ventured in and was able to make out the shape of the last soldier; without wasting time he thrust deeply and ended that cough forever. When he emerged, just as any other man who had not killed before, he was still emotionally wound up, confused by the fact that the guilty men were dead and that revenge had been achieved so quickly and so easily. Unable to come down from that emotional high he rushed about as though looking for more of the enemy, attacking anything associated with them. Meanwhile, Egen ordered the watching back-up man to remove the blanket from the chimney, then help him remove the bar from the gate, after which the smoke was sufficiently cleared from the interior of the building to allow re-entry. Arthfael, having smashed a line of amphorae that were lined up outside now charged in and demolished two stone statues, one of Mithras and the other of Bacchus. He then appeared to regain a measure of self control and calmed a little, although tears of frustration still coursed down his face. Outside again he was still shaking when Egen took hold of him, relieved him of his weapons and advised him to return home with one of the younger men and to show himself to Elvina, who would be waiting anxiously, and assure her that he was well and that young Cara had been avenged.

Arthfael looked back at him with a half-quizzical, half-blank look and said, 'But she has not; it is not enough. Elvina and I have talked and what was visited upon our little Cara was a much greater evil than the killing of those who physically committed the crime can compensate for. It is a crime for which the whole of Rome is responsible, the whole of Imperial Rome; it must be destroyed in its entirety and never allowd to rise again as a power in the known world.'

Egen replied, 'I agree but am of the opinion that it may take a lifetime or more.'

'If it takes forever it must be started now,' answered Arthfael, then allowed himself to be led home.

Josin had entered the courtyard with the remainder of the back-up team and assessed the outcome of their efforts.

Egen congratulated her for her accuracy with the bow and added, 'I do not know whether legend and superstition travels far with these idolaters, but let us see.'

He asked the men to cut and collect a number of long branches complete with foliage, to sharpen the cut ends, then thrust them deep into all the wounds suffered by the victims. All the weapons within the fort were to be collected and transferred to the village as they might well be needed in the future; the bodies were to be left as they lay but decorated with the branches as instructed. He forced the gates as wide open as he could get them and, knowing that tomorrow was the seventh day, arranged for two men to stay hidden on the far side of the track to watch. One opined that at least it made a change from overseeing goats and horses. Egen answered him by saying that in the same way he would make certain that they were well fed, but in this instance continued watchfulnes was essential, so no females would be allowed near; as soon as they saw or heard anything untoward they must report without delay. While he was saying this he privately re-avowed that never again would Josin be asked to commit a violent act; she must from now on be protected from the high emotion accompanying such violence – he must avoid all risk to her and their child. The watch would be changed at regular intervals.

It was late the following day before they heard in the far distance the wail of that looped horn signalling the approach of the relief garrison. It was heard also in the hamlet, and Egen with two others hurried to the vantage point, meeting on the way one of the duty watchers returning to report the sound. When there they settled to observe the reaction of the relief guard as it arrived. That strange wailing signal was repeated as the marchers rounded a bend in the trail to come into full view. The unsuspecting members of the parade were almost at the gates before they noticed them already open. This was totally irregular: the ceremony required that trumpeted salutes be exchanged before they were swung wide. The commander assumed that the current occupants were over anxious to finish their spell of duty, so he called the replacements forward and dutifully had his part of the signal sounded. When nobody appeared from the stockade he became confused and ordered the new men in. They entered in an orderly and disciplined manner, but seconds later emerged in an undisciplined turmoil, shouting, cursing and swearing at the senior officer. He could not understand what he was being told over the howls of abuse from his men, so, to his credit, accompanied by two more men, he entered the post himself to learn whatever it was that had caused this disorder and resentment. It was almost a repeat performance of the first entry, but this time all were convinced of what they had seen but could not believe. The entire company retreated in a halting and fractious manner, cursing anything and everyone, each other and their commander, even the stones over which they tripped and stumbled. Above it all could occasionally be heard shouts of 'dancing trees' and 'flying demons'. The legend had travelled. Order and discipline could not be restored, especially by an officer who was just as shaken and terrified as his men, and they soon fled back the way they had come; even that great circular horn had been thrown to the ground and abandoned.

Having given them enough time to be completely out of sight, Egen ordered the inner building to be razed to the ground and the curtain wall burned; nothing was to be left standing. Then, in accordance with druidical teaching, the bodies were stripped and left for the wolves. What would happen next could not be predicted. It was unimaginable that the Roman hierarchy would ignore the situation, yet at the same time it would be extremely difficult to get men to return to this now bedevilled area; the superstitious mind of the ordinary auxiliary was well known and a powerful obstacle to good order. It was assumed that at some stage a very large force would be sent in the belief that whatever the threat there was safety in numbers, and the situation would be regularised to the satisfaction of the administrators.

From then on a continuous watch would be kept by the community on all access roads until the position became clear. They were not to know, but the military administration in Isca Dumnonorium was desperately short of manpower. Too many troops had been requisitioned to help rebuild Camulodunum and Londinium in the east, and it had been estimated by the administrators that it would require a very large task force, if only to do battle with the superstitions of the auxiliaries, to normalise the situation in Dintagell. Consequently, they thought it best to abandon it altogether. Quite apart from which, to order men to return to what they believed to be a bewitched area could well invite the mutiny which they feared above anything else. Dintagell was quietly obliterated from maps and the region left as an uninhabited void.

Without realising it, Egen and his new friends had won one of the first victories in the battle to free the country from the invaders; they had, in effect, denied land and access to the occupying forces. Day after day the duty watch reported nothing to be concerned about, no Roman patrols or replacements had appeared, and eventually the watch was discontinued, but all inhabitants were exhorted to remain vigilant. For everyone, life in the hamlet relaxed as never before; for everyone that is except Arthfael and his little family. Cara was never to be seen playing outside her home again without the close proximity of both her parents.

In turn, her parents were not seen again with any trace of a smile. The whole village, including Egen and Josin as their closest neighbours, tried desperately to re-engage with them, to return them to some semblance of their former selves, but it seemed a hopeless task. They confided to Egen their fears that a return to normality would be impossible in this place. On the few occasions they had been able to get Cara out of the house all those things which were familiar and unthreatening in the vicinity somehow reminded her of that evil day; they would have to return home and allow her to curl up in a dark corner with her own private thoughts. They were of the opinion that they would have to try somewhere new and far away, somewhere where things were not familiar so as not to bring bad memories back to her. When someone has suffered amidst well known surroundings, to see them again does not bring reassurance, they reasoned.

'Elvina and I have talked,' said Arthfael, 'and agreed that we need to make a completely new start, much as you and Josin did when coming here.'

'If that is your decision,' said Egen, 'where do you intend to look? There is fighting of one sort or another everywhere. You must deliberate carefully.'

'We have,' he answered, and rather surprisingly stated, 'We intend to look to the land of the Silures, if they will have us.'

'But,' retorted Egen, 'that is where the fiercest resistance to the empire since Boudicca's revolt is continuing. The journey between here and there would be long and hazardous, you would have to cross the line of fighting to join them, and, apart from the new surroundings for Cara, would it directly benefit yourselves in any way?'

He answered, 'It is Cara that matters, but we reason it thus: provided we can reach it safely that line of fighting is important. Behind it there should be little hostile activity and the further west one goes the safer it should be, provided of course that we are accepted. If I can get them to accept us there should be reasonable safety for both Elvina and Cara in one of their villages near to the coast; in which case I would be only too happy to bear arms alongside them at the fighting line.'

'When do you intend to start?' asked Egen.

'As soon as we can obtain a suitable cart for transport,' replied Arthfael.

'Give me time to make arrangements for Josin,' Egen said. 'She is still a little distant from her time so, provided she is agreeable, and with your permission, I will accompany you. Two men are required to escort your ladies on such a venture; even the most committed man needs to sleep sometime.'

Josin also wanted Elvina and Cara to be safe and readily agreed, even though she did not wish Egen to be gone for too long or to take unnecessary risks. He then sought out Haerviu and Genovefa and begged that they keep an eye on her while he was away. They readily agreed to do so and added that if she had any physical tasks to perform they would instruct one of their sons to do them for her.

The following day, with the permission of the villagers, Arthfael took charge of a four-wheeled wagon that some years previously had been abandoned at the back of the hamlet. It was in need of serious repair, having been used as a plaything by the older children, and he set about doing that immediately. Although large, it had no steering mechanism other than the independence of its four great wheels on fixed shafts, so turning manoeuvres had to be accomplished solely through sideways pressure applied to the draw shaft by the draught animals, causing it to skid around somewhat – and which probably was one of the reasons for its abandonment. While making turns wider and more difficult, it also made it very stable and easy to keep moving in a straight line, and had the added advantage of being easier and quicker to restore. It was high sided, and the two men constructed a close-woven slatted wood platform just below the top of the sides but not quite the full length, thereby creating a void beneath with a short space behind the driver's bench. That void could, with reasonable comfort, accommodate four persons lying down, yet allow passengers to sit comfortably upright behind the driver, or, if necessary, duck down and be covered by an old cloak, or whatever was to hand. It would be extremely unlikely that all four would need to use it at the same time, except as emergency shelter in very inclement weather. Above the platform would be hay or fuel, piled high to disguise the cart's purpose as well as making it weather-proof and warm.

A few days later Arthfael disappeared on one of the captured Roman horses, only to return much later in the evening leading two cobs which showed signs of having been used in harness; not young animals but satisfactory for the intended purpose. Apparently, he had obtained them by bartering his treasured metal-working tools in another village some distance to the north-east, which few in this commune even knew existed. Once a few personal possessions and provisions had been loaded, and weapons hidden, but so as to be quickly to hand, all was ready for a dawn start.

10

The Search for the Silures

An early morning start it certainly was; dawn had yet to show itself. Cara had been advised that they would be looking for a new home, consequently she was anxious and agitated but still uncommunicative; she had not slept, nor shown any outward sign of being happier. Despite the early hour, most of the villagers were assembled to see them off; they had spent their whole lives there and were well loved.

Arthfael took control of the first leg and directed the line of travel north-east through an area he was familiar with. Cara sat staring at the passing scene but showed no signs of emotion. Once they had got to the hamlet where he had bartered his tools for the ponies, and beyond which he was less certain of the geography, she appeared to show flickers of interest, still silent but somehow less distant and anxious; however, she was with both parents and Egen, whom she trusted, and they tried not to read too much into it.

They had agreed to try not to arouse suspicion by travelling alongside or across farmed land; the load they carried would fit with the topography and, so they hoped, keep them away from Roman roads and their builders, if there were any, for they had seen few signs of such. Nevertheless, the countryside was high and rugged and the going not easy. They struggled on, trying not to over extend the animals, and were thankful when the terrain levelled out into moorland; avoiding the scrub was then the main obstacle to progress. It was late evening when they found themselves trying to make their way through an area of tall, dense shrubs. Egen, using all his skills and instincts as a hunter, had not been able to find evidence of recent human presence, so here seemed as good a place as any to stop for the night. They heated some food over a small fire which Egen sat beside while taking the first watch, allowing Arthfael to rest with Elvina and Cara wrapped in blankets in the snug void beneath the hay.

The following day dawned bright and mist free, enabling them to see far into the distance in all directions, but there was nothing, other than the bright green of the near virgin landscape, a few wild ponies, small birds and mammals – nothing that would give cause for alarm. They breakfasted in exactly the same way as they had eaten the evening before, then extinguished the fire and continued their journey. Little changed in the surrounding scenery as they veered right, keeping the distant coastline in sight to their left; they were navigating by a combination of reputation, instinct and guesswork. After some hours they had the feeling that they were slowly climbing higher and the coastline was easier to keep in view. Towards the summit of a small hill Egen's keen eyes espied a thin, faint plume of smoke rising from just beyond the crest. He indicated to Arthfael to move the wagon a little closer, jumped down and strapped on his sword. He then stealthily made his way forward until he was able to view over the top of the rise. There he saw what could only be described as a hut, such as might belong to a hermit, from which the smoke emanated. Otherwise, the landscape was bare of habitation, not another construction in sight.

An elderly man was bent over in front of the hut tending a small patch of worked soil and did not notice Egan until he was almost upon him. At first he was startled and alarmed but soon calmed as Egen assured him that he wished merely to talk As they started to do so Arthfael advanced the wagon alongside them.

'We only wish to know,' said Egen, 'our exact position. We have travelled far and are not entirely sure that we are where we wish to be.'

'You are really in the middle of nowhere,' said the hermit. 'That is why I am in this place. I have no desire to spend my remaining days living alongside evil drunken mariners, cursing their luck at being ordered here.'

'When you say "here", where do you mean exactly?' queried Egen.

'I mean my home, Portus Abonae, down there,' he said, pointing to the coast. 'About one day's walk.'

'Would you happen to know how many mariners or soldiers are there now?' Egen asked.

'I have not been there recently,' replied the hermit, 'but from reports I receive from infrequent travellers very few remain. If it happens that they all go I may return home.' Seeing they meant no harm he continued, 'Let me explain fully. They came here many years ago, hoping to make an important port for their ships. However, the tides were much higher and the flood much faster than those they were used to elsewhere; they found it difficult to manoeuvre their ships. Some even called the place a hyperborean hell. They got as far as building a small quay with wooden mooring posts and only three stone storage huts; my home was adjacent to those stores. Then things started to go wrong for them. At most they had three ships on station at any one time, but whether they could not handle the conditions, or for some other reason, one or another would disappear. I also understand that there is insufficient reason to keep them here; it was considered a waste of resources. Little more than a full change of the moon past a war galley put out with the master determined to find some booty. It never returned, but some smashed and splintered planking was washed up and identified as belonging to that vessel. I am now of the understanding that only one fat-bellied trader is moored there with about eight crew, and they are in the process of clearing the stores for use elsewhere.'

'And if none returns,' interjected Arthfael, 'you can yourself go back.'

'Yes,' responded the old man, 'but I would have to be certain.'

Clearly it was a relief to the recluse to have had a chance to converse with others, and he cheerily waved after them as they departed.

Both men discussed the situation as they neared Abonae. They agreed there would probably be no difficulty in getting past that port, but wondered whether it would be possible to create some military mischief while doing so. They also calculated that the warship that had so recently been destroyed, had met its fate about the same day that Egen and Josin had arrived in their new home. Arthfael naturally wished not to put his family at risk and they decided to assess the position more carefully when nearer the town.

With the wagon it did not take a full day to arrive at a high point overlooking the port; all was as described. The vessel lay rocking gently, tied to the quay, and by its lines was certainly a cargo carrier rather than a fighting ship. Several men were passing between it and the stone huts, carrying stores of various types, yet they appeared not to be in any hurry and stopped frequently to sip from wine flasks. It was late in the day and the air was warm. One of the crew, presumably the designated watchman, had lit a brazier and placed a package as a seat on the edge of the stone quay next to it and close to the ship. Egen sized up the situation and asked Arthfael to hide himself the wagon and its passengers in some nearby trees, and wait only until first light for his return. He then descended invisibly in the shadows to the single small home near the quayside. By the time he got there the workers had retired into one of the huts and were noisily celebrating the end of the day's work. He waited patiently until all had settled into an alcohol inspired sense of security and sleepiness. While he waited he whittled a small forked branch he had found nearby into a short handle with a hooked projection. He had decided on his course of action which, to be successful, he must carry out with great speed. He further waited until he saw the watchman's head start to jerk back and forth intermittently, an obvious sign of difficulty in staving off the desire for sleep, not that the guard was particularly concerned, other than perhaps for being upbraided by his captain for lack of diligence; after all, nothing ever happened in this back-of-beyond place.

This was Egen's moment and he seized it. He raced out of the shadows and shoulder-barged the semi-somnolent watchman into the water between ship and shore, and, almost in one continuous move, hooked the brazier and hurled it over the rail into the hold of the ship. Drawing his sword, he severed both fore and aft mooring lines, placed one foot on the hull and pushed hard. The tide being at full ebb had already taken hold and the vessel started to spiral out into the racing water. The unfortunate watchman, in desperately thrashing about, had somehow managed to grasp the loose end of a spare mooring line carelessly left hanging from a bollard. The rushing water had also taken a firm grip on him, pulling him after the ship. He was unable to do anything but cling on despairingly, thereby making himself the unwilling link in a tug-of-war twixt quay and sea.

Back in his hiding place in the shadows, Egen again waited and watched. Two befuddled mariners came out of the building, not at all sure whether or not they had heard screams for help, but seeing the craft out on the water it never occurred to them that a deliberate attack had taken place – they assumed that a freak accident of some sort had occurred. The increasingly loud screams of the watchman finally impressed themselves on the foggy consciousness of the emergent pair and, staggering to the quayside they looked down to see their comrade's predicament. At once, they knelt and stretched out for his line in order to pull him ashore. It was a situation Egen just could not resist. Yet again he rushed forward and with two swift kicks caused the would-be rescuers to join their crew-mate below. Their joint yells and curses did not seem to penetrate to the remaining five whom he could hear snoring contentedly through the half open door. He felt more satisfied than if he had cut them down with his sword, but decided to waste no more time. Halfway back he turned to see the ship borne on the ebb tide, blazing furiously.

When he reached the others he found Arthfael sitting beside a small fire with Elvina and Cara wrapped in blankets sleeping peacefully. He related the details of his escapade to his friend who admitted seeing the fire on the estuary and to having been worried. It was while describing his venture that he realised just why he had been content to deal with his enemy as he had, and not to dispose of them more completely. He explained it to his listener. Depending on whether any of the three involuntary swimmers made it back to land or not, there would be between five and eight Roman sailors down there without a ship, and now he had probably presented them with the biggest dilemma of their lives. They were in a part of the land which they hated and had no waterborne way back to familiar territory. Due to their own activities, horses were not available, they themselves having driven off most of the native population, and in any event being lifelong sailors could not ride well; they also knew they would be surrounded by enemies if they tried to travel on foot, not that they would know in which direction to go. There may or may not be a Roman presence somewhere near, but they did not know what or where. Better than all else to Egen's mind, was imagining that if some or all of them found their way safely to a Roman refuge, just how would they explain the loss of a ship, huge quantities of goods and provisions not to mention comrades if that was the case. Would the foreseen punishment be worth going back to face, or would it be better to try to hide away in hostile territory for the rest of their lives?

Arthfael remarked that it would be even more problematical for them than for the three cavalrymen whose mounts they had so recently purloined.

'Yes,' agreed Egen, 'but the odd thing that keeps crossing my mind is that for someone who is a woodsman I seem to be constantly getting involved with the destruction of ships.'

For the time being they saw no danger to themselves, and it seemed unnecessary to disturb Cara. Therefore, Egen again took the first watch while Arthfael carried her and guided Elvina to the wagon. At sunrise they breakfasted quickly, and with Cara being nursed on Elvina's lap they started off once more. Arthfael expressed his satisfaction with the cobs which, although not fast, were stronger and had more stamina than he had expected. They had been advised by the hermit that, in order to slip through the current areas of confrontation, they should try to make for

Venta Silurum and thence to Burrium. This would mean crossing some recently constructed Roman roads, and there was evidence of increasing Roman activity in some areas, but it was the only way to reach their intended destination: any habitation of the Silures that would accept them with friendliness. The greatest caution would be needed at a point where a road crossed the upper river.

As they progressed, subtle changes in the scenery became apparent; the way was more open but still rugged. Nevertheless, by midday they had covered a great distance, unhindered in any way. Eventually, Egen noticed a road to the far right of them which appeared to converge with their own course. From then on both men kept a very wary eye on it. It was, as far as they could see, devoid of travellers but undulated with the terrain and not every part was could be seen at all times. The track fell away quite steeply and they followed it down until they lost all sight of the adjacent road, then slowly climbed the opposite hill, struggling to reach the top. At first, they thought they could hear distant sounds, as of a disturbance of some sort. Surmounting the hill they saw that the convergent road was now close but ran across and down the far side of the incline they had just traversed, and continued to a narrow stone bridge over a fast flowing river in the valley. The river banks were steep, rock covered and treacherous looking. The side of the valley on which they now stood was meadow-like right up to the bridge, and a number of sheep were grazing nearby. Across the bridge the hill beyond was covered in close-packed trees and from there on the road diverged to run parallel to the river in front of the woodland in both directions. Of more immediate interest to them was the cause of the sounds they had noticed earlier and could now hear more clearly. It was not just a disturbance but a confrontation.

A platoon of Roman soldiery was drawn up on the nearest side of the bridge and had adopted their traditional turtleback formation with shields covering their heads, but were unable to advance without breaking that formation into a vulnerable file owing to the narrowness of the bridge. On the far side they could see shadowy movement among the trees and as they watched were able to discern men with ponies waiting for a chance to attack the Roman infantry. They also could not go forward because they too would have had to break into a narrow front to cross and fight a solid Roman formation. A few arrows arced out from the woodland and fell ineffectively onto those upturned shields: it was as firm a stalemate as could be imagined. The only motivational difference between the two sides was that the Romans needed to get to a new post at Isca, whereas the British wished only to prevent them and kill as many as possible in the process. Each time the turtle inched forward in a probing manner it was matched by a similar move from the trees, with just sufficient arrows flying to remind them that they were in an impossible situation. Each side waited and hoped for something to happen to change the stand-off and give an advantage to themselves. It did not, at least, not in a manner or from a direction that either side could have predicted or guessed at. Neither of the protagonists seemed to notice the third group of only four persons waiting high on the hill.

'We cannot stand here for the rest of the day,' said Egen. 'We also need to cross that bridge.'

'But how?' exclaimed Arthfael. 'It would be suicidal to attempt to do so now, you are the ideas man, can you devise a way?'

He could not help but allow a note of scepticism to colour his voice for it seemed highly improbable.

'In my own mind I have already done so,' came the reply. 'It will be a big gamble, but a gamble I feel we should take. Let me explain it to you and Elvina. Then, if you agree, we can initiate it immediately and, I hope, soon be on our way.'

Elvina was dubious and fearful but could see no alternative and hesitatingly agreed. It was a simple plan, but it all depended on those horsemen among the trees being quick as well as comradely. Egen turned the wagon and horses to face the way they had come, and while Arthfael unharnessed them he placed large stones behind the rear wheels.

Elvina stood Cara by her side and held the bridles, while the two men removed possessions and provisions which they laid nearby. After that they pushed a great deal of the load – hay, straw and sticks – into the sleeping compartment. Then, carefully adjusting the stones, they aimed the cart directly at the centre of the Roman formation; they had chosen a path which from where they stood looked reasonably flat and smooth. With practised skill, although it seemed to take a lot longer than usual, Egen produced a flame with the materials from his pouch. When burning strongly he thrust it deep into the pre-arranged load. The hay and straw flared up immediately and it was not long before the thicker sticks were also aflame. One held the draw-shaft while the other removed the stones, and together they pushed until, aided by gravity, the wagon started to roll freely. Swiftly it gathered pace and by the time it was halfway down it was travelling far faster than it was designed to do. It began bumping and jumping but maintained a true course, while the air rushing through fanned the flames so that they burst out in all directions. To the watchers from above it was reminiscent of one of those fiery heavenly bodies that on occasion hurtle across the night sky. When only paces from the Romans, who had been too preoccupied as well as huddled beneath their shields to notice, fate took a hand. The blazing vehicle, now travelling at speed, struck a ridge formed by discarded spoil from the bridge building. which could not be seen from above due to overgrowing grass. Unstoppable, it flew in a high bounce and completely somersaulted to fall in a great shower of flames and sparks into the centre of the Roman turtle... and Cara laughed – not much louder than a giggle, but a definite laugh.

The three adults looked down in temporary amazement and saw a sparkle in her eyes. Elvina scooped her up in a big hug and Arthfael put his arms around the pair of them; even Egen could not resist stroking her arm which hung loosely down her mother's back. It had not been a cruel laugh but, as Elvina explained later, she had always enjoyed watching a fire, especially when it crackled or sparked, and that crashing flaming cart must have struck an innocent chord in her heart and mind, as well as having solidly struck the enemy. That enemy was now scattered in complete disarray, their formation broken, as well as many bones. The horsemen in the woodland, being in a better position to see the open hill behind their opponents, had observed the burning vehicle a few heartbeats ahead of them. They also were startled by this unexpected occurrence, but looking up they saw only the small group and hesitated no longer. Riders and ponies poured out from between the trees and charged across the bridge. The manner in which they rode suggested they were trained and disciplined. Each rider carried his bow in his left hand while the right held an unsheathed Celtic sword. They quickly encircled the platoon, which was so disorganised it could offer little resistance. Many men had escaped the effects of the blazing wagon but had been so scattered that each felt totally isolated, and being on foot with only a short stabbing sword as a weapon did little for their confidence, especially as most had dropped their shields. The circling riders slowly reduced the radius of their enclosing ring, slashing and stabbing as they did so. One or two auxiliaries had managed to escape being so trapped and attempted to flee, only to receive several arrows between the shoulder blades. In a very short time the mood of the horsemen had changed from one of utter frustration to elation: not a Roman had survived, and wounds they had received were few and light. The three adult watchers on the hill were also more than satisfied. They had intended the wagon to strike into and across the centre of the formation, but the high bounce and crash right into the centre was an unexpected bonus. There was now nothing to do except wait as six of the mounted men approached them.

The first, a thickset, shortish man with a wide bushy beard and moustache, looked first at Egen and enquired, 'Who are you?'

But before he could reply a voice from the back of the group said, 'Provided you are not Roman or citizenised he is someone on whom you can rely completely.'

The voice was strangely familiar. It came from a tall thin man in a hooded robe who sat awkwardly on his mount; he did not appear to be as accomplished a rider as those he rode with. As he spoke he shook his head clear from the hood and Egen gasped.

'Athan!' he almost shouted. 'We all thought you were dead.'

'Fortunately for me, so did the Roman infantry,' replied Athan, and, looking towards the bearded man who was so obviously the leader, added, 'With Coellyn's permission, let us sit and exchange news. The passing wind has informed me a little of your experiences but not in their entirety.'

Coellyn answered, 'By all means, I wish to hear all also, but first we must look after the child. She looks famished.' Beckoning to a companion he commanded, 'Bring meat and milk for the girl. No – on second thoughts, bring us all food, the best we have and plenty of it. Let us celebrate this victory. Let the men celebrate but make sure they are all alert through the night and fit for fighting tomorrow. But before they eat make the bodies ready for the dogs and wolves. Now, Athan, I already know most of your story but please repeat it for your friends.'

'There is little to tell,' the druid said. 'When I left the village, using all stealth and care, I reached Mona unharmed. The brotherhood had been assembled and made ready. Unfortunately, although disciplined in thought it is not disciplined in action; it is not an army and when forced to fight no armour is worn. When the attack came the battle was fierce and lasted for several days in attack and counter-attack, but we were overcome by superior tactics and weaponry. For myself I received a heavy blow low down on the spine and another on my head. It appears that in my unconscious state I was buried under several of my brothers, and when the centurions and auxiliaries inspected the field, despatching any who still breathed, they thrust into the body above me but assumed I was already dead. Immediately afterwards, they received a call to turn back to face Boudicca. When I woke fully I was able to extricate myself from the corpses of my brothers and was rescued by Coellyn here and his comrades. Since then I have not been able to walk a great distance without pain, but I can stand and use my staff as well as before. I am now reliant on a beast with a sword blade for a backbone to get about. This makes it impossible to travel unobserved and continue my teaching as I used to do. I have become a permanent resident among my friends here, a constant recipient of their bounty.'

'Your teaching,' Egen said proudly, 'is to a great extent being continued by Josin in Dintagell. Even she is surprised by the amount of instruction she absorbed from you, just as a bowl of sand will absorb water. She is especially proud of being able to calculate and measure so accurately according to your methods.'

He went on to relate in detail all the events since Athan's departure, including Josin's capture by the household overseer, the destruction of the ships in the river followed by the razing of the merchant's home, finding the village destroyed and the consequent trek to join Boudicca, the aftermath and, of course, news of Athan's mother, Berringa. He also told of the happenings in Dintagell which had given rise to their present journey with Arthfael, Elvina and Cara. Athan and Coellyn were particularly amused by the story of how they had dealt with the Roman guard at the river crossing on the route to join the Iceni, and their treatment of the mariners and ship at Portus Abonae.

'You have not exactly been without activity,' observed Athan, 'but that is exactly what I would have expected of you.'

Coellyn was greatly impressed by the courage and skill demonstrated by all of them and said, 'We have our habitation on a hill just south of Burrium. It is large, well fortified and encircled by a great palisade with sufficient accommodation for all of you, and you are of course very welcome. We will escort you there tomorrow at first light.'

Egen responded by saying, 'With all due respects and gratitude I wish not to travel further. I have already been far too long away from Josin and I would make haste to return. I would be eternally grateful if you allowed Arthfael and his family to join you as part of your own tribe.'

'I understand your wish to return quickly,' said Coellyn, 'and for these three you may have no fear we would be proud to accept them as our own. But there are two things before you go. In gratitude for your actions today I give you one of our strongest and fastest horses; it will help you back speedily. Secondly, please stay long enough to see this bridge destroyed; I should have done it long ago. The river, with its difficult banks, makes a formidable barrier. If they wish to search us out they will have either to build another, which I will not allow, or go the long way round where we will also be waiting for them.'

Egen expressed his gratitude and stayed with them through the night, spending a great deal of it conversing with Arthfael and family, while at the same time many of Coellyn's men started weakening the west side of the construction by digging at its base. Before they had completed the digging and had filled a deep hole with inflammable material to further weaken its structure, he crossed alone to the unwooded side and waited for dawn. He was agitated and restless as he now wished to start back to see Josin as soon as possible. The material was ignited and as it flared he stood and watched; he could feel the heat even from where he was standing. It was not long before the cracking and creaking sounds of disintegrating stonework were heard, whereupon men reached over with stout poles and pushed and banged at the footing just below them. Suddenly, with a soft groan it came away from from the bank, curved down and broke in the middle. The entire structure then crashed into the river below, restricting the flow only temporarily until it swirled over the top. Looking across to see his travelling companions and new friends watching him, he gave them all a cheerful wave, mounted his new steed and galloped off.

The bearded Coellyn was as good as his word, this horse was strong and very fast, and without anything to slow him he was back near Abonae far sooner than he could have expected. He decided to risk going down into the port to see what the situation might be there now, but as he jogged warily he kept his hand close to his sword hilt. He turned off the narrow track towards the harbour, where he was not surprised to see the quayside completely devoid of vessels. There were, however, two or three groups of people talking animatedly and one or two individuals going about their business. As he approached they tended to edge towards shadowy corners away from him. He could see distrust, even fear, in their eyes, so he called out that he only wished to speak with some of them. Receiving no response but complete silence, he banged his sword firmly into its scabbard, raised his arms high in the air and called out that he meant no harm to anyone, he merely wished to speak.

One well-built woman, either with less fear or perhaps more defiance than others, left a group and walked slowly towards him, her arms encircling and bracing a large basket of shellfish against her stomach. When she got close he noticed a long wood-handled knife lay on the crustaceans, presumably used for gathering and opening the shells, within easy grasp of her fingers.

'What is it you wish to know young man?' she asked.

'When I was last here,' he said, 'a ship lay moored to the quay. I am curious about its whereabouts now.'

'That vessel,' she replied, 'thanks be to the gods, mysteriously disappeared during the darkness a few days ago. I say "mysteriously" because three of its crew were found washed up further down the river, their bodies severely battered by the rocks.'

'What happened next?' he asked.

'Exactly what one would expect,' she said. 'The remaining five awoke from their drunkenness to find no sign of their mates or ship. At first they were bewildered. They ran in circles in a panic, shouting and cursing each other and anyone or anything in sight, striking at any within reach. Eventually they sat and talked, or rather shouted. From what we could hear and understand, without their commander who was one of the missing men, they were completely lost; they had no one to tell them what to do. They had no idea whether they should go, or where to go if they did. Their possessions and weapons had disappeared with the ship.

Two only had a seaman's knife each; they had no outer clothing and were truly terrified. Should they encounter any in authority, their punishment for loss of a ship, as well as other failures, would be of the severest. Still arguing and cursing they fled along the track by which you arrived.'

'Thank you,' he said. 'I will leave you to enjoy your peace and hope it may be a long one.'

She called after him, 'If you see an old man who lives the lonely life of a hermit, would you please advise him that he can now return?'

'Of course, it will be my pleasure,' he called back.

Then, smiling and waving, he retraced his steps along the track to where he had turned off. Remembering his promise to the basket woman, he picked up the trail to the hermit's hut and jogged along happily. He was on his way back to Josin and Dintagell. But on approaching the hut he had a feeling of disquiet, a feeling that all was not as it should be, and as he got closer he saw that the ground was greatly disturbed and the vegetable patch trampled upon. The door was open and the few necessities that would have normally been stored inside were strewn about. He dismounted and made his way to the far side of the hut where he found the old man's body lying face down with a deep wound in his back. Before disturbing anything, he examined the ground closely with his hunter's eyes, and his first thoughts were confirmed to his own satisfaction. The trampling and individual footprints suggested that about five persons had been involved in the disturbance. The wound in the old man's back was inflicted by a knife rather than a military sword or similar weapon.

He had just been acquainted with the story of events in the port after his first visit, and he was certain in his own mind that this was the work of the five seamen. He felt very, very angry. He had not been exactly happy with some of the things he had seen when involved in the sacking of towns, but at least, he thought to himself, that had been in the heat of battle, provoked by the need for revenge. This, however, was unprovoked, cold-blooded murder of a defenceless old man who had desired only peace and quiet. Gently he transferred the corpse to the hut and laid it inside, then closed the door and piled rocks against it so that the body would not be disturbed. He now wrestled with three problems: should he in compassion return to Abonae to inform the hermit's earlier neighbours of what he had found, which would delay and possibly make impossible a second self-appointed task, that of tracking down those seamen to make them pay for their evil act, or should he pretend that it was not his concern and continue on to Dintagell, which of course he longed to do. He reasoned that the man had chosen to be alone and perhaps would have preferred to remain that way, or that someone from the port would eventually search for him, discover his remains and pay their respects.

No matter how much he wished to be home he could not ignore what in his conscience were the demands of justice, and so determined to hunt them down there and then. He reflected on what he had with him to ensure a successful trail: a good horse and a bag of provisions, including a water flask supplied by Coellyn, a long rope or lead always attached to the saddle for use as a long grazing tether, a blanket and leather cape, and his sword and knife. Satisfied that he was sufficiently well equipped, he started to re-examine the spoor and set out to follow it. Whatever had been the actual relationship between the five he could only guess at, but it soon became plain that they had not at first remained physically close together, and he imagined that they would have been spread apart, arguing and insulting each other. Then the signs indicated that they had closed to follow behind each other in a single file, yet he felt sure that they would have still been berating each other. The path they had taken was not straight, not easy to follow, almost as though they had been searching for something, possibly for shelter or something to eat. Water was no problem as small streams abounded. However, to them red wine would have been preferable. It continued this way for some time, alternating between the metalled road to the left and the high cliffs to the right. He calculated from their meandering that they did not wish to be seen or stray far from the road, and were looking for a coastal village or town to enable them to be taken on as crew to a ship, obviously without admitting their identity, but this was all conjecture while he rode and looked.

He slowed and advanced quietly when he smelt smoke, and soon came upon a small farmstead comprising two roundhouses and lean-tos with picketed enclosures. The whole site had the appearance of not having been worked for a considerable time. It was ramshackle and completely overgrown, giving the impression of having been abandoned, yet smoke was being emitted from the roof of one. The trail had led here; therefore, the occupants must be his quarry. He did not go close immediately but waited and watched, and while he did so he looked about him and surmised that it had been abandoned owing to its proximity to the new road, and the probability of interference from travellers. This thought brought to his mind a number of courses of action, perhaps slightly wild but, with luck, satisfying and possible. He thought about them and gradually grew eager to put them to the test.

He tied his horse to a tree well away, then crept quietly in the shadows to the house from which voices and the smoke issued. At first he positioned himself where he could hear but not see the men. It was not difficult because, as he had imagined, they cursed and screamed at each other; how they had managed together in the confines of a ship was difficult to understand as none seemed to have any regard for the other. They were all complaining of being cold and hungry, and four seemed to be blaming the fifth for this state of affairs. They cursed him for calling himself the ship's cook when he was unable to strike a fire. His defence appeared to be that he rarely needed to make a flame as he had always ensured that one burned constantly, that they in any case should be grateful because, although it had taken most of the day, he had succeeded, and as a result his fingers and hands were extremely sore and painful, but the fire was now burning well and beginning to warm them. Going to the lean-to, Egen found a crumbling portion of wall, and by pushing aside a long coil of rope hanging there, mildewed and tangled tightly with bindweed, he was able to peer in. They were each trying to toast a piece of meat on a pointed stick over the contentious fire. The smell was not very appetising and he assumed it had come from something they had found already dead. Nor was it to their liking, as after a couple of mouthfuls each threw the remainder into a corner and settled into a dissatisfied and noisy slumber.

Egen still waited patiently until, as he had hoped, one stirred and with crude remarks left the hut to relieve himself against a tree. He stayed his hand until the man was adjusting his dress, then leaped forward and with his open hand banged the sailor's head hard against the tree. His victim dropped unconscious and he quickly removed the sash which held the sailor's smock-like shirt close. Cutting it lengthwise he had more than enough material to bind his hands and legs and provide a gag; he then threw him into one of the nearby picketed enclosures. He returned to the house and noted that by now the other four were completely asleep. Even in sleep they were apparently not comfortable for no one had attended the fire which was beginning to go out, and each was unconsciously trying to pull his garments closer about him, wriggling and grunting as he did so. The door did not fit well and earlier they had all worked their way to the farthest point from it to escape the draught. He fully intended to capture all alive; the problem was to get them to face him singly. The solution was to use a trick he had employed as a hunter, seemingly many seasons past, which had enabled him to guide game animals into a single file. He quietly made his way back to where he had noticed huge clumps of sweetbriar and cut four large bushes from low down on the stems. He dragged them back and was satisfied to see that they billowed out as expected and whipped without easily breaking; he had also cut a long, forked branch for later use. Approaching the house he eased the door wide open and saw as he did so that the sleepers involuntarily shivered as the cold air entered, the fire now being only lightly smoking embers. Stem first he pushed the initial clump through the door, shoving it with the forked branch to compress it as it entered and allowing it to spring out again when inside. Having guided it well to the right of the room he followed it with the second and third and mentally debated whether the fourth would go; he decided that it would and shoved that in as well. He stepped inside and saw that it had arranged itself well; the room was more than half full of briar extending well past the central fire and only just short of the sleeper's feet. Effectively, there was only a narrow passage around the left side of the chamber, and should anyone attempt to force their way past or through the shrubs they would suffer multitudinous and painful tears to the skin.

He stood in the entrance with drawn sword and, holding the mildewed coil of rope which he had cut away from the lean-to wall, he suddenly emitted a piercing howl. He knew it was possible for a fit person, when alert and ready, to jump from a prone position directly to his feet, but in this instance he saw four people almost achieve that feat straight from sleep and simultaneously. In reality they all found themselves totally startled and fell about in confusion, cursing wildly as they lurched against each other, then letting out their own howls as they rebounded into the unforgiving thorns. It was some time before they were fully cognisant of the fact that somehow they were in a trap, a trap set by someone they did not know. In their bewilderment and fear they growled, grimaced and spat, the normal reactions of vicious thugs who find themselves cornered. Then in the dim moonlight filtering through the doorway and gaps in the roof, hesitation and increasing fear took over as they made out the threatening figure before them, and realised there was absolutely nothing they could do. Egen let that realisation gel in their minds before ordering the first two to move forward. While keeping his blade in a menacing position he tossed the rope to the second and ordered him to bind the wrists of the man in front tightly behind his back, but to leave an initial tail on the rope of about three arms' length. He kept a sure eye on the binding to make certain it was done effectively, and the same with the following two. Thus three were linked together by the single length; the last he tied himself, a little awkwardly because of having to keep him under threat of the sword; this also left a long tail of spare rope. Satisfied that all four were now very secure and linked, he pulled them out to the enclosure where the fifth murderer still lay. He cut the bond on the man's legs and linked him into the chain. This was almost a relief to that man as he had never before been so cold and frightened, but at least he was still alive and had not been left to rot alone.

Egen then fastened the group around a tree, wrapped himself tightly in his cloak and half dozed. As the sun rose and started to warm the air he made sure his prisoners were as they should be. Then, with exaggerated sounds and movements, he opened his provisions and started to eat and drink; he did this with a great smacking of the lips and showily wiping his mouth on his arm. When he had finished he removed the long tether from his saddle and looped it, to the absolute terror of the first man, around his neck in such a manner that it would neither slip tighter nor become loose. This procedure was repeated until all were linked by both hands and necks. The long tail of the neck halter he wrapped around his wrist and started to ride slowly to the Roman road. Once there he advanced his near hysterical group until he found a tree on one side of the road with a young sapling almost opposite on the other. It now remained only to tie one long tail of the wrist rope to the tree and the other to the sapling, thereby ranging the five fully secured murderers across the road facing east. He then retrieved the long tether and replaced it on the saddle. The day was now warm and he sat and waited until midday at which time he repeated the feasting performance; he could hear his captives' stomach responses from where he sat. It was late in the day before he heard and saw what he was waiting for. First it was the ghastly wail of that familiar great horn, then, approaching from the east, a company of auxiliaries flanked by two outriders. He mounted his horse and rode sufficiently far away to be reasonably well hidden and yet able to watch events. As the company closed upon the bound group it slowed – they could not believe their eyes. The outriders warily cantered forward to assess the situation and tried to make some sense of it.

Egen was too far away to be able to hear all that was said, but as a great deal was angrily shouted, most of the rest could be understood by coupling that which could be heard with the body language of the captives and the military. The first questions were how they came to be in this situation, and who exactly they were. All five from the moment of capture, were too distressed and angry to concoct an agreed story, which they should sensibly have done at the time their ship disappeared, and now they were close to mental as well as physical collapse. They wailed and moaned and begged to be released. This the senior commander was not inclined to do, not until he had some coherent answers. The only thing they appeared to agree on was that they had been set on by overwhelming numbers. None wished their identities to be known, for by now the the loss of the ship would be common knowledge to Roman authority and to be connected with that loss would be disastrous; their stories differed so wildly that nothing could be believed and suspicion was increased. They had obviously not been left there by Hibernian slave traders as a punishment for resisting capture, to be collected later, as one claimed. Nor were they being traded and transferred between native tribes as claimed by another. He was not going to get a sensible answer; there was clearly a great deal they were trying to hide. He therefore ordered the rope to be exchanged for chains and to keep them under guard. He would let higher authority decide their fate, which in his own opinion would result in their being chained to the oars of a galley for the rest of their lives. It was now getting dark and the decision was made to set camp for the night by the side of the road where they now stood.

Egen watched it all, and, although desperate to get back to Josin, he could not immediately pull himself away; there might yet be a chance to perform a little more anti-Roman mischief. He did not wish to get embroiled in any sort of fight. To do so in these circumstances would be foolish, but there must be a way to inconvenience or discomfort them beyond that which he had already done, even if it was merely to satisfy himself.

He studied the situation carefully. Two small tents had been erected and in front of one was a fire over which hung a cauldron. The main force was bivouacked a little further on to the west, and the two horses on long tethers grazed on the nearside. A sentinel stood close to the fire holding a pilum; all except him were soon asleep, and he was not far from it. Egen decided that somehow he would acquire those animals, leaving the outriders, who were also the commanders, to walk to wherever they were bound. Getting close to the horses with his skills was no problem, but to walk them away would require a diversion of some significance. He ensured that his own mount had enough fodder to keep it quiet and happy for a while, then, under cover of the trees, moved along well past the extremity of the camp on the far side of the road. At a place a satisfactory distance away he selected a tree with a strong high branch reaching near to the road and set about constructing his diversion. He gathered a quantity of small dry branches, hay and straw which he tied into a very large ball-shaped bundle, binding it together with thick tendrils of ivy which abounded in the vicinity. Purely to amuse himself he pressed a piece of bark into the centre to represent a nose, but this in turn inspired him to enhance his original idea. There was plenty of time and he worked quickly. He collected some long thicker branches and, using the ball as a head, put together a large man-like figure, which he padded and proportioned using twigs, hay and straw with ivy ties. The whole thing when erected would be nearly as high as the overhanging branch. He added a long tail and fixed it to the back of the figure. The moonlight was not so bright as the previous evening, for which he was thankful as it enabled him to work without being easily seen. A rope of twisted creeper was then thrown over the branch and attached to the neck of his creation and he hauled it into a standing position, making sure that the added tail hung in a continuous gentle slope upwards from a stone which held it to the ground. A flaming ball of fire hovering over the road, as he had first visualised it, would, he thought, have been sufficient diversion, but now he looked at the giant effigy and hoped it would be much more effective, appearing at a distance to hover and dance as it blazed over the road in the dark of the night.

He struck a flame and set it to the extreme end of the tail. It caught readily. In the shadows he quickly but quietly made his way back and crossed the road well past the camp, then crept up to where the horses were standing. No one, including the guard, appeared to have noticed anything untoward. He saw the faint glimmer of flame get to the figure and start to catch and spread. The guard had still not moved. He appeared to be sleeping on his feet, only the pilum preventing him from falling flat. Lying close to the ground he picked up a pebble and aimed it accurately at the sentry; it struck his helmet with a faint metallic ring, but to the wearer it must have sounded much louder, startling him into wakefulness to such an extent that he dropped the javelin and nearly fell. As he staggered to recover his equilibrium he saw the burning shape in the distance illuminating the empty area around it. Confusion and fear in equal measure engulfed him. He needed to alert everyone to a danger he did not understand and ran forward waking all, including the officers, and directing their attention to the spectacle. Even as they struggled to don their upper armour, from within their tents they ordered men forward to investigate. The figure was now burning entirely and brightly and displayed its outline very much as Egen had hoped; none of the spectators could take their eyes from it as they obeyed orders, but advanced only slowly, fearing what they might encounter.

Egen now quickly released the horses and quietly walked them across the road to where he had left his own hidden in the trees. Attaching the loose bridles to his own saddle he watched with a broad smile the chaotic performance played out before him. Orders were screamed and auxiliaries moved hesitatingly forwards with drawn swords. The supporting vine burned through and the whole fiery mass dropped to the ground; this made the warriors advancing on it jump, then creep forward again even more nervously. Finally, two got close enough to poke at it with their weapons and discover that it was a man made object, but by whom, and why and how it had been ignited was still a mystery. A careful search was instigated around the site but nothing was found; it remained a mystery that left the entire company nervous and agitated. They retreated to their campsite and the standing guard was tripled. Only then did they discover that the horses were missing. Egen moved on happily, engrossed in his thoughts and speculations; those speculations were remarkably accurate, despite his being unaware of the intended destination or route of his victims.

Unlike their Celtic tormentor, the Roman leaders of this venture were not happy. They had somehow lost their mounts and, unless the result of animal ill-health or military action, this was a serious punishable offence. They were only too well aware of this as they happened to be on the presiding panel that had passed judgement on three cavalrymen whose horses had mysteriously disappeared not a considerable time ago, and the men they were now commanding were fully aware of this. There was also the unavoidable fact that they were now going to have to complete the journey on foot marching alongside those men; forward scouting would also have to be done by runners which would not be nearly so rapid and effective. The chained prisoners were not happy, not only because of their present predicament and the events that had brought them here, but also because they knew the vindictive nature of the military establishment and that they would unjustifiably be blamed for any mishap that befell the expedition from here on in; in consequence, they would suffer unlimited physical and verbal abuse. The company itself was not happy. It had been marching for two whole days with very little sleep at night and very little good hot food during the day, and it still had a long way to go. Any one of that company would have been glad to be serving anywhere in the empire than here in this cold, bedevilled province.

Unhappiness was about the only thing not in short supply, and now it had started to rain. As if that were not enough more was to come. They were not to know that the bridge they were hoping to cross no longer existed. They were yet to come to the meadow before that non-existent bridge and behold it littered with the remains of their comrades, and wolves and dogs more hunger sated than they had ever seen before glowering at them; that the warm soft bed, hot food and bathing facilities they were looking forward to, by the time they had marched around the head of the river, were going to be a great deal further away – and, certainly, none of this boded well for the miserable, chained prisoners being dragged along behind them.

11

A Chariot Acquired

Being alone and unhindered, he made remarkably good progress and, other than dozing while he allowed the horses to rest, he kept on going as far and as fast as possible; he was now really anxious to get home to see Josin. He only slowed when avoiding any place where he might meet with unfriendly strangers, and it was the following evening when he cantered straight into the centre of his village. He slid from the saddle outside of their home and Josin, who had been waiting anxiously for his return and happened to be standing there when he arrived, asked two youths nearby to take charge of the horses while she took him in for a rest and a good meal. The older looking of the youngsters jokingly remarked that if Egen was going to continue to capture enemy mounts for the village in this way, it would be necessary to extend the paddock and build more stables.

While she was preparing the meal he related the details of the venture to her. She was only too happy that he was safely home again but gently scolded him for taking risks on the return journey, as when he had captured the five seamen, then set the army on a wild goose chase. She was excited and happy to learn of Athan's survival and current safety. His meal that evening seemed better than anything he had eaten before and he fell into the most satisfying of sleeps.

The following morning he sought out Haerviu and Genovefa to assure them of the safety of Arthfael and his two dependents, and to give details of the journey; but he also wished to discuss several other things that had passed through his mind while on the mission. It transpired, however, that during his absence things had not stood still here, and Haerviu had also been waiting to speak to Egen about several items. Deferring to the older man, Egen held back until he had heard his anxieties. A small number of strangers had been seen on the Roman track near to the now destroyed fort; although not members of the occupying forces, it could not be ascertained whether they were hostile or not, and Haerviu had reinstated the continuous watch. Josin had continued to amaze people with her inexhaustible memory of the old druid's teachings, and in particular her understanding of his principles of mathematics and measure. He would be grateful if she would continue to expound on them, especially to the younger persons in the commune. He had cogitated on whether it would be a good idea to re-construct an observation post where the Roman fort had previously stood. He also wanted Egen's ideas on teaching the young men the techniques of battle as they had very little experience in that respect.

This all took a great deal away from those things that Egen had wished to talk about, for his main concerns had been his and Josin's role in the community. They had received only kindness from all, but it still lurked in the back of their minds that they might be viewed as interlopers. Haerviu's attitude made it clear that they were entirely mistaken in that suspicion, that they were being relied on by the whole village. This then gave Egen the confidence to comment truthfully on Haerviu's actions and ideas. He tried to get a more definitive description of the strangers seen, but nothing more was evident. He knew Josin would be pleased to continue the work of teaching, but requested that at this time not too much strain be put upon her. He was sure that the re-institution of the watch was a good thing and would be happy, if required, to oversee the running of it. He also agreed that an observation post be erected as proposed, but it should as far as practicable be used by the restored watch to see but not be seen, at least from any great distance. However, he would first wish to examine the site; he had been advised by Josin that great lumps of it had crashed down into the sea. He also reminded Haerviu that he himself, as far as teaching fighting techniques was concerned, was not a trained expert though he would be happy to show whatever he knew to the younger men.

The response took the form of a rhetorical question: 'What is an expert, but one who has knowledge of a subject from the accumulated experiences of others? In this case you have developed your hunting skills into those of battle by way of experience with little need of instruction. From observation it is known that none can equal you in thrusting a javelin far and accurately. It would seem that you are equally adept with a sword and, despite your damaged left arm, are also reasonably useful with a bow, certainly proficient enough to be able to teach others who have no impediment.'

Egen thought about this for a while before suggesting that if he were to pass on his acquired skills it would be better it were done at some distance from the village; he was of the opinion that should it attract attention from elsewhere it would be better not to bring that attention close to their homes and families.

'That should be no problem,' replied the old man. 'You have not resided here long enough to know our environs well, but if you proceed along the path towards the paddock, but at the point where the path drops down turn left, you will see a narrow track leading up to higher ground and curving around a rock face. From there continue walking for about four hundred paces and you will discover a very large open space fronting a small cave in the cliff. This space is quite level up to its edge, then drops away very sharply. From there the terrain can be observed nearly all the way around for a great distance. It is for you to judge, but I think it would suit the purpose well.'

Egen and Josin set out to assess the fort site and the practice ground early the next morning, having to travel more slowly than they would have liked owing to Josin's condition. But he was glad that she was accompanying him, not least because he valued her opinion highly. When they arrived at the burned out fort he saw for himself that most of the grass-covered area that had been alongside the ruin, including the space where Cara had been found by the villagers, had indeed collapsed and lay on the beach below, where it was being swept away by successive tides. He did not know how suddenly it had happened but shuddered at the thought that one of his neighbours, or even several of them when Cara had been found by them, could have been standing there when it gave way. There remained a large rock headland jutting out over the sea, connected to the mainland by a stone bridging piece which could be used for access. It would be possible to build an observation post there with the advantage of its being easily defended if necessary. The disadvantage was that it would be difficult to re-supply should it be cut off by attackers. It not only looked out to sea but was also a good vantage point over the approaches to the hamlet, which of course was the main object of the exercise. Provided it was used solely for its intended purpose and a constant watch kept, the probability of surprise attack would be small. The advantages seemed to outweigh the disadvantages, and they decided to support the idea. They then turned back and followed the directions given by Haerviu towards the second site.

It was nearly midday before they found themselves crossing the meadow-like space close to the cave. The area appeared to be near ideal for their purpose and much larger than they had expected. The ground was level and generally clear of tall growth, and beyond its perimeter dropped almost vertically as described. It was possible to see for a very great distance over the beautiful, verdant countryside, with the desirable feature that they themselves would be almost impossible to see from lower down. Egen was sure that a settlement in the far distance was the one from which Arthfael and himself had rescued three Roman horses. Turning to face in a slightly more northerly direction, he noted a wisp of smoke rising from between two small hills, just a little nearer than the first settlement.

'I wonder what lies there,' he muttered to Josin.

'I do not know for certain,' she replied, 'but somehow I have the feeling that it could be one of those itinerant sites.'

Seeing his puzzled expression, she continued, 'I see that you have not absorbed all that Athan communicated to us.'

He reminded her that as he was more often away seeking food when Athan was lecturing it could be difficult to understand all. She then began to explain his teachings. 'Before the arrival of the Romans these islands were the lawful inheritance of our own people and race, even though divided into tribes and families large and small. As would be natural, some lived in friendly tolerance while others existed with a certain amount of friction and animosity. With the arrival of the Romans leading the biggest war machine ever known, and relying on riches stolen from other peoples, our land was not only subjugated but could be broken down into different factions. As you know, there are those so bedazzled by the fine buildings erected and the Roman lifestyle that they succumb completely and try to be an integral part of it. There are others, such as ourselves, who have seen the darker side, the evil and the cruelty, who are determined not to accept their arrogant and wicked governance. Then there are those tribes who live the old way, but to avoid excessive bloodshed of their own people co-operate with Rome, and whose lands are described as client-kingdoms – a meaningless term. That was the way of Prasutagus and Boudicca before the death of the former and the brutality inflicted on Boudicca, her family and her tribe. Tyrants never seem to learn that when inordinate pressure is applied the subsequent reactionary force is usually far greater than that applied in the first instance. Other small family and tribal groups, scattered far from the occupational forces, strive to live the old way by trying to ignore the fact of the occupation. Which brings us to itenerant sites. It is not a good description but serves the purpose; they are small groups of outcasts or undesirables whose main object in life is self-gratification without responsibility. It is only the common interest of self-preservation and greed that allows them to come together in small groups. They take pride in seeing themselves for what they actually are not – hard, tough and fearless. They live by taking by force anything that answers their needs, refusing to show loyalty to anything or anyone. They move around constantly from one place to another, not staying long enough to allow local resentment to build into retaliatory action, hence the term itinerant. Their methods include travel and attack by chariots similar to that which we formerly devised, and the lance and sword. Their hamlets, if you can call them that, are badly constructed as they are intended for temporary accommodation only, and they do not have the restriction of dependent families. The only thing they do diligently is practise their fighting skills and develop an unlimited contempt for others. They do not fight Rome because that would be futile; neither do they care to become citizens, for the discipline and order of that lifestyle would not be to their taste. Their most despicable attribute is that they allow themselves to be used by Rome to gather information on their own peoples, for which villainy they get well rewarded; not that it would prevent them, if it suited their purpose and without detection, from cutting an imperial throat with as little compunction as any other.'

Thus enlightened, Egen was filled with admiration for her accumulation of Athan's knowledge and understanding, acquired as it seemed so very long ago. They both turned and retraced their steps, passing close to the cave entrance.

Josin, showing herself to be the true daughter of a metal worker, pointed to a large boulder with a smooth flat top standing near to the cave and said, 'That would serve well as an anvil to straighten bent practice blades or spear tips. You must remember to bring a good hammer with you.'

They returned to the village elders to impart their views. Soon a picket fence had been erected around the intended instruction ground, for no one wished to see another hurl himself over the edge in a show of excessive exuberance. After which, Egen set enthusiastically to his task of instructing the young men of the hamlet in the skills of martial arts, and between times supervising the design and construction of the observation post. Josin settled in very easily to her job of instruction in the old ways, before the unwanted intervention of Rome and according to the beliefs of Athan and the druidic brotherhood. Soon they were such an integral part of the community that they could imagine they had lived their entire lives there. In consequence, the days passed quickly into months. There were no reported sightings of anything untoward, although it did concern Egen that an increasing number of young men from other villages would appear requesting training as fighters. Whilst he was happy to do this, it was essential that knowledge of the existence of his activities should not reach the ears of any who would wish them harm. He therefore instigated a rather convoluted system of interrogation and vetting and secrecy. The last thing he, or anyone else, wished to experience was a repetition of the fate of his first two home hamlets. It seemed to him that the passing wind that saw all and sometimes spoke of it not only existed but that he was becoming a part of it.

The fast moving months saw Josin give birth to twins, a boy and a girl, who were as like to each other as reflections in the still water of a sylvan pool. They named them Gwain and Mirim in honour of Josin's father and Egen's mother. The event aroused a great deal of excitement and activity among the women of the village, so much so that Egen was at the same time proud and irritated. He was perfectly aware that the seemingly superfluous activity was well intentioned, but he felt that it denied him a great deal of time he wished to enjoy in quiet intimacy with his little family. It did, however, allow him to continue his training activities in the knowledge that Josin would have all the necessary help while he was away from her.

One afternoon he was particularly concerned, as he descended from the training ground, to see what appeared to be the entire population of the village trying to gain access to his home. Stepping rapidly forward he roughly pushed aside many and stepped inside. To his astonished delight he saw Arthfael, Elvina and Cara sitting there talking to Josin deliberately loud enough for all to hear the conversation. They were equally pleased to see Egen. The two men greeted each other warmly and he was quickly brought up to date with what had been related to everyone else. It transpired that the Silures had not only welcomed them, but treated them as generously as Egen and Josin had been here. While there Arthfael had been instructed in the fighting methods of that tribe, including the use of chariots. He had, like all in this place, been familiar with the more mundane business of driving carts for agricultural purposes, but not the fast and very manoeuvrable fighting vehicle for which this immediate area was eminently unsuitable.

One morning, Cara suddenly appeared to snap out of her torpor. It was as if something had suddenly severed her isolated inner self from the memory of that day when she had been so savagely abused by depraved Roman soldiery. Maybe it was just that her very young mind could not hold it any longer, or equally it could have been effected by her innate delight in sparks and flames, for that morning, just as she had opened her eyes, a camp fire seen through the entrance of their abode had crackled loudly and momentarily sent flames and sparks skywards. She gave a squeal of delight, not the hesitant little laugh that she had emitted when the cart somersaulted and burst apart in a shower of flaming bits on their way to seek the Silures, but a loud, long unsuppressed laugh. From that moment on she was able to accept and return the affection of both her parents. She was not entirely the carefree child she had been, for in the presence of others, not fear exactly, but a faint shadow of wariness could be detected in her bearing, but she appeared to be happy again. It was she who first expressed the desire to see again the friends and people of their old home. Assuring themselves that this was not just a passing whim, Arthfael and Elvina readily agreed, for they too had been longing for their first home and their neighbours. Although they had been back only a very short time Cara did not seem unduly disturbed by anyone or anything.

The following day the interest of the village seemed to be fully satisfied, although the subject of their return remained the sole topic of conversation. Now Egen and Arthfael had the opportunity to talk more closely and intimately as they walked to the training ground together.

It transpired that Arthfael had won a reputation among his hosts as a relentless and fearless warrior, almost certainly as a product of his overwhelming anger and hatred for all things Roman. His methods, however, were traditional, the same as those adopted by Boudicca, to rush in with a sword in one hand and a lance or spear in the other, slashing and stabbing furiously. He appeared almost to relish cutting down anyone who in any way represented Rome. His desire for revenge seemed insatiable. Egen recognised that this might be successful against small patrols, but disastrous if, as the Iceni had already demonstrated, it was used against mass formations of disciplined soldiery. He then guiltily confessed that he had neglected charioteering in his instruction to the young of the village. Most young men had experience of handling farm carts and, being young and self assured, assumed that they would be able to handle a fighting vehicle. This was as much an error as thinking that anyone who could handle a coracle on a mere or small river would be experienced enough to control a tall-masted vessel with sail on the open sea. He put his lapse down to the psychological impact of not being able to imagine that type of warfare in this locality, despite the fact that he believed that any serious fighting man should master all aspects of combat. A serious fighter would not necessarily know where, or when, or under what circumstances he would have to confront an enemy; this applied even more so to those who made their way across country from outside communities.

He excused himself by saying, 'We just do not have a suitable vehicle.'

'We could acquire one,' was the quick, almost mischievous, response.

'Where?' asked Egen.

'At this moment I cannot say, but within striking distance are small bands of those treacherous, thieving itinerants of whom Josin has spoken. They rely entirely on chariots as an essential part of their way of life. It would be only right and just to make some of them taste the fare they dish out to others. We need only to wait and watch.'

It was obvious that Arthfael was aching for further action. He had developed a taste for retribution against any he saw as enemies of his family and people.

Within days, information was gleaned from the passing wind that a new travelling group was seen to be throwing together a rudimentary round house shelter. It was sited a little over a half day's ride to the south-east. They did not act immediately, but waited two days to allow the wanderers to attain a certain sense of security. Together with two of the most trustworthy trainees from their own commune, and mounted on two former imperial horses and two ponies, they set out to find their quarry. It was not difficult. They traced it to a large area of moor-land below a thickly wooded knoll. Hidden among the trees as near as they could get to that shelter, they saw that it was indeed rough, barely adequate to keep out the worst of the elements. Dirty smoke filtered through the ill-made thatch. Attached to it on one side was a hastily erected paddock of picket fence and brushwood, within which were two horses, still wearing full Roman riding equipment, and four native bred ponies. But what really caught their eyes were two of the most magnificent chariots seen by any of them, or perhaps anybody, in the islands. Against the crudeness of the campsite they were truly incongruous. One was being raced furiously around in a large circle, drawn by two cobs, the driver obviously practising his turning skills, while the other, unattached, stood close to the hut entrance. They were designed like those used in Roman circuses: high and rounded at the front, sloping low to an open back, light but strongly constructed with every piece of exposed woodwork covered in brightly coloured decoration. The high and round front and sides appeared to glow dully with a yellowish, metallic shine. But it was not metal; it was un-tanned leather, stretched tightly over the shaped wooden frame, repeatedly soaked and dried and further stretched and smoothed until it was hard without a wrinkle or bump marring its surface, then polished with a mixture of wax and oils until indistinguishable from moulded metal. No indication of ownership or origin could be seen on them, and how these itinerants had acquired such magnificent vehicles would remain a mystery. Similarly, what the two Romans who were undoubtedly inside were doing there would never be known, but it was clear that it would not be official business but more probably some sort of nefarious deal. None of that really mattered for the object of this exercise was to obtain one of these chariots. They edged further back into the trees and Egen laid out a hastily conceived plan.

Arthfael muttered, referring to the chariots, 'Why not both of them?'

Egen replied, 'We have two young men with us from our own village, not yet fully adult. Should anything befall them through our lack of care we would not be welcome home. They have mothers who love them as much as you love Cara, and we must take the utmost care.'

Returning to the edge of the wood, they waited. Egen tensed and at the precise moment urged his mount forward until, within seconds, he was alongside the head of the outside flying cob. He grabbed its halter and, matching its pace, forced it into an ever decreasing circle. The driver, startled and confused, unarmed and not expecting trouble, dropped the reins which were now having no effect and was flung against the outer side of the carriage. As the outfit bounced and lurched he had the utmost difficulty retaining a hold on the upper edge. Egen then pulled hard and, without slackening speed, turned the team round in the opposite direction. This was just too much for the occupant who could not prevent himself from being catapulted over the opposite lower rear corner to crash as an untidy, silent and motionless heap. Now Egen hauled back and stopped the fretting ponies, climbed into the vehicle and attached the reins of his former mount to one of the long straps fitted inside for the purpose of retaining the driver's choice of weapons. He then cantered off to the narrow track between the trees. Arthfael and the two youngsters recognised their cue when they saw the team hauled to a halt. Immediately, they charged in across the intervening heath either side of Egen, making straight towards the simple paddock. With a previously prepared length of rope Arthfael looped it onto the rickety construction and heaved it aside, out of the ground and away from the house. The other two, whooping loudly, chased the enclosed and panic stricken animals through the opening and out onto the open moor-land.

The occupants of the hovel were so engrossed in the intricacies of whatever evil agreements they were trying to accomplish, that it was far too long before they realised that the commotion outside was more than the excited exclamations of a trainee charioteer. Two centurions and four social outcasts emerged swiftly to see the empty corral and fleeing horses and riders. The profanities they screamed would have offended even the ears of a long-serving galley master. Pursuit was out of the question; not only would it take time to round up their mounts, if they were able to do so at all, but they would not know in what direction to start, all the raiders having taken entirely different directions into the far distance. There was no point whatsoever in remaining. Their animals were not going to return to them of their own volition; they would have to go and find them on foot. All negotiations were now null and void.

Having arrived at the agreed muster point it was not long before the two boys joined Egen, but of Arthfael there was no sign. They waited with increasing anxiety as time passed, earnestly praying that no misfortune had overtaken their friend. Just as Egen had decided to go back to look for him, he arrived with a contented smile on his face.

'As far as I am aware,' Arthfael said, 'we now own the only example of such a vehicle.'

He went on to explain that, having put his share of the conspirator's animals out of reach, he had looped back to the point in the wood from which they had first watched the house. Even from that far he could hear the cursing and see the rage that was so great it was on the point of developing into fighting. He waited until they had finally set out to try to retrieve the fleeing horses and were sufficiently far away, before carefully moving on to the site. Taking up great armfuls of brushwood that had formerly graced the paddock, he forced much of it below the chariot and a further amount inside the house against the crude uprights where the roof was at its lowest. He then took two burning brands from the central fire and thrust them into each of the bundles of kindling before racing back to the cover of the trees, delaying only long enough to see the flames take a firm hold and observe the frustrated searchers turn towards the conflagration. By this time they were so far away he could only imagine the crudity of the words they were undoubtedly screaming. By the end of his story the two youths were grinning broadly, but Egen was not quite so amused. He was glad that the property had been destroyed and the enemy discomfited, but Arthfael had not acted in accordance with the pre-arranged plan. In actions against a foe it is essential to stick to agreed arrangements and maintain discipline. That way complete success was more likely, less risk was involved, and, if nothing else, it caused less tension and anxiety for colleagues. In this particular instance Arthfael could have caused one or more of them to go unnecessarily in search for him and suffer unforeseen consequences. He had often reflected that had the hotheads at the battle of Manduessuedun been gifted with a little more discipline and waited for an authoritative order the outcome could have been vastly different, and the invaders may well have been on retreat out of these islands. While saying nothing now, he determined to have a word on the subject with Arthfael at a later date.

They made their way home in a lighthearted and leisurely manner, discussing the events of the day. It was late evening and nearly dark before they found themselves climbing the track to the lower paddock, and glad that they were seen and recognised by the boy whose turn it was to keep watch. He opened the gate for them but his eyes were full of wonder at the chariot they drove in. He was instructed to disguise it as best he could until they had time to prepare a more suitable shelter for it. It had been decided on the way back that this was where it would be kept. The area was just large enough for training purposes and it would be unnecessary to dismantle the chariot for manhandling up to the higher site over a narrow uneven path. Practice would require that the current occupants of the meadow be penned for a short while for their own safety. The youngsters would have less time to perfect their techniques for other activities, but with the opportunity to learn to drive, race and fight from such a vehicle they would consider that a small price to pay. From then on Egen concentrated his efforts on the higher ground with sword, shield, javelin, bow and other aspects of close quarter fighting, while Arthfael instilled the skills of chariot control into his more than willing pupils.

12

The Past Revisited

Within days a routine had emerged, Egen demonstrating the slash, thrust and parry, the javelin launch and release of an arrow, while Arthfael familiarised his trainees with the skills needed for fast and controlled driving. This routine would continue unaltered for an indefinite period.

Egen had not felt so satisfied and content for a very long time: Josin had a comfortable and comparatively safe home, and both were accepted and respected members of the community, which in a strange way raised a feeling of contradiction within him, for he taught war but lived peaceably. That trouble and conflict existed outside the bounds of this place was confirmed by information blown in on the passing wind, and evidenced by the increasing number of young persons from far and wide wishing for instruction. Yet somehow it did not intrude on the life of this hamlet. It was to him almost as though they were being watched over. When time and the elements permitted and help with the children was available, they would climb to the cave entrance and relax, leaning against the rock wall. When the breeze from the sea was too much, he would stand his sword upright in a small fissure in the rocky ground, supported by the anvil stone just a step or two from the cave mouth, and stretch his great cloak from it to a broad shrub adjacent to the cave itself, thus forming a very effective wind break. Owing to the feeling of seclusion and privacy it provided, he did this almost ritually. The view from there was incomparable; it ranged across the varying green shades of the hills, meadows and trees, with occasional stretches of rich, red soil between them. Snug behind that cloak, they would rest and recall their journey and all their adventures.

It seemed not long for the days to change to weeks and the weeks into months and years. The twins thrived and were happy; they were popular with their fellows and practised all the skills taught by their father and his friend. The close resemblance of their looks was constantly remarked on, but it was not only in looks that they were alike; should any of those things that affect a person's life in one way or another happen to one, very shortly a similar occurrence would befall the other. Any incident affecting one was expected to repeat itself to the other with such reliability that their parents were often prepared for the repetition. There was therefore no surprise when Mirim and a youth from the training squad having approached them wishing to become betrothed, a similar request from Gwain and a tall attractive girl from an outside tribe followed close afterwards. There were no objections in either case. The only difference between the two situations was that whereas Mirim's suitor was the son of an elder to a small hamlet just a short distance to the south, Gwain's intended was the daughter of a chief of a large and influential tribe some considerable distance to the north. Paradoxically, it was this difference that was the cause of a similar circumstance between the two.

At the appropriate time, and in accordance with normal practice, Mirim would leave home and go to live with her husband in his village. In the case of the young lady from the north, her father as chief of a respected and large community, was regarded as a minor king. Thus the practice was reversed where Gwain was concerned: he also would have to leave home to live with her family. The line from his bride's father had to continue and be seen to do so by his tribe, which meant that both departed from their home within a very short time of each other. Despite frequent and happy visits among the three families, this change in lifestyles affected Egen and Josin quite profoundly; they had less to do and worry about in their own home and more free time.

Egen could not help but reflect that were there more interactions of this type between the lawful inheritors of this land and a little less friction between tribes, the coming together of indigenous peoples from the extreme length and breadth of the island to form a united total population might soon be brought to fruition, with the result that they would be more able to resist invasion and usurpation. That might eventually happen, but it would be far into the future. For the time being he would use what little skills and influence he possessed to prepare the way for that future. They filled the extra free time peacefully enjoying the warm evening sun whenever possible, in relaxed idle conversation outside the cave mouth, snug behind their windbreak.

At first it was quite strange and satisfying, until he noticed occasional slight withdrawals on Josin's part, a sort of temporary wistfulness as though she were dealing with an inner and secret problem Initially, these lasted only for seconds, but as time passed they became more frequent and longer in duration. Eventually, he grew concerned and demanded to know what was troubling her.

'It is nothing serious,' she replied. 'Quite ridiculous really, but as we sit here I sometimes look down towards the village and see not our current home, but the first we fled from with Athan. The surrounding terrain is different, but in essence the hamlet is the same. It is a little larger and we have gained some years, the hunter has become the warrior, and Athan's pupil is now the teacher, but the attitude to living and working is the same, the friendliness and co-operation between neighbours is the same. Strangely, it is this sameness that stirs within me a longing to see our first home again. I know, of course, that it no longer exists, that it is a burned out site, but it is the same site beneath the same stretch of sky and beneath the same cliff edge, by the same sealed cave concealing our kith and kin. Perhaps it is part of the spirits of those people and that place that still lives within me that calls me back, still makes me wish to see it again and breathe its air for a short while once more. I know that, unless something extraordinary has happened, it will have remained unmolested and must be entirely overgrown as if nothing had existed there, but the call still draws me.'

He moved himself into a more comfortable position and responded, 'I wish you had told me before. I too have had similar desires, perhaps not quite so compelling as your own, and I could not have expressed them in the same words or as well as you, but that spirit which in part dwells within you is also within myself. Somehow it seems there is a need to prove one's memories. I have never spoken to you of it for fear of putting unnecessary and possibly dangerous wishes into your mind. I want nothing to happen to you. However, it is now certain that your longing will only get stronger. It is not ridiculous; provided you are well aware of the difficulties and dangers involved, we will go. It would depend on those difficulties how long such a trip would take, but I am sure we are not so essential to the lives of our neighbours that they would miss us for whatever number of moons such a journey would take.'

The change in Josin's demeanour was dramatic; it was as if a great weight that had been bearing down on her had been suddenly lifted.

'To hell with the danger,' she said. 'You and I have fought side by side far too long and often to worry about that. If all goes well, so much the better; otherwise, provided we are together in our final moments, I will be content.'

The decision had been made and neither wished to go back on it. Even so, Egen expressed his opinion that there was no great rush, that there was little point in making difficulties and dangers greater than they need be. It was now late in the year and it would be wise to travel as unencumbered as possible, so he suggested the best time to depart would be in late spring. By then the seasonal rains should be over; after all, they would be relying for shelter on the type of temporary cover they had used on their way to the Iceni. She readily agreed. Now that they had made their decision she was as happy as if she had been on her way to festivities to celebrate the summer solstice. They informed Haerviu and then their more immediate friends. They had the entire winter to plan and arrange things for the venture. A simple farm cart piled high with hay and kindling, drawn by two ponies, would be their mode of travel. They hoped that inquisitive eyes would assume they were simple crofters. They had, however, every intention of being seen as little as possible, and would try to travel through, or near, forest and woodland. Over the winter they concentrated on fitting a false bottom to the cart, somewhat similar to that used on Arthfael's journey to the Silures, but this time shallower, to contain their weapons which they had no intention of travelling without. There would be access points front and rear, the front one under the seat by the foot well. They also made certain that the hubs and spindles were in excellent condition for a long journey but, in keeping with the guise adopted, ensured that the wheels and other woodwork were well scuffed and untidy. In their eyes the only risk they were taking in its appearance was that the animals chosen were much stronger and more reliable than the average crofter would require, but they hoped this would not be noticed by others, especially from a distance.

Finally, the days began to get warmer and the rains diminished, and Josin became more eager. So much so that he was convinced that if the entire Roman army stood before them she would cut her way through it alone. On a morning when the first rays of the sun arose so bright and silvery it appeared to offer a gloriously warm day, they set off. They were determined to cover as much distance that first day as humanly possible. Relying on Egen's almost faultless sense of direction, aided by a clear sky, they travelled on undulating wooded tracks, weaving a path away from home.

They met nothing to perturb them. The only people they saw were far in the distance and nothing to do with the forces of occupation. They left the higher hills behind them and approached more level ground. It became necessary, in order to retain the cover of the trees, to veer northwards and, follow a curving route around the plain, they eventually arrived at a tree-lined valley which they agreed would be their first overnight stay. It was very much a compromise between the need to find somewhere soon, and the desire to be safe, warm and comfortable. It was not ideal insofar as mist and damp would tend to drift down onto the site, but they had under the false floor warm and waterproof cloaks made from skins. It would also be possible to make a small fire without it being noticed above the valley sides, not that they had seen anything, other than animal spoor, to suggest there were eyes to watch them for many miles in any direction. After seeing to the horses' welfare they erected a small lean-to shelter, this time using the wagon side as the primary support. Taking it in turns to watch, they spent a less than comfortable night, and Josin, during her turn to be alert, mused to herself that she was glad they were making the trip now while they were both comparatively young, fit and agile, for one never knew when the burden of years would overtake a person, making such a venture much more difficult.

Nevertheless, they had at least gained enough rest to rise early, even before the rays of the sun had started over the horizon promising a clear day ahead. Egen used the side of his hand against the sun to estimate direction and time, and they made good, uneventful progress until, emerging from the protection of a thin line of trees at the edge of woodland well before the sun had reached its zenith, Josin emitted a sudden squeal. 'That is Berringa's hill,' she said.

It was still far distant, but the distinctive positioning of some large rocks partly buried in its northern slope made it unmistakable, even though the trees on its summit had grown and changed.

'That is what I was hoping to see, and thankfully it is,' Egen replied.

As he allowed his gaze to slide down the western side to more level ground, he was sure that he could make out the staging post between him and the hill – merely a small grey blob silhouetted against the skyline. He needed to get much closer before making a decision on what action or direction to take.

When they were close enough to make out the shape more distinctly, they climbed down from the cart to reduce their height and walked the outfit carefully through the already long grass. No flag was raised and no sign of life was apparent. As they drew nearer, they saw the great gates were not only open but they hung at a twisted angle, indicating that neither hinges nor supports had recently been attended to. He withdrew his sword and instructed Josin to remain there while he investigated. Should there be the slightest sign of trouble, she was to mount up again and flee. She did not argue. She would remain a while and watch, but was secretly determined not to run away. As he got nearer he got bolder and walked through the opening, while keeping his left side close to and protected by the gate post, thus allowing his sword arm full and free movement. By now he believed the post to be abandoned, and a quick check at ground level confirmed this. He returned to the gate and signalled Josin to join him. Together they examined every room and space – everything portable had been removed. The same applied to the upper level, from where it was possible to gain views in every direction. Unlike the condition of the gates, the roofs on both levels, including the stable block, were sound. But no provisions remained, nothing to attract even the hungriest rodent looking for sustenance.

'If you agree,' he said to Josin, 'here would be a good and safe place to stay this evening. I have scanned as far as possible from the highest point and there is no sign that anything other than small mammals have been anywhere near for a very long time. It would save us having to build a shelter, and the ponies would have a well deserved rest in those stables. We could bring in the wagon now, so that it cannot be seen by anyone who may have extremely long vision – it is well always to allow for the unlikely. It is not late. We will have time to climb the hill and explore whatever remains of Berringa's home. Unless condemned to live forever she will no longer be there, but it would be only right to pay our respects to her memory.'

This had been Josin's only thought and desire since they first sighted the hill, but the logic of doing things in the order he had suggested could not be argued with.

He continued, 'Depending on what we find, we should return here and spend a more restful night. We are now well into our journey and there is no great need for rush.'

Hand in hand, they worked their way up. As they neared the line of trees which prevented the site from being easily watched from the Roman tower, they saw only a vixen sitting not a great distance away; it did not seem concerned by their presence as her two cubs played, each rolling one over the other between her forelegs. Maybe it judged the distance to be safe enough for rapid escape, or perhaps had decided that no threat existed from these interlopers; it just sat contentedly, satisfying its own curiosity. However, the animal's appearance served to remind Egen that he would soon have to revise his hunting skills for the days ahead. Nearer still they were assailed by the rattling sound of a magpie's warning call, then the chatter between it and another. This was followed by the repeated slow, lazy, superior-sounding caw of a large crow. The sound recalled those that had warned Berringa of their arrival there long ago when Egen was so badly wounded. Rounding the opening that had allowed approach to the dwelling, they gasped. Nothing was there. The ground where her hut had stood was just a matted tangle of hardy grasses and creeping ivy. Stretching, overgrown branches from the adjacent trees occupied the space where the thatched roof had been.

Neither uttered a word but searched all around for clues. Egen pushed with his toe and kicked away sections of ground cover, finally remarking that the soil beneath held evidence that the former house had been burned to the ground a long time ago. They both thought deeply about possible explanations, none of which could be proved, though some were more probable than others. Had they but known it, one probability that they had agreed to was more likely than any other sequence of events, and turned out to be almost exactly what had happened. The local consul had revised the viability of certain forts for their logistical value and vulnerability, and it had been decided that this one near Berringa's hill should be decommissioned. To evacuate it safely a large contingent of auxiliaries was sent, complete with ox-carts, to remove anything of use or value, which meant in practice everything other than the walls and roof. The resident garrison, emboldened by the arrival of numerous colleagues and the fact that they would no longer be staying there, requested the senior officer to destroy the house on the hill, offering the spurious excuse that it was believed to be a resting place for insurgents. The commander needed no urging; to him it would be a light-hearted diversion.

'If that was what happened, I hope that Berringa was not harmed,' declared Egen.

'It is extremely unlikely,' responded Josin. 'When we were here previously and you were mostly sleeping recovering from your wound, I learned a little of her ways. Her friends, the wildlife in all its forms, by its behaviour kept her aware of danger. In that way, as she looked after them, they looked after her; it was not unusual for her to refer to them jocularly as her animal infantry. I am sure she would have been forewarned, and by the time the soldiers arrived she would have been gone.'

What actually happened was this. Even before the appearance of the clearance platoon on the far side of the valley on its way to the tower opposite her home, Berringa had realised that this was not a normal stopover operation and hastily collected a few of her most precious possessions, to which she added some food. She then tied two blankets, shawl-like, over her cloak and continued to watch. When the entire platoon started to climb the hill towards her, one of their number bearing a flaming torch, their intentions were obvious. Quietly, she slipped away from the house and made her way unseen down the southern side of the hill by way of a covered track she had used many times before. She then circled around to the far side of the tower and waited. As the last soldier left to climb the hill she pulled herself through a small drainage arch, never guarded as it was presumed too narrow for use by an average person and unpleasant. Their duty done, the house having flared up quickly and nearly as quickly died down again, the soldiers moved off, while she settled into the tower for two days, contemplating her next move. To have stayed longer despite, the shelter it afforded would not have been in her nature. She disliked being enclosed by Roman stone walls. Having decided in which direction to travel, she set out to live whatever little time was left to her far from the invaders' influence, and perhaps to lie down for the last time.

Having seen and adjudged all they possibly could Egen and Josin turned back to descend the hill; it was then that Josin noticed something half buried near the root of a bush; it appeared to be unnaturally smooth and round. Stooping to examine it, she recognised it as one of Berringa's unguent jars and picked it up. How it had escaped the flames and came to be there could only be guessed at. Perhaps it had dropped from her bag as she fled; maybe it was the very one which had contained the evil smelling mess with magical powers that had helped cure Egen's wound. Who could tell? Now it held nothing but dusty soil from beneath the bush. She carefully cleaned and wrapped it to put among their belongings in the cart. It had previously been agreed between them that souvenirs for their own sake were merely an encumbrance, but in this instance they deemed it would be ungracious, if not actually sacrilegious, to discard it.

On reaching the bottom of the gradient Egen looked around for something to use as a substantial lever. He found a long, stout pole lying under the steps leading to the upper floor which he was able to insert under one of the gates to heave upwards and pull. With Josin pushing from the other side they were able to reset it almost in its intended closed position. They repeated the procedure with the other gate. Now they were effectively closed, and with almost superhuman effort he dragged the locking timber to the gates and balanced one end in one of the sockets; with Josin struggling and pushing to help they managed to lift the other end to drop it squarely into all the remaining sockets. They now felt as safe and secure as they would be anywhere and decided there would be no need for either to stay awake to keep watch. The following morning, well rested and having searched carefully in every direction, Egen deemed it safe to light a fire and cook a substantial breakfast. Opening the gates no more than was necessary to allow the wagon to squeeze through was only slightly less difficult than closing them, and they had to be careful when they allowed the heavy locking bar to crash to the ground, as a damaged limb at this stage was the last thing they wanted.

As they passed between the gates they were filled with a curious confusion of emotions: they were well aware of the tower's oppressive purpose and the evil reputation of its garrison, but they had just spent a secure warm night within it. That mixture of emotions did not diminish as they progressed along the valley; they could not help repeatedly raising their eyes towards the hilltop as if hoping to see some trace of Berringa's home, as if their experience the previous day had somehow been at fault – but nothing changed. All they could take with them was the harsh, mocking caw of the crow from high up which slowly receded into the distance. The ponies, on the other hand, appeared eager to be on their way and pulled strongly as they were turned diagonally to climb the opposite hill.

On reaching the summit, Egen directed them as near due east as it was possible to get and yet remain within the cover of trees. The route led over undulating countryside and sometimes they had to break cover to cross from one woodland to another. On one occasion they passed over a metalled road without seeing any sign of its being used. They seldom spoke as both were filled with their own private thoughts, except when Josin thought she recognised parts of the way taken from the great battle, but Egen kept steadfastly on, trusting in his own navigation. On those occasions he felt nothing but admiration for her courage and determination on what must have been a nightmarish journey, especially in the dark and rain with him curled up delirious and tied to prevent him sliding out from the confined space at her feet. He was convinced that no other woman could have done it. At midday they stopped for a quick cold meal and resumed the trek as soon as they had finished it. They stopped for the night, making a shelter against the wagon, as they had done before, and set off again at first light. Later in the day he recognised an opportunity, and leaving her for only a short while returned with a wild duck which he rapidly gutted and plucked; it would provide them with several meals. The debris he buried carefully – their tracks could not be totally hidden but he felt that there was no point in allowing their passing to be broadcast far and wide on the wind. Towards evening both arrived at an emotional low; from the morning they had set out they had not encountered a soul. This is not what they had expected. They had been ready to deal with danger and hostility, yet their experience so far seemed to suggest that their precautions had been unnecessary However, they were not about to abandon them. To relax now could be their undoing.

That evening their chosen spot was perhaps the darkest and dankest yet; it appeared to fit with their current mood. It was therefore with some surprise that Josin awoke to see Egen sitting cross-legged by the fire chatting to a middle-aged man dressed in the fashion of a Celt. He saw that she was awake and passed her a warm beverage that had been readied on a flat stone over the low flames.

'This,' he said, is Drust. 'He happened upon us while searching for mushrooms. Apparently. his village is a little beyond that lower hill, but experience has taught him that here is the best place to search.'

The subsequent conversation was an exercise in finding out as much as possible about each other without giving too much away. Drust was allowed to know only that they were travellers, but from where to where they were careful to keep to themselves. He, however, was more loquacious and the apparent dearth of people soon became the main subject of the conversation.

'It seems you have travelled far from a very different environment,' said Drust. 'It is true that not a great many people are to be seen hereabouts, but that was not always so. I have lived here all my life and before the coming of the invader it was as many others. Hamlets large and small were distributed widely over the surrounding countryside, existing in various degrees of co-operation and rivalry. Then came the slaughter. Roman savages in shining armour seemed to appear from everywhere, killing stealing and burning. It was too much for most. They were not prepared, so they razed their own homes to the ground and fled. In time, only a few of us were left, and we were in constant hiding. Quite suddenly, the persecution diminished. I do not know for certain why that should be. Maybe it was something to do with the two great battles: the annihilation of the entire druidical brotherhood and the slaying of the inimitable Boudicca. Otherwise, I can only assume that even Romans can tire of murder when there is nothing left for them to steal. All the time they were indulging in the bloody destruction of our homes and neighbours they were also building fortified towns with strong stone walls, about one day's march between each. At the same time, one or two rich merchants built their own villas on sites where some hamlets had existed and there lived in extraordinary luxury served by slaves which they treated with unnecessary harshness. The military increasingly retreated into the towns behind their high stone walls, which made the villas ever more difficult to protect; as a result, the merchants followed and the villas fell into ruin, hastened by the efforts of resistance groups. The Romans frequently transfer or exchange troops between centres, their mounted scouts being sent well ahead of the main body, and, while waiting for the infantry and its commanders to catch up, they re-acquaint themselves with the pastime of attacking any native residents they may happen upon. The few of us left scratch a living from the ground but always keep a sharp eye for any signs of military excursions outside those walls. Sometimes, as a youngster grows towards adulthood he or she will disappear to join the resistance, which in many parts still harasses the occupier. Who can blame them? There is little enough to keep them at home: no life and no future. We seldom hear of them again. As far as I understand, the situation is similar over vast swathes of the land, although I am told that if your journey takes you towards Londinium more of the populace may be seen. More and greater re-building is being done there. The military needs workers; to that end citizens and others are not persecuted, even though local Celts are looked down on, but you will see them working together, each for their own purpose.

Life is both cruel and complex, and each must make his own choices.'

Then Egen was able to surprise Drust. 'I can assure you,' he said, 'that the entire brotherhood was not destroyed. Athan, one of the greatest of them, survived. He no longer travels, but his teaching of the ancient truths, measures and mathematics are still broadcast. Equally, Boudicca was spared death at Manduessuedun. She fought as one possessed. Trapped by the wall of dead she had herself built up, she was facing death when she was rescued by others from outside her following. She no longer has a great army, yet fights still with the resistance. It is said that, should the occupation last to the end of time, she will also, fighting against it, instilling in her countrymen the persistence and fury that only she is capable of. Any story you may have heard of the destruction of these two leaders is untrue. It is Roman propaganda. They do not know the fate of either of them, but they could never admit the truth; it would diminish their reputation for supposed invincibility. Even as they spread the story of her end, they were sending out search parties for her, for after the battle they could find no trace of either her or her children.'

His listener was perplexed. He had no reason to distrust or disbelieve what these people said – they seemed honest and well informed – but he and everyone he knew had for so long believed that Boudicca and the brotherhood were finished and now part of the past, that he found changing that belief extremely difficult. Almost certainly, when he passed the news to his neighbours, they would be convinced he had been gathering and eating the wrong mushrooms.

They watched their visitor wend his way home in a southerly direction until he was out of sight. They had no reason to doubt him, but they had given little away of their intentions and were not about to relax their caution on the basis of one conversation. They turned the team north for a short distance before turning again to pick up on their original route. The day was much as the previous, except that they talked more and were more light-hearted. They felt they were now deep into their quest, and the sadness of Berringa's hill was more than a day behind them.

The anxieties that each had nurtured within themselves concerning the few people they had seen, had been reasonably answered and alleviated by their conversation that morning. They were well aware that when they reached their destination, it was unlikely that anything recognisable would exist, yet they were still anxious and determined to get there. They travelled onwards, using cover wherever possible, and seeing perhaps just a few more people than yesterday, but none in military garb. If they had been seen by any of those persons, and Egen was sure that they had by one or two, there was no sign of it. They had been completely ignored, which in its own way was reassuring. They stopped late in the evening in a spinney close to the top of a small hill which they judged suitable for a night's rest.

Again the day dawned bright and warm, which encouraged them to be on their way quickly. Emerging from the trees to look around from the highest point, Egen gave an exclamation of half surprise and half satisfaction as they looked down at the far side of the hill. It seemed to reach a much lower level than that from which they had climbed last evening. Down there was the place where they and a group of villagers had literally swept a platoon of imperial soldiers off their feet. Despite the changes over the years, that great bow in the river with its boisterous and chuckling falls at either end of a much wider and shallower stretch at its base, was unmistakable.

The hillside below them had been cleared of a great number of trees, presumably to give the guards at the checkpoint a much wider and earlier view of any approach to the ford. That fortified checkpoint itself had been rebuilt to at least twice the size of the original, catering for double the number of personnel, a fact evidenced by so many moving about the building. Two lines of posts had been set into the ground before the fort in order to prevent a repetition of the fiery destruction of the original. It was too early in the day to expect to see travellers or merchants seeking to traverse the river. Egen sat there for a short time thinking that he would like to cause some other form of mischief today. However, he had Josin alongside him and the last thing he wished was to put her into unnecessary danger yet again, so he immediately cut short the string of ideas that had begun to enter his thoughts. He drew saatisfaction from two facts: first that his group's actions all those years ago had caused the occupiers to go to so much trouble to rebuild and defend the post, and secondly that they were south of the river as he had intended, and much closer to their objective than expected.

He turned the outfit towards the bright early sunshine which cast elongated shadows at them, the proportions of which made them aware that the landscape was getting gentler. It was as though a giant hand from far ahead had grabbed, pulled and stretched it, thereby depressing the hills and causing the inclines to be less arduous, creating a more rolling aspect. Large and small areas of woodland in contrasting shades still mottled the vista, and in many places linked one hill to another. As they rode forward they wondered how many simple hamlets and how many determined freedom fighters were hidden deep in those forests. Although not close, they began to notice more people travelling in roughly the same direction as themselves, some driving ox-carts laden with stone slabs, others in wagons similar to their own. These latter mostly carried balks of timber, meat carcases or vegetable produce. It had earlier been in their minds to alter the load they were carrying, but now it seemed to fit quite well with the other traffic – the kindling would have been quite normal and the hay could be protection and bedding for almost any produce, such as small game, for trading.

So far all were dressed similarly to themselves, as people who had not elected to submit to Roman citizenship but, in order to survive, worked for them, condemning themselves to being but a step or so above slaves. On occasion, other vehicles would join the trail until all began converging towards the same objective. They both tried to call to mind, in case they were questioned, reasons for being there which they had rehearsed before starting out. It proved unnecessary, all those around them exuded a total indifference to anyone else. They appeared utterly morose and concerned only with their own thoughts. This suited Egen and Josin and they quietly continued their progress.

Before long, they passed two small gangs of workers marking boundaries of some sort; soon they were among many such gangs, each working on its own part of an enormous construction project, and each having its own mustering point in the form of a site fire. Those fires, as shown by the debris around them, were kept burning day and night, indicating that many were not allowed to leave their particular site even after dark. One by one, their fellow travellers dropped out to make pre-arranged deliveries to particular workings. As casually as they could manage, they drifted on along passageways between workers, desperately hoping that they looked as if they knew exactly where they were going and what they were doing.

It was hard to appear casual while taking in the fact that they had never seen so many disparate throngs of people mingling together without actually fighting each other. There were high officials in full togas, ordering and questioning lesser mortals, who, dressed in simpler Roman robes, tried in turn to look important as they passed on those instructions. Wealthy merchants strutted about, attended by servants and slaves who were kept in order by a senior house servant wielding a switch. And there were very many dressed like themselves, either working with the gangs or trading with overseers. Also among them were military personnel of every rank, from senior commanders to auxiliaries guarding slaves and prisoners. It was difficult to distinguish between these last two categories for all were wearing little more than rags; the difference was only apparent by the weight and length of their fetters. Prisoners who were regarded as dangerous to the empire wore much heavier and shorter chains and were beaten indiscriminately by their captors according to their whims, when perceived shortcomings or defiance were not necessary. The lighter and longer chains of slaves enabled them to labour more freely.

Totally absorbed in trying to translate the unexpected sights and sounds into some sort of meaningful picture, and at the same time trying to be an unnoticeable and integral part of the scene, they were startled to be challenged by an irate guard waving a spear in Egen's face. They had just passed a stacked pile of stone slabs behind which the man had stationed himself to oversee his quota of slaves, and he emerged screaming insults.

'You stupid, stinking, misbegotten Celts! Where the hell do you think you are going?' he screamed. 'Can you not see we are building a sea wall here?' As much to demonstrate his importance and knowledge as for any other reason he continued to scream at them. 'Beyond that mark is the most glutinous and treacherous morass you will ever see. At low tide it will consume anything and everything within a few moments, at high tide it has been known to swallow entire ships. Would it not interfere with and delay the work, I would be happy to allow you to continue, and laugh as you disappeared below the mud. Now take your stinking produce to where you are expected – to that gang of prisoners below the hill. Because of your tardiness they are overdue to be fed and if you do not reach them soon they will die of hunger.'

There was nothing to be gained by protesting that they were not the expected cart, or that they had no food; either could have proved fatal. Egen instead contrived to look sheepish and muttered incoherently as he turned towards the direction indicated. He did not hurry. He knew that a man of that temper, having projected his sense of his own superiority, would not bother to watch them go, but his next move was also important for their safety. When well out of earshot, Josin reminded him that the hill they were advancing on was the same as that they had used on the night they had attacked the ships, and those ships probably lay beneath the mud, not too far from the new sea wall being built today. As they spoke both were relieved to see another wagon, somewhat similar to their own, emerge from a clump of trees to the right and canter towards the prisoners some distance away. The driver dismounted and after an exchange with the gang master proceeded to distribute near rotten meat and vegetables to the workers, and allowed them to slake their thirsts with dirty water from lidded wooden buckets. Nevertheless, the chained men seized the food and gulped and swallowed greedily, each hoping that by finishing quickly he might be able to acquire more.

Egen felt sickened that a fellow native could profit by treating his own kind in this manner, especially as they were probably only criminals according to Roman military law. The scrabble for sustenance was so frantic that the guard and driver were fully stretched to control it, which allowed Egen and Josin to slip by unnoticed. As they did so he noticed the soldier's own wine flask hanging by a strap from a forked stake. He was sorely tempted to lean sideways and take it but, realising that an auxiliary separated from his wine would certainly result in extra unearned beatings for those in chains, he allowed it to slip through his fingers and remain hanging. He had already acknowledged Josin's remarks concerning the hill, and he now reminded her that there should still be a depression near the top. If unoccupied it would be a good place to spend the night again. It would hide the wagon and allow a small fire to be used without being obvious. It was not late, but he had calculated that the final trek could be completed in one day if they had an early start. They were in luck. Not only was the hollow not occupied but the remains of recent camp fires were evident, which meant that their own fire, if seen, would not be considered unusual or suspicious.

The eastern skyline was a mere streak of grey when Egen roused Josin from a deep slumber; it would be some time yet before it brightened into a summer dawn. He handed her a warm drink and then bustled about preparing for the onward journey. He looked down at the riverside and noted the large number of individual fires for each work gang, effectively delineating the overall shape and size of the construction site, which, although nestling within the deep wide curve of the river, was enormous. Both, having eaten a little, mounted the cart and drove carefully towards that slowly brightening streak. He could just make out the start of the long high ridge with its grass, reeds and marshes on the river side and woodland on the landward side, which he recognised as that which stretched on almost to the estuary, and under which their childhood homes had been protected and hidden. As they skittered down they thought that they could not have chosen better ponies: they did not look out of the ordinary, but they worked well together in harness and never seemed to tire.

They crossed a deserted metalled road at the base of the hill and made straight for the forest opposite. Entering the trees was at first difficult as the fringe was close packed birch, but they managed to pick an erratic path through into the main body where there was less undergrowth and the trees comprised established oaks and ash, having greater distances between them and a high spread canopy. The main problem was that the mature trunks often had elongated exposed roots which, approached at speed, jarred the wheel rims and hubs mercilessly. Despite this, they made satisfactory progress, seeing no-one and, hopefully, remaining unseen. The forest stretched on and on, but by the time the sun was high Egen began to recognise areas that were once part of his old hunting grounds; here and there he would point out items of particular interest to him as part of his past. He now knew that, provided they kept close to the base of the ridge, they would eventually come to Athan's refuge, that half cave or depression in the rock, protected by a high overhang and hidden by trees, to which he had taken them on the night of the destruction of their hamlet. Soon he could see the distinctive overhang straight ahead of them. They reached it without difficulty, despite the undergrowth having increased greatly in the intervening years, thereby hiding the rocky depression even more effectively. This was part of the past and, despite its associations with that fateful day, it was something they wished to respect for Athan's memory and the shelter it had provided. They unharnessed and tethered the ponies in a sheltered spot and provided them with hay from the load, then dragged the wagon deeper into that hollow. They could now safely heat a meal and reflect on those events of so long ago. Afterwards, there would be ample time to walk to their former home. They rose hesitantly and, hand in hand, traced the way to where the village had once stood. As they walked a feeling of warmth and welcome came over them, even the air smelled differently, although they knew that was only memories welling up within them of childhood and their first homes. Walking clear of the tallest trees, they entered a very overgrown space which had been the clearing where their round houses had once existed. The changes were such that it was hard to orientate themselves properly, but as they looked towards the ridge where the yellowish-white rock was just the same and the stone-blocked cave discernible, though the stones themselves were totally obscured by massive ivy roots, they were able to locate where the various homes had been and remember the occupants, all of whom now lay within the cave. When they were endeavouring to re-discover the main square and its centre, Egen suddenly shouted that he would not be very long and disappeared into the trees at great speed. While he was gone Josin made a re-appraisal of the environs of the site. As they had noted earlier, the ridge face was recognisably the same, but somehow had a less tidy look about it and this she put down to an increase in the quantity of tufted hanging plants. Water droplets still exuded from fissures in the rock face and came together to form the same stream, but the pool it created below was now full of forest debris and overflowed in a different direction. The encircling saplings were young and encroached deeply.

It seemed no time at all before Egen re-appeared carrying one of his father's finely crafted javelins. He did not himself quite understand why, but it just seemed right and respectful to mark their visit with a sign. Josin fully understood and as he removed the metal tip from the weapon she removed a small shawl from beneath her cloak and tied it to the blunted spear head; then, having pulled away part of the covering ivy and stones, he projected the metal barb into the cave, hoping that in the unlikely event someone discovered the area, they would not be able to use the shaft as a viable weapon further to defile the site. Having decided as near as possible on the probable centre of the village he rammed the spear upright into the soft soil. They looked around and felt their hatred for all things Roman flare up again with a new intensity; as Josin later described their emotions, it was akin to pumping air into a metal worker's hearth, causing the glowing fire to erupt into leaping flames. There was nothing more to do, nothing sensible they could do, other than make a last circuit of the space and stand before the hidden cave to make their final spiritual communication with their sleeping kith and kin. Then, without looking back, they returned to Athan's refuge. The sun was now low, so they made a fire, ate and settled for the night. They were tired and satisfied: their mission was complete and they now desired only to return to their family and friends. In doing so, however, they would need to renegotiate the journey and its dangers.

The morning dawned grey and overcast. It almost appeared that even the weather did not entirely approve of their leaving. There was no desperate hurry so they took advantage of the shelter provided by the refuge and breakfasted in a relaxed manner, after which Egen went in pursuit of game for the return trek. This he did using his old method of quickly fashioning a temporary spear from a nearby sapling. He did not wish to employ any of the better-crafted javelins from the wagon on the basis that they all had now been used to kill Romans, and to do so would somehow defile the meat they would later need to eat. Slowly the sky cleared and the air started to warm. They re-connected cart to horses and, with a last look around, drove south.

They had no desire to return via the vast building site or meet its workers again. Egen was sure he would be able to by-pass it by taking this southerly route for a while and slowly curve around to the west. They were genuinely surprised at how soon they arrived at the forest edge and faced open, meadow-like country. It soon explained itself: there, not far ahead, was the Roman road which in their memories had been unfinished and a very long way back to the east. In the intervening years it had been completed. A great part of the woodland had been destroyed to allow the road to follow a straight route. He remarked that, even allowing for the military's predisposition to build roads as direct as possible, in this instance the distance between the new forest edge and the road appeared to be excessive.

Josin smiled mischievously and replied, 'Perhaps that is to allay travellers' anxieties regarding the legend of the Green Man of Kent.'

The terrain from there on was mostly level, so it was possible to see for a very great distance along the road in either direction. They crossed over it into the very long grass on the far side, but even as they veered slowly to the right there were many low decaying tree stumps to be avoided. Very soon they were in the vale in which Egen had had his first experience of chariot fighting, the same valley where he had first heard of his being the mythical Green Man and had deliberately expanded on the legend for practical advantage. They slowly climbed the rise to that ridge which connected the north and south woodlands, and which was not far from the second hamlet home to which Athan had introduced them, also now destroyed. Although they had made many friends there, they had not lived there for a great length of time, and it was not the place of their childhood and as such did not have the draw of childhood memories Accordingly, they carried on past without too much regret.

The next few days were much as the outward journey. They saw very few people and those whom they did see paid them little heed. Drust had been correct: the ethnic population remained largely hidden, and the invaders stayed mostly within their stone walls. The weather turned even warmer and drier, making overnight stops that much more comfortable. Eventually, they found themselves near the brow of a hill with Josin's nightmare forest, south of the battle site, on their right. According to Egen's estimates, Berringa's hill would be some distance to the south-west. Further calculations, based on the position of the sun combined with his innate sense of direction, indicated that their home lay diagonally through the woodland. To take that route would certainly be quicker, possibly by as much as one day, than circling all the way around on the southern edge, even though they would be travelling on smoother grass-land. Such was their desire to be home, especially as they were now so near, the forest route was the one they agreed on. This, they hoped, would also be their last overnight stop before reaching home. They therefore moved into the cover of the trees and prepared for yet another early start. They had throughout the venture settled on a routine whereby whichever of them had taken the last watch would also be the one to drive away, since the one already wide awake would be more mentally alert and ready to take the reins. Consequently, while he was still finishing his breakfast and rubbing the sleep from his eyes, Josin had harnessed up and was already aboard and waiting, anxious to be on their way.

They jogged and bumped through the forest, keeping as close to the diagonal as the conditions allowed. When they left the trees, they saw, laid out before them, a great rough moor rising to a height about level with the tops of the trees. Rocks and stones were strewn in every direction apart from the land between the forest edge and the start of the moor proper. It would be possible to ride a horse solo over it but it was not suitable for a wheeled vehicle, Their only choice, therefore, was to drive slowly and carefully close to the trees, scanning the moor for smoother ground to move out onto. The closer they got to the higher part of the rise the more promising it looked, but that was yet a considerable distance away. It looked greener and more inviting but as their hopes rose so they were immediately dashed. The skyline they had been looking towards was suddenly marred by the sight of three horsemen some distance apart meandering over it from the far side. They were immediately identifiable as forward scouts for a body of infantry on the move, their relaxed manner indicating they were well ahead of the main body. It was too late to hide; each had seen the other at almost the same moment. It was no use attempting to race away; they would have easily been overtaken. The riders were instantly alert and interested, and moved slowly at first as they uncovered their swords, then broke into a trot.

Egen muttered, 'It is not fighting ground and this is not a chariot.

Our only advantage is reliable animals. We have no choice; it is back to the Boudicca days.'

So saying, he fumbled beneath the seat and handed a lance to Josin which she took in her right hand, passing the reins to her left.

She answered, 'We were so near to home and safety. It is a shame.' Then, with a stern face, continued, 'However, if need be, let us go down fighting.'

She watched him retrieve his sword and allowed him to move over to her right side. He placed his left foot on the crossbeam pivot and his right knee onto the seat; he was now braced to swing his sword arm freely. As he had said, this was no chariot, but she manoeuvred the cart to line up with the smoothest approach for her intended charge. The scouts kicked their mounts into a gallop and she was about to respond, then hesitated. They were not completely sure whether they felt rather than heard a movement just above their heads, and involuntarily ducked and glanced up to see three small dark clouds of arrows speeding their way towards the riders. They were close packed and as they cut through the air seemed almost to be jostling for the privilege of being the first to strike. Only two did not make a hit, missing only by the width of a finger. The force of the impacts threw all three victims from their saddles, and one whose foot had somehow tangled with the saddle straps was dragged about one hundred paces before his horse stopped. Had the missiles not killed him the bouncing of his head over the rocky ground would certainly have done so. It was only then that they were able to look back in complete amazement to see from where those arrows had been loosed. Closing on them just clear of the trees were a dozen men on sturdy cobs, each clutching a bow in his left hand while his right was free, and controlling their mounts with leg movements only. All but one passed on either side, making for the bodies.

That one man came near and said, 'It is well that we were close. You might have had a difficult time.'

'Many thanks,' replied Egen. 'That is certainly true, but who are you, and where did you come from?'

'My name is Edmund and I lead this band against murdering invaders. As for where we came from we have been with you for most of your journey, from its very start. Your work is too valuable to us to allow harm to come your way. You were watched over and guarded until just beyond the river crossing. For very practical reasons we could not go far beyond that crossing; from that time on you were truly alone and at your greatest peril. Thanks to the passing wind we were able to pick up on you again in that valley that separates your first home from your second.'

'We are truly astounded,' responded Egen. 'We saw no sign, no trace of your presence.'

'You were not meant to,' was the smiling reply.

While they spoke, Egen watched the arrows being removed from the dead and recognised two of his previous trainees grinning sheepishly at him, but what really startled him was the fact that as the arrows were being withdrawn they were replaced with sharpened branches still retaining their leaves.

'Where did you learn that?' he enquired.

'From that same passing wind. Surely you are aware of your own legend and the fear it instils in idolaters? We use it often. I can assure you that it will probably be a very long time before soldiers can be persuaded to come this way again. No matter what punishments are meted out for refusal to obey, to them fear of the unexplained is greater than all else. It has given rise to a new practice among them: those few that return to Rome wear a badge depicting a dancing tree. It is meant as a sort of boast, a sign that the wearer has served here and survived the unknown. Not a great tribute to their invincibility, for it also implies that very many have not survived. Did they but know, a single rootless tree has ever symbolised not strength but decline, decay and disintegration.'

They watched as swords were returned to their scabbards and the horses held until they were ready to leave, then allowed to stray wherever they wished.

Edmund added, 'I would like to be here to watch as the detachment comes upon them, but that would risk their belief in the myth.'

They moved nearer the trees and Egen, looking up and around, received his second great surprise of the day. The sun had moved hardly at all and the shadows were almost unchanged. The whole episode, from the sighting of the enemy to the displacement of their bodies, had taken very little time, although it had not seemed that way; the impact of the threat and the unexpected intervention which had counteracted it had impressed itself upon them so forcefully that it had stretched heartbeats into a lifetime. It was still early. If they pushed hard they might yet be home that day. They thanked Edmund profusely, and he advised them that once over the ridge the ground was more suitable for travel. They would thus be able to move away from the woodland and follow the path of the sun directly to their village. He also assured them that the rest of the way was clear from danger.

It was as he said and, eating what little food they had left as they travelled, they arrived at the paddock as the evening light was fading and the hamlet was illumined by cooking fires only. The youth on watch was alert and released the gate for them, but, as they bumped over the deep rutted ground at the opening, they were all three surprised by the noise of a loud crack as one of the rear spindles snapped and the cart leaned sideways over the wheel which moments earlier had supported it. They could hardly believe their luck; it had held through that very long journey, through all sorts of country and difficulties, giving way only when they they were safely home. They almost collapsed in laughter and relief. They retrieved their weapons from the cart as the lad willingly took charge of it and the animals, and walked up the long path to a welcome from Arthfael and Elvina who had been watching out for them from the day of their departure.

In truth, they had not been away for very long and after initial welcomes they fell back into the routines easily. The only thing that was different now was that they had no pulls of doubt or duty to the past nagging at them. That conflict continued in the outside world was not in doubt: Romans still built walled towns, but more than ever remained within them; indigenous tribes still attacked them when outside those walls, and recruits for training did not abate. The immediate vicinity, however, was not greatly troubled. This enabled Egen and Josin to enjoy freedom of movement as never before. Over the next few years they were able to explore the nearer surroundings, but liked nothing more than their previous habit on warm afternoons of just sitting near the upper cave and reminiscing, enjoying the view and breathing the clean, warm air.

13

A New Journey

Arthfael grunted as he tried to hurry. Once more his smooth-soled sandals which had taken on a shine after an afternoon scudding about in the paddock, slipped off yet another tuft of grass or stone. He wanted to discuss with Egen a change in the routine and, as was his way, wished to do it at once. On a warm, late summer afternoon such as this he was sure he knew just where he would find him.

He rounded the last bend in the path to the cave and looked up. As expected, he saw the improvised windbreak hanging limply on its supports. From where he looked its angle effectively hid the cave mouth. Anxious to get his ideas agreed, he moved around the obstacle and saw them seated together against the rocky wall adjacent to the opening.

He started to apologise. 'I am sorry to...' and abruptly stopped.

They had not moved in the slightest, not even looked up as he approached. With a suddenly pounding heart and a sob he could not stifle, he realised that they had, hand in hand, already started a new journey towards a new future. They had always sworn to do everything as one, and in this fate had conspired to grant them their wish. He rushed forward to confirm his suspicion, but there was no breathing. So sudden and unexpected was it, that he was momentarily stunned. Recovering his wits, however, he leaned back, seized the great cloak and covered them with it, weighing the edges down with large stones. The sword, which he knew meant so much to Egen, he thought to lay beside them. He stood up and went towards it, but yet again his sandal slipped on a smooth stone and he fell uncontrollably. In order to protect his ribs from the pommel, he managed to thrust his hands over it, thus cushioning the impact. Cushioned it may have been but it still had the full weight of his body behind it and the blade, with a low screech, sank deeper into the small fissure in the rock. Cursing his own carelessness, he stood up and pulled at the hilt to remove it; it would not budge. He tried again with both hands but it was no good. He re-positioned himself with a foot on either side, grasped the cross-guard firmly and heaved with all his might. His shoulders bulged and his leg muscles quivered with the strain, but he could not move it. He did not wish to leave it unguarded but, remembering that he had the reputation of being the strongest man in the village, he thought the weapon would be quite safe. As he stumbled down the path to report to Haervieu, he met one of the youths from the village who volunteered to watch over the bodies until relieved.

A meeting of the elders was immediately called and messengers sent to advise Gwain and Mirim. It was concluded that the most appropriate and respectful tribute they could make would be to lay the couple within the cave they loved so well, then seal it in the manner they had used for their own parents far across the land. This, it was felt, would give them some kind of spiritual communion with their kith and kin. The sword would remain standing; apart from the fact that it could not be removed, it would be a suitable memorial and marker until such time as someone of appropriate lineage, ordained by the gods, at some time in the distant future should be able to withdraw it.